FOUR STONES

by

Norman Hall

Deux Voiliers Publishing

Alymer, Quebec

This book is a work of fiction. Names, characters, businesses, organizations, places, events, and incidents are either the product of the author's imagination or are used fictitiously. Any resemblance to actual persons, living or dead, events, or locales is entirely coincidental.

First Edition

Copyright © 2015 by Norman Hall

All rights reserved.

Published in Canada by Deux Voiliers Publishing, Aylmer, Quebec.

www.deuxvoilierspublishing.com

Library and Archives Canada Cataloguing in Publication

Hall, Norman, 1942-, author
    Four stones / by Norman Hall.

ISBN 978-1-928049-32-6 (Ingram paperback)

    I. Title.

PS8615.A39243F68 2015   C813'.6   C2015-903356-X

Legal deposit – Bibliothèque et Archives nationales du Québec, 2015

Cover Design – Ian Thomas Shaw

Distributed by Ingram

To my children, Angela and Christopher, and to Karen.

Chapter One

Rita Brickston looked like shit. She could see it in the stained mirror in the toilet at the end of the hall. She had had enough of looking that way. More importantly, she had had enough of being hunted, enough of expecting death around every corner. Then again, it was all built into the job description.

Only a few days ago she had looked like a million bucks. Turning heads as she glided across a floor, her long blond hair glistening in the lights of the crystal chandeliers of the Turkish Embassy in Bern, Switzerland. She had gone to the reception to meet her contact and pick up the information on a mole hidden inside the CIA.

Earlier, Rita had also turned more than a few heads as she had played tourist in the 820-year-old City of Bridges. She had arrived in Bern three days before her performance at the Embassy, hoping to convince any followers that she was actually vacationing. It didn't take long before she realized she was being followed and her plan had failed. She spotted the tail as she strolled around the UNESCO World Heritage Site of the old town.

She was standing in the tourist crowd at the base of the almost 500 year-old clock tower waiting for the figures to revolve while a mechanical joker's arms reached up and alternated the ringing of the two bells above his head. There was a man in the crowd pretending to be interested in the beautiful clock but was actually watching her. Doubt began to set in when the man failed to follow her into the crowded Kornhaus bar. The bar was part of the original city granary and still possessed the colourful pillars and ceilings adorned with musicians and women in traditional costumes accompanied by mythological figures—a mermaid, man in the moon and a dragon. Rita was impressed with the richness of the mahogany banisters and the bar surround where she sat and had a Schweppes Bitter Lemon while she waited for the man who never came. As far as she could see.

Occasionally being paid to stay at four and five star hotels was one of the few perks that Rita's job brought her. There was little pleasure that night however, as she wrestled with her doubt about the man and began to question her own instincts. She slept little, but by morning she had won the wrestling match.

Instead of eating breakfast in the Hotel Savoy Bern's dining room she walked straight through the lobby and down Neuengasse and found a nice bistro a few blocks down. No one followed her. At least that's what she thought. She spent the day taking advantage of the excellent tram service and the six kilometres of Lauben—the all-weather protected promenades and arcades. She finally found what she was waiting for at the Flohmarkt, Flea Market, on the banks of the Aare. Across a stall of delicate porcelain there was the man, supposedly examining a table of what looked like wood-working tools. Rita looked down and picked up a blue and white porcelain cup, turning it over and holding it to the light as if to inspect its genuineness. This action gave her another opportunity to glance at the tool table, but the man was gone.

This time the doubt didn't come. Not a believer in coincidence, even in tourist infested August Bern, Rita knew she was being followed by the opposition. Making her way back to the hotel, she went down the ancient Kramgasse. The alley had been full of traders and merchants plying their wares for hundreds of years. In spite of feeling she was being followed and using the tricks of her trade, Rita never caught sight of the man again that day.

That night she continued to play the flush tourist. Dressed to the nines, long blond hair up, she took advantage of the table she had booked at the Bellevue Terrasse with its view of the Aare and the snow-covered peaks of the Eiger, Monch and Jungfrau. She doubted that the man following her could afford to eat at the Bellevue, even if he could get in the must-reservation restaurant. She was confident he hadn't gotten a table. The next day she rejected a boat tour on the Aare for one of the many swimming spots on its bank and the rest of that day she swam and sunned herself. She recognized no one.

* * * * *

Alexei Petrovsky had been hunting Rita Brickston since before her arrival in Bern where he was sure she had spotted him at the Clock Tower and again at the Flea Market. From a distance he had appreciated watching her swim in the Aare and admired her body as she lay sunning herself. He had left early, confident in his belief that the exchange of money for information he was waiting for would take place that evening at the Turkish Embassy reception. While he thought she had recognized him in his tuxedo at the reception, he appeared to perform his diplomatic function believing, mistakenly, that she wasn't sure he was the same man she had seen dressed as a tourist around the old town. More by instinct than by observation, Alexei knew she had made contact and acquired the information on the CIA mole. Information that he desperately wanted her not to have.

His plan to take the information from her had dissolved when Rita had brazenly and unexpectedly walked through the lobby of the Hotel Savoy and out the front door, onto Neuengasse and into a taxi. His reaction had been too late. That was five days ago.

CHAPTER TWO

David Stone had never seen a body by emergency flasher light before. To add to his confusion, this particular body happened to be sprawled inconsiderately over his spare tire. He reacted quickly. He closed the trunk.

It had been a reflex reaction. Much later, when he analyzed it, David knew he was in shock and denial. Subconsciously, if he closed the trunk the body wasn't there. That was post-event analysis, however. At the time, David went and got the flashlight he carried in the glove compartment and decided to examine the right rear tire. It was flat alright, no doubt about it.

* * * * *

Only ten minutes before he had been under high powered halogen lights. A welcome to interrogation central. Or so they seemed to say to him as he had approached the Canada/U.S. border.

David had crossed the border hundreds of times in his life and the only time he had had any difficulty was the time when he was seventeen and the customs officer decided his long hair, age and messy old car made him a likely candidate as a druggie. Both he and the car were searched, including the ashtray, looking for signs of marijuana. The customs officer had been right. David did smoke dope frequently in those days, but hadn't been stupid enough to take it across the border since one of his friends had been caught with marijuana seeds in his ashtray. Still, for reasons he couldn't articulate, crossing the border made him uneasy.

As he pulled up to the "Stop here until vehicle in front has been inspected" sign, thoughts of home and Mary dominated his mind and he eagerly moved up to the inspection booth when the car ahead of him pulled away.

With the border behind him and home calling, he began to creep over the speed limit as he drove along Highway 405. It wouldn't be long now and he would feel the warm embrace of home. David was wrong. He knew it when his car began to mishandle and a strange road noise assailed his ears. The car had a flat tire. As he had pulled off the road onto the soft shoulder, it had not taken David long to use up the appropriate number of four letter epithets that people utter under such circumstances.

It was a humid and moonless summer night. Dark as pitch, except for the vast array of stars and the lights of passing vehicles. It was a pleasant contrast to the starkness of the border crossing. But it hardly had been appreciated by David as he already felt the sweat forming on his upper body as soon as he had gotten out of the car. He had still been muttering to himself about his ill fortune as he had opened the trunk and found the body.

* * * * *

The tire inspection over, David told himself quite seriously, "I guess I better get to it." Again David opened the trunk. The woman's body was still there. The sweat sheen coating his body froze. His jaw fell, making a tunnel out of his mouth. Resisting the competing needs to close the trunk again or vomit, he summoned up enough courage to shine the flashlight on the body. He wasn't sure why. There were no apparent injuries though he did notice that the corpse was not wearing any panties as the dress was askew on the left side. Without thinking he reached into the trunk and pulled the dress down. For all intents and purposes the woman could just be asleep. His weak light had left the staring eyes in shadow.

Shock and horror, unfamiliar to the normally calm, in-command David, were threatening to eradicate any rational thought as a debate began to rage in his head at high speed, frantically searching for direction.

"I'll call the cops," he decided.

He pulled his cell out of his pocket, and turned it on. The time it took for the phone to chime active was just long enough for hesitation and second thoughts to come on the scene. Doubt about calling the police inserted itself and an inner voice told him he had better think it through before acting precipitously. The analytical part of his nature was asserting itself.

Still staring at the body, his next thought was to change the tire and then drive to the nearest Ontario Provincial Police detachment. That thought was soon countered by the realization that he had smuggled a dead body over an international border. That was immediately followed by an image of himself back at the border and under the "interrogation" lights for real.

The debate raged until David left it hanging, unresolved. He lifted the body out of the trunk and laid it on the grass verge of the embankment that ran along the shoulder. Perspiration once again began to coat his skin. He was surprised there was no blood and only the faintest odour. Irrelevantly, he realized it was the same perfume that Mary wore. Turning back to the trunk, David began to take out the spare tire, jack and cross-wrench when he heard a funny rustling sound in the dark behind him as if there was something moving through the long browning grass of late summer. The sound of twigs snapping as something put pressure on them came to his ears and played on his increasingly active imagination.

Momentarily, David was afraid to turn around. Forcing himself to turn, he shone his light in the direction of the sound. There was nothing there. Silence had returned. A car and a truck went by on the highway, catching David momentarily in their headlights.

It took a few seconds for David to realize what was wrong. The body was gone. A shiver moved up David's spine with such skill that he no longer felt sweaty. Goose bumps broke out on his back in concert with the rising hairs on his neck. Panic began to lurk in the back of his mind. Shining his light rapidly back and forth over the grass did not help. The body was not there. Rational thought returned, laced with hope, and it fleetingly occurred to him that maybe the woman had been unconscious and not dead. After all, he had not had the courage to look for a pulse.

Cautiously, he moved toward the place where he thought he had left the body. Shivers and goose bumps forgotten sweaty palms and upper torso were now the regimen of the day.

He looked over the embankment edge. The body lay on its back at the bottom, its legs apart but the dress neatly in place just below the knees. For several seconds David stared at the unknown woman's dead, pale face and turned away and puked on the grass verge near the side of his car.

A man who always carried a handkerchief, David wiped his mouth and a spot off his tie and went back to his spare tire, jack and cross-wrench. Methodically, almost trance-like, David began changing the tire, only vaguely aware of the traffic periodically whizzing by. Occasionally he wiped the beads of sweat from his forehead with greasy fingers. Certainly he did not notice the OPP cruiser pull up on the shoulder behind.

"Good evening," said the constable, "everything alright?"

Startled, David jumped, the cross-wrench just missing his foot as it fell to the shoulder. "Officer, oh, er, yes, thanks, just a flat tire," David hoped the guilty look he knew was on his face didn't show in the flashing red lights and headlights of the cruiser.

"It might have been a good idea to put out flares, sir," said the constable, apparently not noticing David's nervousness. "Sorry to startle you."

Still a little too hesitantly, David managed a "Yes, thank you, you're right, of course," as he picked up the wrench and bent back to his task loosening the last lug and yanking off the wheel with its offending tire.

"Well, please give it some thought next time," the constable said. "I'll stay around until you're done. Funny how most people notice my red lights," he smiled.

David didn't look back, just nodded and began to lift the flat up toward the trunk before he realized he hadn't removed the spare. With the spare in place, he began to tighten the lug bolts in tune with his stomach. He did summon the courage to glance in the direction of the police cruiser, but could see nothing through the glare of the headlights. He heard the police radio squawk and assumed the constable was doing a CPIX check on his license. David found no comfort in this knowledge and in his current state of distress he couldn't remember if he had any outstanding tickets. In response, he picked up the pace of his work.

"Well, I'll be on my way. Good night," the constable said as David again jumped at the sound of the voice. He had not heard the constable walk up to him as he replaced the jack and tossed the flat tire into the trunk, all the time telling himself to calm down. "Thanks for stopping," he said, now amazingly calm and controlled. "Good night," he said.

He couldn't believe he actually waved as the police car pulled onto the highway. David slammed the trunk lid, got into the car and drove away.

It came as a surprise to him that he had decided to leave the body at the bottom of the embankment staring with unseeing eyes at the moonless, star-filled sky.

8

* * * * *

Bern was a few days ago. Seven to be precise. Since then, Rita's long blond hair had been cut to shoulder-length auburn and even more recently, since last night, it had been hacked to a very short black. The revealing forest green gown with the slit to mid-thigh she had worn to the Turkish Embassy reception had been replaced by faded jeans and some kind of generic, baggy black hoody with a faded Roots logo on the front. The six inch heels had suffered a similar fate, having been replaced by well-worn sneakers.

In the same time period she had gone from the four-star Hotel Savoy Bern to an old dorm room at the University of Geneva. For the first two days Rita had been able to risk eating in some of the old student haunts, until one evening from her small table in a back corner she had seen a familiar face pass by the window. It was the face of the man who had almost caught up with her in Bern, the man who had spotted her too late passing through the Hotel Savoy lobby, the man who had stood fuming and gesticulating on the curb as she had ridden away in the last cab outside the hotel. Now he was in Geneva, searching for her around the student areas.

She had left the bistro along with a group of boisterous students and believed she had made it back to her dorm room undetected. From then on it had been two days of sneaking in the middle of the night to get food from the vending machines in the snack room on the ground floor until her small change had run out.

A few hours ago she had seen the Russian again, this time standing talking to students on the grass outside her dorm window. It was only a matter of time now before he kicked her door in. The chair propped under the doorknob notwithstanding, it was time to break ground while she still had a chance, if she did have a chance. It was a three-quarter moon and she had waited for an hour just inside the rear fire exit to the dorm until a wayward cloud had covered it, enabling Rita to run to the trees across the lawn.

* * * * *

Alexei had driven to Geneva based on some expensive information from a Bern taxi driver and a station conductor. It turned out to be worthwhile information, though it had taken him three days to be sure. On day three he realized he had seen someone that could be Rita sitting in the back of a bistro in the student district, but by the time he had done an about-face and entered the bistro the table in the back was empty, a half-eaten meal still on the table. The woman he was now sure was Rita could have gone to the toilet, but he didn't think so. There was a line-up. The thought was confirmed when a woman clearly not Rita came out the toilet door. Alexei was convinced. He had found and lost Rita again.

When he had silently sprung the lock and opened the door to her dorm room on the third floor at the University of Geneva, he had every expectation that she would be there. She wasn't. Once again, he knew he couldn't have missed her by much—the indent in the bed where someone sat was still there. Briefly, he cursed himself for waiting until the building was quiet before entering and going up to Rita's room. He had had to choose between risks—being identifiable to the police or Rita vacating the room. As he watched the front and rear exits from his cover half an hour previously, a random cloud had blocked the moonshine and Alexei had thought he had seen movement on the lawn to the trees opposite, but he had decided it was a case of very active imagination. Now he suspected he had been wrong.

He had retrieved his car and driven to the train station, arriving in time to see a train leave for Lyons. At the nearby bus station he had just missed a bus to Basel. Alexei made a decision—she was going to Basel. That's what he would do, what any well-trained experienced professional would do. It was the least likely choice, the choice that was slower and exposed the agent to danger longer. Alexei had enough respect for Rita that based on her past decisions she would do the least likely. Basel. So, the hunt was on again.

CHAPTER THREE

David Stone loved Boston, though he would have felt the need to qualify the statement with some reference to Toronto, a city he loved unashamedly. He had gone to school in Boston—Newton really—and had lived in the suburbs of the old city—Dedham, Medfield and Walpole. "South Walpole, actually," he'd say in order to try and disassociate himself from the infamous Massachusetts State Prison.

    David was attending a social service administrator's conference and while he had found the conference agenda worthwhile enough to justify the expense to his agency, he had also been attracted by the opportunity to spend some time in Boston. He had enjoyed the day-long session on the use of innovative technologies in NGOs, had attended another on charismatic leadership (reminding him of his seminary days in Newton), and another on staff supervision techniques as well as a panel presentation on foundation fundraising. In the off hours he had seized every opportunity, along with a couple of other attendees and a friend from Marblehead on the Northshore, to visit some of his old haunts.

Jacob Wirth's—a long famous German restaurant with sawdust on the floor and waiters in tails, was a must, as was the Golden Dragon in Chinatown. They also got to watch the Red Sox beat the league-leading Blue Jays at Fenway Park, as well as take a ride south down Route 1 to South Walpole and stuff themselves on the clams served so plentifully at the Red Wing.

All in all, David had found the conference helpful enough to justify the costs to his agency. He was not one of those administrators who would waste agency money for the sake of a travel op. He had thoroughly enjoyed Boston again and the opportunity to see old friends, but he had had enough. Now back in his hotel room overlooking Copley Square, David hung up the telephone after talking with Mary and their daughter Sara—son Michael was at work. Five days away from home was all David could take. He missed Mary and the kids and wanted to be home again. At six thirty the next evening, Friday, he would board his flight home at Logan airport. Already he could sense his distancing himself from his second favourite city.

Until he'd met Mary and her kids seven years ago, David had moved around a great deal, not really settling down anywhere or to anything, let alone anyone. He even moved within the same community many times as if born with a natural aversion to possessing the same address for any long period of time. Not wanting to be trapped with a label of permanence, always wishing to be in transition. There had also been a few changes in profession along the way as well, clearly marking change as the constant in his life.

Raised in England as a child, in Canada as a teenager, and living in the United States in his twenties, David possessed an interesting cross-section of English-speaking culture and education. David possessed very little accent in his speech, though there were occasional snippets of Bostonian and Yorkshire. Not to mention a Canadian "eh."

As an only child, David had a kind of independence and self-sufficiency which tended to scare some. Mary, on the other hand, had all kinds of family with the accompanying disagreements, arguments and blow-ups. David never did understand these. He only had friends who, if they treated him the way family treats you, would not remain friends overnight. David's understanding of this aspect of family relationships was purely clinical, not experiential.

An introspective, overly analytical person, David was often hard on himself and those around him. In spite of at least quarterly pledges to calm down, relax and lower his standards, he usually failed miserably. "J'essaie," he would say, "I try," and shrug his shoulders until the next quarterly self-examination and self-flagellation.

The inner peace David sought had always eluded him. A good administrator and clinician, David could not always stop himself from opening his mouth and letting the blunt truth, as he saw it, escape his lips. Even if the timing was just a tad off. He fully realized that Mary was probably one of the few women in the world who could live with him for more than a month.

David opened the book he had picked up and began to read. But his mind wandered back to Mary and the kids and his longing to be home with them—his family, where, for the first time in his life he actually was finding a measure of peace and contentment. Indeed, one might even say a feeling of safety and security. With Mary and the kids in his life, David had softened and become more realistic in his expectations and more relaxed and open to enjoying life. He was also more vulnerable.

"Less than twenty-four hours," he said out loud and focused his mind on the novel open before him. He had no inkling of what the road home would bring.

* * * * *

Not very good at being predictable, Rita had gone on the train to Lyons, getting off at Pont-d'Ain, a few stations down the line from its destination. Two more days and a series of buses and milk trains finally took Rita to Amsterdam where for the first time she had been able to place a call to Joel Jerrow, her control back at Langley, or wherever he was States-side. When the call had gone through, Rita was shocked when she was told that Jerrow was not available, but that he had left instructions that she should avoid Schiphol airport and make her way to England by ferry and then to an airport and fly to the northeast U. S. The conversation had been cut short by the Langley man with the unfamiliar voice. Rita had had no time for discussion or argument. The people at Langley were supposed to know where it was safe, but she really only trusted Jerrow and had to struggle to overcome her suspicions. Given all that, she had no choice but to trust the information she was given, no matter how strange it appeared. How plausible was it that the Russians had the resources to watch all the international airports in Europe? Then again, what she carried was vital. She was bright and experienced enough to avoid Frankfurt and Schiphol. The latter, Rita had been to before and was happy not to watch the mice scurrying around her feet late at night while she had a drink and a simple sandwich at the Cone Bar.

For her part, Rita would have preferred a train to Copenhagen, a flight to Oslo and then New York, but someone at Langley in Jerrow's name wanted her in England and she was not given a chance to argue or question why. Ferries take a long time. It had occurred to Rita that that would make them least likely to be watched. She would learn she had been wrong. "Do as you're told," she had ordered herself and looked for ferries to Britain.

The ferry from the Hook of Holland to Harwich would take about seven hours, the train from Amsterdam another couple, followed by another train ride from Harwich to Liverpool Street Station. "Then what?" she wondered. Which airport—Heathrow or Gatwick in London, Manchester, or Prestwick in Glasgow? Probably north would be safer, but then again, the Russians could have figured she might think that. She would decide on the long ferry ride.

* * * * *

When the phone call came, Alexei was in Frankfurt, hoping to see Rita booking a flight to the U.S. He had lost her trail yet again. Indeed, he had lost, period. Now a phone call had changed everything. Rita Brickston was going to England by ferry and he had ample time to arrange a welcome for her.

CHAPTER FOUR

Seven a.m. was not her favourite time of day. In fact, ten a.m. was only considered marginally better. Nevertheless, Mary Stone left the comfort and warmth of her water bed for the hard, cruel realities of the wooded bedroom floor and a trek to the bathroom to get herself ready for work. She was too late. Sixteen-year-old Sara was already there ahead of her. The daughter reluctantly admitted the mother and another day began in the Stone household. Except, of course, David was not at home. A fact highly resented by Mary, now having gone four days without her morning snuggle.

Dark haired and dark eyed, Mary Stone, at the age of forty, was still a good looking woman by any standards. At a svelte five foot five when she dressed to the nines, which was almost daily to go to work, men still stared as she swished down the street. Not overly endowed with self-confidence and a good self-image when she first met David, Mary had thought David was nuts when he regularly called her beautiful and sexy. She firmly believed that David saw her only through the somewhat jaundiced eyes of love—for which Mary daily gave thanks. She was equally thankful that David very clearly felt the same way in reverse, that is, he could not really understand his good fortune in finding and having a woman like Mary.

Mary had met David some seven years before when she had finally got up enough courage to extricate herself from what had turned out to be an unhealthy marriage. Sara had been nine at the time, Michael ten. Mary had not wanted entanglements. She had been feeling trapped for eight years and was not about to yield an inch of the freedom she had just recently attained. David was in no hurry, nor was he interested in a legalized entanglement like marriage. He too had had his share of distorted and distended relationships. David found Mary confronted him with regular doses of down to earth common sense from which he was kept by his sometimes analytical and philosophical head trips. He gave Mary the shots of self-confidence that she first needed to cope as a single parent clearly adored by her two children.

Slowly, carefully, their relationship grew. They bordered on the punctilious in controlling its evolution—a primary concern being the well-being of Sara and Michael. The two children liked David but living with him was something else again. It all came together, however, five years ago when Mary and David, with the children's blessing, got married and bought an eighty-year-old house on a large lot with three black walnut trees they harvested each fall. The house was in Stoney Creek, an historic town just southeast of Hamilton and at the beginning of the fertile fruit growing crescent of Southern Ontario.

Stoney Creek was famous for its Winona Peach Festival and the Stoney Creek Dairy to which families came for tens of kilometres for the famous ice cream, and an annual reenactment of the Battle of Stoney Creek. In June 1813, an inferior number of First Nations warriors, Canadian militia and British troops routed a much larger force of American invaders in what was at the time an unorthodox night attack. Every June, David and Mary dressed up in period costumes and participated in the mock Battle—Mary as a camp follower and David as a surgeon. The experience, while exciting and enjoyable in its own way, also exposed them to the often cruel and brutal lives of early nineteenth century Canadians.

As she went upstairs to wake her son for school before leaving for work Mary smiled and told herself, "David and the kids and I are doing okay." Still smiling, she tripped over Michael's bow in the upstairs hallway near his room. David and Mary had gone out for dinner the Saturday before and Sara was staying overnight at a girlfriend's. Michael, as was his wont, had been left alone and laid his trusty bow and arrows beside him on the couch—"just in case." The bow and arrows had, in the intervening six days, found their way to the upstairs hallway. That was unlike her own bow, which Mary had hung in its place along the basement stairs.

Archery was something Mary had taken up many years ago and had become something she could do with her son, who was yet to best her.

After saying, "Shit," Mary, not the world's most avid house cleaner, left the bow where it was and went into her son's room to wake him for school, only to discover that this was his late day for classes.

"That'll teach him to clutter up the hallway," she smiled to herself and thought as Michael fell almost immediately back to sleep.

"When's David coming home?" asked Sara. The children—reaching young adulthood now—had always called him by his first name. They had a father whom they loved and who saw them regularly.

"Tonight," answered Mary, having given Sara this information at least twice a day since David had left.

"Oh good. I need help with my Math. I wonder what he's bringing us from Boston?" she said in a mercenary tone with a twinkle in her eye.

"Clam chowder or maybe beans," said Mary over her shoulder, excited herself about her husband's return and wondering what he would bring her. Custom in the Stone household demanded presents all around, though David was firm in his refusal to bring any back to Minnie and Mustard, the family's cat and bird.

*　*　*　*　*

Rita changed her mind. Before leaving Amsterdam, she had taken the time to buy the clothes that would radically change her image. She had always loved Amsterdam. It was the only city she had visited where when you left the train station there was free parking for at least two thousand bicycles, whereas cars shelled out Euros for more distant underground parking. Rita loved the beauty of the canals and admired the endless bike paths.

Memories came flooding in. Cyclists everywhere in the frequent rain, their multi-coloured umbrellas in one hand as they navigated their way over the tram tracks, along the canals, over the bridges and down the city-wide bike paths. The night she had nearly died in the line of duty. She had killed a Russian who had gotten too close and returned to her room in shock. It was in the former canal house, the Hoksbergen Hotel, on the Singel not far from the Flower Market. When Jerrow had entered the room enveloped in dejection obviously thinking her dead, sudden relief and joy whipped across his face at the sight of her. They had found themselves in each other's arms. A still unresolved sleepless night had followed. They were old memories apparently still easily made fresh.

There was no rain in Amsterdam this day as she did her shopping. Rita avoided the multitude of shops at the Central Station, opting for De Bijenkorf department store located at Dam Square. This department store, translated as The Bee Hive, was at least two levels above The Bay or Macey's. There was no doubt in Rita's mind that De Bijenkorf would have exactly what she needed. She was right.

Once on the ferry, she would doll herself up, making herself look like a businesswoman with a conservative suit jacket and skirt and medium heeled pumps, white silk blouse, colourful scarf and the popular wide-brimmed hat.

What saved her life in Harwich, however, was the black beamer she had rented. At Harwich, her reception party quickly ogled the good-looking dark-haired woman with the floppy hat in the BMW, but hurriedly moved on to surveying the discharging foot passengers headed for the train station. As she drove by, Rita noticed her reception committee, smiling to herself as she left them behind. She was curious however, as to how they had known where she would be.

With seven hours to plan, and with a good highway map of England at hand, Rita decided to leave the car at Peterborough where she would buy a ticket through to Edinburgh on the northbound train. To mix her trail up more, she would get out at Doncaster in South Yorkshire, leaving the train to continue north without her. From Doncaster, an old rail hub, she would catch the next train to Manchester airport where she would take the first available plane to North America.

* * * * *

The two men fucked up. They had been given the simple assignment of "helping" Rita when she arrived at Harwich. On the surface it was a no-brainer, the CIA agent was to be, had to be, on that particular ferry, a very expensive bribe to a security official at the Hook of Holland had shown Rita on CCTV boarding the ferry. Unless she had jumped overboard into the North Sea, decidedly unlikely even in the summer, she must have gotten off at Harwich. They had a good, though slightly grainy, picture of their quarry.

It seemed that the briber at the Hook of Holland terminal had failed to keep watching the video replay. If she had, she would have seen Rita disembarking the ferry five minutes later. If she had watched the footage from the CCTV camera covering the parking area—something she would have done had she not seen Rita walking onto the ferry, she would have plainly seen Rita emerge from a BMW and walk to the ferry. It was to the BMW she had returned when she disembarked and drove onto the ferry wearing the broad-brimmed summer hat—something, according to the saleswoman in De Bijenkorf, was favoured by European professional women of means making their way to and hopefully through the glass ceiling of the corporate and banking world.

* * * * *

Forty-three minutes elapsed before the missing of Rita was reported to Alexei's boss, General Zukarov. No slouch, even when enraged, after carefully noting the names of the two men who had missed their prey, he contacted the SVR floater not far from the Hook of Holland Ferry Terminal and had her review the videos from all cameras. To ensure that Rita stayed on the ferry, he told her to watch the CCTV covering embarkation until the ferry took in its lines in preparation for departure.

It hadn't taken long, just five minutes and there was Rita fighting her way against the flow of boarding passengers and walking quickly away. A few minutes later the SVR floater witnessed Rita climbing into a bimmer and follow the last two cars onto the ferry. It was immediately obvious how she was missed disembarking at Harwich. The unimaginative, soon to be unpleasantly reassigned, watchers in Harwich had easily been deceived by a talented professional.

When he had learned the story on his arrival at Heathrow, Alexei had had to rely on the proverbial Plan B, in this case the last of his resources—the two person teams he had already dispatched to Heathrow, Gatwick, Manchester and Prestwick. The four person team outside the U.S. Embassy in London were the best he had. If there was one thing about which Alexei was certain—Rita had not gone to the Embassy nor had any Embassy staff left it to meet her. Because of the SVR mole somewhere in their midst, Alexei knew the CIA team around Rita was small, very small. In fact he knew it was just four people, including Rita.

Rita Brickston, or whatever name she was using now, in Holland it had been Maureen O'Driscoll, was going home. The microchip, which revealed among many other things the identity of the highly placed SVR mole in the CIA, was being delivered personally. It seemed Alexei's bad run of luck might still have an opportunity to change.

Leaving his airport teams to do their best against a very skilled adversary, Alexei, trusting his instincts, had stayed at Heathrow where, after checking with the team there, had taken the first available flight to the northeastern United States. He ended up in Philadelphia. It had been a terrible flight—he had been incommunicado for seven and a half hours with no way to check out his hunch. The female agent, he had been assured, had gone to England to come to America. Alexei knew there was always a risk, however slight, that her plans had been changed and she might pass the item in England. Such an act, once done, meant the chase was over, and the hunter would go home without his prey. Mother Russia would have lost another one. A SVR mole brought into the light. Notwithstanding the risk, Alexei trusted his gut, more than his source, and that told him Rita Brickston was going home, microchip and all. And he would be ready to greet her.

Once through customs at Philadelphia International airport, Alexei looked for and found the coffee shop. After asking if it was alright, he sat down next to a rather portly man in a three-piece suit, briefcase safely ensconced under his chair—the image of the American corporate executive in transit. An agonizing ten minutes passed while the executive mentioned the local weather and his fear of flying, finally making his departure insisting that Alexei keep the copy of the Philadelphia Inquirer which rested on the table between them.

Alexei, of course, had had to stay several minutes pretending to read the paper's first section which had been separated and left on top of the others. Finishing his coffee, Alexei was able to walk out of the coffee shop, paper in hand. He had detected no tail and identified none on the man in the business suit with whom he had shared the table. After pitching the newspaper in a trash can in a men's room, Alexei went to another coffee shop where he opened the envelope which he had found in the Enquirer's comic section. Someone had a sense of humour, Alexei thought to himself.

There was no change in Alexei's facial expressions or in his body language but he felt relief, nonetheless, as he read that the target had left what amounted to three hours prior for Toronto. The second team member at Manchester had been spared the fate of her colleague by using the toilet at the time Rita came through the airport. She had been smart enough, however, to catch Rita boarding an Air Transat flight destined for Toronto. Rita's going to Toronto was a lucky break. Toronto had well over a hundred thousand Russian ex-pats which meant the Consulate there had more than the usual number of SVR and FSB undercover officers to keep an eye on them.

Gambling that Rita wasn't going to Toronto to hand off the microchip but because it was the first flight to North America she could catch, Alexei arranged a reception team whose job it was to follow, observe and let themselves be seen. If done correctly, Alexei's arrangements would keep Rita away from booking a flight to the U. S. If the plan worked, Rita would have to resort to a bus, a train or a car rental. Based on Rita's proven abilities so far, Alexei expected she would choose the latter—a lot safer than being trapped on a bus or train and ultimately a lot faster. The U.S. border is not that far from Toronto. More importantly, Alexei's directions guaranteed that Rita would be successful in her quest to lose any followers. The two people assigned to the car rental agency area would not be so easy to spot, in part because they would not be expected.

The plan had worked. Rita rented a car at Avis, arranging to leave the rental in Buffalo, New York. Revealing her destination was a potentially fatal exhaustion-induced mistake. Within minutes Alexei, now in New York City, had Rita's destination. He was now sure that Rita was going to deliver the microchip personally, not hand it off. Buffalo would be his last chance.

General Zukarov had been explicit when Alexei reported in. There was a grudging compliment on his foresight in being in New York—not anything like the length of comment he would have been subjected to had he been in Northern England scouring the back streets of Manchester using his non-existent Lancashire accent. "Get to Buffalo, before that bitch gets there!" Alexei had already made the necessary reservations, but he had learned that giving the General a chance to sound authoritative was a good management strategy.

For once, Alexei had been lucky. There had been a Pinnacle Airlines flight with vacant seats leaving JFK for Buffalo in forty-five minutes. Once in Buffalo he would rent a car at Hertz—he loved driving big American cars, especially when they were being charged on his Chase VISA card under a name he would never use again once the mission was over.

In New York he had met up with a "pig" by the name of Mikanovich foisted on him by Zukarov. Together they would go and get the microchip. As for the "bitch" Alexei had far too much respect for the so far elusive woman to have anything but admiration. "Bitch" would be the last word he would have used.

Chapter Five

David Stone hadn't driven so slowly since he took driving lessons. This was a slight exaggeration, but not by much. He was discounting the time fifteen years before when at two in the morning he was driving home on what was, even for Massachusetts, a particularly narrow and winding road with three centre lines. Any sane, rational person would have driven slowly under those circumstances. This situation was a little different, of course. In Massachusetts the cause had been alcohol. It didn't take much reflection to realize that it really didn't compare with finding a dead body draped over one's spare tire. He was still in a state of shock and avoiding the possible consequences of leaving the woman's body at the bottom of an embankment.

A reputation as a slow, patient driver was not something which would ever haunt David Stone. If anything, his driving habits were the antithesis to this. There was little doubt in anyone's mind that if driving habits and attitudes could be used as an accurate measure of personalities, David would never have an ulcer. Without driving recklessly, he habitually travelled at ten to fifteen kilometres an hour over the speed limit, often banishing other drivers to the side of the road with the help of some well-chosen four letter epithets. His driving did reflect an aspect of his personality. He was known for being a quick and decisive thinker. A quality that was eluding him at the moment.

David had spent his professional life helping others work through personal crises, but had never really had a serious crisis in his own life. Sure, he had had his moments of emotionally fraught situations just like everyone else, but never a real crisis, until now that is.

Under these circumstances, the normally thirty-five minute drive to Stoney Creek from Highway 405 and the Queen Elizabeth Way—the main highway between Buffalo/Niagara Falls and Toronto—took David forty-five minutes.

By the time he pulled into the driveway of his and Mary's red brick house with the Niagara Escarpment in the background he was no longer in a state of shock but still not able to decide on the next step, even though he had tried to put the drive home to good use thinking things through.

"First of all," he had lectured himself, "you're in serious trouble. You've smuggled a body over an international border. Secondly, you've not reported it but have dumped the body at the side of the road. Third, you're in serious trouble." This was pretty much how the internal monologue went. One big circle, with no end. This lack of decisiveness was very unfamiliar territory for psychologist David Stone.

David was lucky. When he arrived home, the children were not there. This was only lucky in retrospect because he had hoped to delay telling Mary about the body until they were both in bed—clearly the most propitious place for such announcements.

"After all," he rationalized "it hardly seemed appropriate to bring up, in casual conversation, in front of one's children, the startling fact that you had just come from leaving a dead woman's body in a ditch at the side of the road." He could hardly slip it in between telling about the deterioration of Boston's Tremont Street and the excellent clam chowder he'd had at the Red Wing.

"Oh, by the way, a funny thing happened to me on the way home tonight."

David, who prided himself on his ability to "think things through" walked into the front hall of his home to be greeted enthusiastically and lovingly by his wife. With Mary's arms around him, David discovered his well-thought-out plan of action, so seriously pondered during his slow drive, consisted of playing it by ear.

One of the things David consistently forgot was that he did not fare too well when he chose to play things by ear with Mary. Before he knew what was happening he was back to the "Oh, by the way..." approach.

Mary was kind. She allowed David a chance to open a Waterloo Dark and present her with the piece of scrimshaw he had brought her. And since neither of the children were home he hauled out the long, dangly earrings he'd bought for Sara and the Red Sox baseball cap he'd got for Michael. The earrings never to be worn, after the obligatory one time to please David, because "long and dangly" didn't fit with the current self-image, just David's wishful thinking. And the cap? It would go on the wall with the twenty or thirty others—clearly put to better use than the earrings.

Mary was magnificent as well as kind. She smiled and nodded her way through what were to her the preliminaries—she was one of those greatly feared and admired women who always knows that there is something important to be told, and she possessed the patience to go through the ritual necessities of pretending that everything was normal. A quality which had made her a great success as a mother, a quality David also needed from time to time. For David, avoidance worked well until a brief silence fell over the conversation.

"Well," she said, like an all knowing mother seeking explanation from a potentially errant child.

Before he knew what was happening, David spilled his guts. He told her everything, including the fact that the woman had on no panties and bra but did have on long dangly earrings. "Very similar to those I got Sara," he added irrelevantly with a weak smile.

Several minutes passed while Mary absorbed the information, struggled with the shock and believed David wasn't having her on. She then commonsensically put her finger on the immediate problem.

"You've got to go back and get the body." There were no flies on Mary. Later she would panic and have diarrhea. For now, she would be calm and precise.

"Say what?" David was not going to make this any easier having increased his own shock in the retelling with panic once again beginning to well up.

"The body David, you can't leave it at the side of the road. It's not right. It just shouldn't be done." David got the kind of look across his face which indicated that he had no idea that there were clearly demarcated rules of etiquette which applied to the leaving of bodies. An Emily Post list of do's and don'ts.

"Besides," Mary pressed on, "they'll find it in the morning and you'll be in deep shit. Good Christ," the enormity of it all beginning to hit her, "we'll all be in deep shit," the calm was beginning to crack. "The Children's Aid Society will take away the kids!"

David hauled himself out of his own fears and clutched at fact and reason, his quick thinking ability surfacing just in time. "First of all, it's not exactly at the side of the road, it rolled down a pretty steep embankment. And so what if they find it? They can't connect me to the body. I'm hardly a likely candidate for the crime of murder," he chastised, feeling sure of his ground.

Mary experienced relief. It flooded over her like a hot spray on weary muscles, tension began to leave her. Of course David was right. After all, if she thought it through there was hardly anyone she could think of who would suspect David of murder and none of them counted for much in the community—she was being really honest. For a brief instant Mary realized she was actually making a mental list of all the people she could think of who would either believe David capable of murder or would accuse him of it. By the time she had come up with five people, only one of whom would accuse him, she realized she was missing the point of it all. Temporary avoidance by focusing on the non-problem among the real ones.

The brief respite over, the really dangerous problem hit her. The tension returned and she could feel her muscles tautening in preparation for action as the adrenalin began to flow freely again into her system and the calm returned to her mind.

Instantly, David sensed, then saw, the danger signals. The look of calm spreading over her face, a strange, intense sparkle coming to her eyes. Panic, the sort associated with impending doom, once again began to infiltrate its way back with an insidiousness which would soon give it a fair measure of control over him unless he checked it quickly. David opted for speech—the kind that might bring forth information, information bringing enlightenment and knowledge which everyone knows are the death knell of panic.

"What is it?" he asked, a little more tentatively than he would have liked.

"Oh! Nothing," said Mary out of a fear of being right than an attempt at female coyness.

"Don't do that, it must be something. For God's sake spit it out." Speech wasn't helping to stop the spreading panic—it was not resulting in information, but creating more tension and uncertainty tinged with anger.

"Well," pause.

An expectant look, an encouraging nod of the head, a slight opening of the mouth to hint at speech and a gentle beckoning motion of both hands for further encouragement.

"Well," previously stated but this time more positively, more self-assurance backing it up. "It's the police, David."

Warning bells began to ring in the temples, flashing lights—red—blinking incessantly in the frontal lobe, not behind the eyes, the stomach starting to behave as though it just discovered a basketball size piece of suet. All of this happened to David simultaneously, of course, and in a mere three seconds. Somewhere deep in one of the dark recesses of the mind David knew a monster was stirring, a quickly repressed truth, not wanted in the conscious mind, but one he was beginning to understand was going to come inexorably marching forward until recognized in all its horror. David waited. Mary would share the meaning soon enough, throwing a bright white light into the corner and revealing the unwanted information in all its ugliness. "The police," he thought and waited. Then light dawned.

They started to talk over each other. The message was always the same. The OPP constable that stopped David would remember him when the body was eventually found. The details of the CPIX would be revealed and the police would soon come knocking on the Stones' door.

"Shit," David threw into the silence that followed the truth. Inside, David experienced the shriveling which takes place when daylight sweeps in through a crack in the armor and a feared truth is exposed. "Oh! Shit. I didn't think it through," he said. "I was in shock and denial and I've really fucked up."

Mary smiled. "I love you," she said simply and wrapped her arms around him. Of the three main choices: castigation, panic and support, Mary chose the one most needed.

There they stood, for a time, holding each other, rocking a little, giving love and getting strength.

"OK," he said suddenly, "let's go."

"I don't want to go to bed right now," she kissed him and walked toward the mud room. He mostly wasn't thinking of going to bed either. Clearly, they had no option, they had to go back and get the body before it was found. At that moment the idea made sense—after all, what other choices did they have?

All the way back to the north side of Highway 405 where Rita's body lay spread-eagled at the bottom of an embankment, David and Mary talked it over.

The biggest temptation was to call the police. It was an action which had a great deal to commend it. There was no disagreement between the two of them that dealing with such matters was the police's responsibility. A valiant attempt was made by them both to convince themselves that "this sort of thing happens all the time."

Quickly, they realized, when more reasoned arguments came to the fore, that an average citizen finding the dead body, indeed, the not-overly dressed dead body, of a woman in the trunk of his car especially after bringing it, albeit unknowingly, across the Canada/United States border was not par for the course in the daily routine of the average police officer, at least in this particular section of North America.

Mary was able to recount a number of television docudramas and news reports of late addressing themselves to the number of innocent people who were charged and convicted of crimes they did not commit, but only reported, to a suspicious, insensitive and overworked police department, crown prosecutor and judiciary. All with the help of an insensitive and ill-informed headline and sound bite seeking media. The sum total of all their discussion had the net effect of putting reporting to the police in the close to insane category.

No doubt existed, whatsoever, in their minds that the body was a matter for the police. David was an innocent victim of someone else's crime. The fact that he had knowledge of the location of a dead body and had even moved it didn't count. Ordinary, everyday, understandable human panic could easily explain that away. Couldn't it? Again, they were not convinced that the police would necessarily see it that way. Finally, they agreed that they would call the police with an anonymous tip about the body's whereabouts as soon as they had moved it elsewhere.

As they reached the Queen Elizabeth Way—called the Queen E by the locals—cut-off for Highway 405, David realized that he had no idea where, along the other side of the highway he had had his flat tire. His best guess was that it was nearer to the border than to the Queen E.

CHAPTER SIX

Alexei Petrovsky was uneasy. It was the kind of unease that crawled up to the mind through the lower intestines—the kind that cannot be shaken or rationalized away. It sat with sharp teeth slowly gnawing away inside him. There was nothing he could do but note it, like he did almost everything else in his life.

Alexei was an expert at noting things. Filing away this tidbit of information here, that face there, this fact someplace else, that opinion in that box. His mind, like all minds, was an intricate rabbit warren of nooks and crannies jammed to the rafters with data. The difference from most other people, however, was that Alexei Petrovsky could find what he wanted in his mind when he wanted it.

While there were some good reasons for him to be uneasy this night, he knew that these were not the source of the feeling of impending disaster which was waiting to flood over him whenever his highly disciplined mind relaxed.

Twenty minutes into the seventy-five minute flight Alexei turned toward his seat mate and said: "Seven o'clock. We'll be in Buffalo about seven o'clock." There was no reply. Alexei looked more closely, disgust coming over his face as he realized that Piotr Mikanovich was asleep.

"There sleeps one of the identified reasons for my unease." He told himself. "Mikanovich is a pig, and a vicious but not a very bright one at that. But one with important political connections," he reminded himself. A fact which made Alexei dislike him all the more.

Since he had been ordered to not work the mission alone, Alexei had tried to have an agent other than Mikanovich assigned to the mission. The official word was that none was available. Alexei knew differently—Mikanovich had high placed support, and after a couple of years abroad he would be brought back to a desk in Dzerzhinsky Square where he would be better suited to some of the terror tactics of some of the departments in the FSB.

Alexei did not trust Mikanovich. He was not a man motivated by success in the profession, for unlike Alexei himself, Mikanovich saw a successful mission as a way to get promoted, a route to a cushier job, more power and much less danger—in Mikanovich's case, it would be the power of the bureaucrat. On the other hand, there was a reason Mikanovich relished a field assignment—his way of making the best of an otherwise unpleasant situation. He saw it as an opportunity to unleash his sadistic tendencies. This had not escaped Alexei's assessment of his associate. On a sensitive mission Mikanovich's proclivities were dangerous. Very dangerous. A man motivated only to serve himself makes mistakes, too many mistakes because his judgment is always coloured by his desire to meet his own needs. A man whose mind is too full of himself and his desires misses things—little, important things; a man like this pays scant attention to a mission or cares little for the well-being of his associates. Alexei knew that working with such a man he must be careful or he would be dead.

Alexei had had to deal with someone like Mikanovich before—his own father. Surely more wily and intelligent than Mikanovich, Boris

Petrovsky was no less a vicious thug. Also like Mikanovich, he desired climbing the KGB ladder.

When Alexei appeared on the scene in 1977 his father had moved up the KGB ranks while having successfully escaped the purges of Khrushchev and Brezhnev. It was his father's brutal nature that impacted Alexei, however. The regular vodka induced beatings he witnessed his mother receive along with those of his older brother. When it became his turn, Alexei learned how to grit his teeth and bide his time. It was when his father began to brutalize his younger sister following his mother's early death that Alexei decided that enough was enough. He knew that his brother, who was already eyeing a career in the KGB, had learned how to successfully mimic his father's cruel and brutal lifestyle. If anyone was to save his sister it was going to have to be Alexei.

It had been more than a year since Alexei had been a victim of his father's brutality and Alexei was confident that the beatings had stopped. After all, his father knew he was in danger of being beaten himself. Alexei understood that while repaying brutality for brutality might temporarily feel good, it wasn't beyond his father's capacity to have him arrested and charged with assault. In the end, Alexei opted for a more subtle approach, and if it worked, an approach that would be permanent.

Alexei knew his father had enemies—everyone in the KGB had enemies and Alexei set up cameras to catch his father brutalizing his sister. Taking the pictures, Alexei was able to paste on the face of an obviously young teenage male where his sister's face had appeared and left the picture array on the desk of his father's deadliest enemy. It hadn't taken long before Boris was arrested as a degenerate. He could hardly claim that it was his own daughter in the bed which was clearly in a room easily identifiable as Boris's own bedroom.

It had only taken forty-five years, but Boris Petrovsky followed in his own father's footsteps into the gulag wasteland of Siberia. Besides the positive result of Alexei's baby sister being spared more brutality, the fact that their father was now considered a proven degenerate meant that an intensive investigation and interrogation had been launched into every detail of Alexei's and his brother's lives.

As a straight "A" highly competitive athletic student with obvious aptitude for computer technology and foreign languages, Alexei was soon cleared. His brother, however, who had remained unmarried and spent many hours in the company of men and in visiting whore houses, required a more prolonged investigation, one which ultimately plateaued his career.

All of this was eighteen years ago. For Alexei it had made him seek the underground life of the field agent, a job which kept him mostly out of the political intrigue of HQ and Embassies. It meant not much of a social life and no family life. Based on personal experience Alexei had little desire in that direction. Hot passionate no-strings-attached coupling was his preference and such coupling was readily available for someone with his rugged good looks. He knew that in a different world Rita Brickston was a woman he would have liked to bed. She had beauty and brains. He had had enough exposure to this attractive highly intelligent American CIA agent to know.

As he thought about his quarry, Alexei easily admitted a grudging admiration for this clever and resourceful American agent, who had repeatedly slipped through his fingers and those of the agents he had sent to capture her. It now looked as if he had finally outwitted her, however, and avoided the serious consequences of her escaping with the microchip. If she got away, the whole SVR net in half of Western Europe and much more importantly the identity of the greedy mole they had so carefully nurtured in the CIA would be exposed. The microchip had to be retrieved or destroyed.

There would not be very much time, Alexei knew, to get the information back and kill the American before her support arrived—if they hadn't already. Alexei was certain that she was still alone, however. For the CIA this had been a very special mission to acquire information and expose a mole which would mean only a very small select group would be trusted; hence, extremely limited human resources. Alexei already knew from his CIA source that Rita Brickston's support was minimal. He was counting on being able to get to the target before her support could arrive and he was counting on the four and a half hours difference between his flight and hers, since it would only be at the very last minute, if at all, that she would have revealed her destination to Langley. Or so Alexei hoped.

Agents with the hunter sniffing at their heels do not have time to sit around international airports waiting for the right flight. This had been particularly true in Manchester. In this case, Toronto must have seemed like a good choice, typical of the target, because on the surface it was unlikely that the SVR would have any coverage there. Of course, the downside was that her support would also have to come from out of town. It was only luck that the surviving SVR agent had been coming out of the toilet in time to catch site of Rita leaving the Air Transat reservation desk and hurrying for the now boarding flight. There was another downside that Rita probably didn't consider—the large number of SVR agents at the Toronto Russian Consulate, not to mention the SVR and FSB undercover agents in the large Russian community there.

Except for the gnawing intestinal unease, Alexei felt confident. He could smell the scent of the prey and knew he was closing in. He looked over at Mikanovich as a prelude to waking him up and telling him the plan. Again Alexei allowed a look of disgust to cross his face as even in sleep Mikanovich looked like the sadistic thug he really was. A sadism Alexei would use, however reluctantly, to recover the microchip.

Chapter Seven

For the second time that night, Rita registered under an alias in a two-star Buffalo, New York hotel. Rita Brickston of New Haven, Connecticut, signed the registration card as Judith Johnson, Seattle, ICO Industries. As Rita registered the night clerk smiled knowingly, or was it flirtatiously? Rita wasn't quite sure which—exhaustion, physical and mental, was taking its toll. Rita looked again. The night clerk certainly did not look like the kind of man who knew anything, on closer scrutiny he was obviously a different type altogether.

Black hair slicked down, with the kind of face that probably had a five o'clock shadow at birth, the man wore a dark blue paisley patterned tie which clashed dramatically with the pin-stripe in the shirt and dress slacks. A plaid jacket was on a hook behind him. It was the smile. A twisted smile with a slight curve upwards on the right side, which made Rita believe he was the kind of man who would drill holes in bathroom walls so he could watch women guests take showers. Following the fantasy to its conclusion, Rita saw herself as a "psycho-type" victim in a fourth Hitchcockian remake. Realizing that her thoughts were closer to reality than she wanted to admit, Rita turned her back on the denuding eyes of the night clerk and walked to the bank of elevators.

An elevator door opened instantly, making her involuntarily lean back in surprise. She was tired. It had been a rough seventy-two hours. Indeed, the three weeks prior to that hadn't been any great shakes either. Nevertheless, she could ill afford to be startled by elevator doors that open when you press the button—unusual though that may be.

"Get a grip on yourself, lady," she told herself, almost out loud, as she stepped into the elevator and pushed "seven"—the top floor. Two star hotels don't have penthouses. While Rita loved her luxury, a better hotel was totally out of the question. Much harder to find her in one of many two-star places than the few five-star ones.

Rita was not startled when the elevator door opened on the seventh floor. She had gotten a grip on herself. She stepped out into a deserted, somewhat grungy threadbare burgundy carpeted hallway.

"Well, I've picked the right hotel," she thought to herself. There was no little sign facing the elevator pointing the way to the various rooms. She turned right on the assumption that the rooms were numbered in ascending order from the left and 716 would be almost at the end on the right. She was wrong. When she finished cursing herself, she realized that her error was a good thing—someone looking for her just might make the same error—an error which could save her life.

It was your typical cheap hotel room. Two double beds with those atrocious white knobble bedspreads. A blond dresser/desk/suitcase shelf piece. A blond matching desk chair and a blond easy chair with a slightly discoloured cream vinyl-covered foam seat. The focus of the room was a nineteen inch diagonal silver plastic colour television set with a Home Box Office pay converter on top. On the wall over the beds were two unidentifiable seascapes practically big enough to be billboards. One seemed to represent sunrise, the other sunset.

Rita did not search the room, though not without a brief internal struggle.

"This is America," a voice told her, "you don't have to search rooms for listening devices here."

"Bullshit!" another voice replied, "All the more reason. You think America is a free country?"

Rita did not search the room because the opposition couldn't possibly have known she would pick this hotel. Twenty-five minutes ago she didn't know it herself.

A look at her watch told Rita it was nine p.m. which meant another two and a half hours and it would all be over. The three-person debriefing and protection team would be arriving. The chase would be over, the hunted safe. The mole exposed.

Rita was good, very good, at what she did, but this mission had been a close call all the way. Her cover had been blown. She knew that once the debriefing was over she would spend more than the usual amount of time out of circulation—visiting New Mexico, having a little nose change, perhaps a mole or small scar added.

She looked at herself in the dresser mirror and could see the fatigue she was feeling.

"A shower," she thought, "a hot then a cold shower." Visions of cool drinks beside aquamarine-coloured water began to impose themselves on her mind—the fatigue once again reasserting itself. She smiled at herself as she unbuttoned her dress letting it fall to the floor at her feet. She stepped out of it and unhooked her bra, tossing it on the bed nearest the door. The one with the picture of a sunrise over it. Her nipples went hard as the conditioned air hit them. She massaged the ridges her ample breasts had forced the bra straps to dig into her skin. Leaving on her panties, she pulled down her pantyhose and stumbled a little as she used her feet and toes to free herself of them, leaving them in a crumpled mess on the floor beside the dress.

Having dropped her overnight bag down on the suitcase shelf, Rita took out a change of clothes—a pair of jeans she had only worn four times and a top only three. She had not spent a lot of time in England, or Geneva for that matter, doing laundry and the business outfit she had bought in Amsterdam was in a washroom trash can in Peterborough. She laid the clothes next to her bra—it was going back on after the shower—her other one was even dirtier. Pulling down her panties she laid them on the bed next to the bra—they too were going back on. She took one look around the room and with a toss of her head went into the bathroom to shower, her cloisonné earrings swinging in time to her hips.

Rita did not have to use the toilet. That was the first thing she did at the other hotel, just before she called the special number. The one that was a Keene, Vermont number but went to a switching station in Erie, Pennsylvania where the signal went on its way through a scrambler to Langley, Virginia, and then it continued further to ring a telephone in an old Brownstone on 74th Street in New York City.

"This is Red," she had said when the sound of the ringing stopped, indicating someone had answered the phone.

"I'm feeling lazy," came the reply.

"Don't be a brown dog," Rita said to the voice she didn't recognize.

The line went dead. Rita spent the next five minutes going through the hotel listings in the yellow pages picking the hotel where she would shower and wait. The five minutes up, the hotel chosen and a reservation made, Rita dialed the number again. The signal's circuitous route now went to a New York airport hotel. There was no noticeable delay before the indication of a ringing phone came through the ear piece. The phone was answered on the tenth ring. That was the understanding.

"J. Jerrow speaking, who's this?"

"R. Fox," said Rita.

"Thank God you're alright," came the response. "Tell me."

"Buffalo, the Broadway," she said.

"Two hours." The line went dead.

Rita smiled, picked up her unopened suitcase and walked out of the hotel—by the back stairs. She had appreciated the "Thank God"—it was against the rules, but it felt good to be missed, especially by Jerrow.

Rita had felt the fatigue sapping her alertness as she crossed the street a block down from the abandoned hotel and rental car to go into the foyer of another and into a phone booth where she called a cab. Originally, Rita had driven down this street because it had several cheaper hotels. She had purposely picked the first hotel because it was only a block from the one she was now in. She could ditch the car, use the phone, call a cab and when the cabby arrived complain about mislaid reservations and surly desk clerks while asking about the Broadway. A reservation she had actually made herself while waiting to talk to Jerrow.

All that was thirty-five minutes ago. In the bathroom, Rita turned on the bath water. The prescribed procedure called for baths. Rita hated baths. The book said that a bath was to be taken with the bathroom door full open, the agent sitting facing it. Gun to hand. The book didn't mention what to do with the taps which seemed to always face bathroom doors in hotel rooms. It did happen to mention what the agent should do with her gun—place it on a dry towel on the bathtub rim. Rita hated baths, besides, her gun was in Geneva and the only person who knew where she was was Jerrow and his team if he told them. Rita trusted Jerrow. A good thing since her life literally depended on that trust.

When she had the mix of hot and cold she wanted she pulled across the shower curtain, turned on the shower and stepped under the streaming hot water. She felt her body relax. "Just two more hours," she thought.

Rita closed her eyes and let the hot water pound her face and exhausted body. The visions of aquamarine water returned as she felt her remaining energy draining away. In another minute it would be time to switch from the hot to the cold water. It was far too soon to let dreamy relaxation take over. Rita neither heard nor saw her hotel room door open.

Chapter Eight

Joel Jerrow stared out of the window into the darkness, the only sign of life his own reflection staring back. He was tired. He had barely slept in forty-eight hours, managing a restless sleep of a couple of hour's length in New York. That had been yesterday. Jerrow's body had no idea what time it was and it was only by an act of will power that he knew he was on a CIA private jet heading for Buffalo.

His mind began to wander. He knew it was the exhaustion. He could not give in to it, let it take over. Jerrow knew the limits of his self-control. Rather, he did not know the limits, he had never reached them. He let the fatigue lap over him, toying with it as though it had a persona all its own, deceiving it into thinking that it could have its way with him.

Years ago Jerrow learned to work with what he had. Right now he had exhaustion. If he used it correctly he could get some rest, trick his body into thinking it was relaxing. Through this practiced self-delusion Jerrow knew he might gain a morsel of energy. Later this energy morsel could create a chemical reaction in a synapse leading to a thought that saved his life.

There were two basics in Jerrow's trade, sleep and eat whenever you can. He was too far gone to sleep, but he could do the next best thing, deceive himself into relaxing, the prelude to sleep.

As he stared into the darkness beyond the window, Jerrow let his mind wander. He was flying, but not to Buffalo. The airplane was heading east, to Cape Cod. To home. The summer home owned by his family for three generations. It was no longer a large jet engine aircraft, but a single engine propeller driven craft. Jerrow could feel the tension dropping off his face muscles. It was a few years ago he had just come back from a very difficult mission in Amsterdam. Out the starboard window, he could see the narrow spit of heavily populated sand that was the Cape, with Martha's Vineyard and Nantucket beyond, as the plane banked and dipped into a landing pattern. Through the windscreen Jerrow saw the colourful wooden harbour buildings, wooden docks some piled with lobster pots, the bare masts of ketches, yawls, and sloops, the tiered layered cruisers of the Cape Cod rich and a smattering of fishing boats come into view. The pilot chuckled, obviously enjoying the challenge as the warmer air of the land hit the summer cold water of Cape Cod Bay.

Jerrow turned away—he had seen it all before. He knew his brother could land the plane, indeed, had been with him facing much choppier waters than that in the sheltered harbour now coming up fast and in conditions which made this breezy, warm summer day seem tranquil in the extreme. His brother knew his business.

As the seaplane landed, spray from the green water of the harbour splashed against the window. Jerrow was transported to another time. He was smiling as sunlight glistened off the spume thrown up by an outboard slicing through the water. He opened his mouth to let the foam fall into it. He closed his eyes against the salt sting as his face was drenched in the spray—suddenly she was there, blond hair plastered to her face, almost golden in the sunlight. He reached out to her, pulled her down. His mouth covered hers as the cold green water washed over them. He felt Rita's breasts harden from the cold, her lips soften to his.

Jerrow blinked. Self-control brought him back from the brink. There was the sound of jet engines in his ears and in the window was the reflection of a tired man who for a brief instant almost looked happy.

When Rita's cover had been blown in Bern by that "bastard Russian" and she had gone to ground in Geneva, all Jerrow could do was worry. When after five days with the Russian sniffing ever closer she had run, Jerrow was beginning to think she was dead. He had no idea that Rita had just gotten out by taking a series of buses and milk trains to Amsterdam. Nor did he know that once there she had called in and was shocked when she was told that Jerrow was not available. The only instructions he'd left were to wake him the minute she called in. He had certainly not left instructions that she should avoid the airport and make her way to England by ferry from the Hook of Holland heading for Harwich, and then to an airport and fly to the northeast U. S.

It wasn't until another day had passed, after Jerrow had spent a ragged night full of dreams and nightmares, that Rita had called in from Manchester. It seemed there had been a novice SVR man waiting for her at Manchester airport and she had been forced to kill him. The Russian had been young and green and very shocked when he felt the needle enter his neck, its sharp point plunging deep. For the briefest of instances the Russian agent felt the hot liquid shooting inside him. It was his last thought.

Rita had left the body slumped on a seat in the main terminal. It could be ten minutes or ten hours before someone screamed to announce that the man next to them must have had a heart attack and was dead. They would have been right, the drug Rita had injected did give the man a heart attack; that's how tanghin works. She had left her hypodermic syringe in the trash container in the ladies room, hoping that if it were found the finder would assume that some junkie had used the washroom to shoot up. She didn't know another Russian agent was in a nearby stall.

Jerrow listened. He had let her talk because she had just killed a man and she had to do something with the now useless adrenalin coursing through her veins.

"You're alone," he told her, "you've done well. You're almost out of the hole. Take the first flight to the northeast, in fact, anywhere on the continent. Just get out. Call me at the number seven," he paused. There was silence.

"Alright?" he asked meaning it in both senses.

"See ya," came the flippant reply and he knew she had regained control.

No mention had been made of the instructions to take the ferry or of Jerrow's apparent unavailability. There had been no time. All that would come out in the debrief. For now, what Jerrow didn't know wouldn't hurt him, though it might kill Rita.

That conversation was yesterday. Now he knew where Rita was and he and his two-man team would be with her in an hour and a half. Back to wakefulness, Jerrow remembered how close he had been to declining this mission, certainly something he would have done under normal circumstances. His feelings for Rita were not clear or rather they were too clear. They had become involved ten years before on Rita's second mission. Even back then Jerrow had a reputation for getting the job done—for demanding more of the Company than it was willing to give, for pushing his team further than they could safely go, for pushing himself as far as was necessary, and for not playing the internal political games that went on around him. Jerrow had been a man working on becoming a legend, and didn't even know it—a fact which simply added to the legend.

At the time, ten years ago, Rita had had a secondary role—a diversion which, while risky, was not considered by anyone to be dangerous to the point of lethal. Anyone was wrong. The Russians had followed the diversion further than expected. Either they honestly thought they were onto something or they knew better but wanted to take out what they must have known was a novice agent anyway. By the time Jerrow realized what was happening he was impotent to intervene. Rita was alone—for the first time—on the end of a long string.

In Jerrow's enraged mind, Rita was dead. Jerrow was wrong. Which meant he was not as bad off as the Russian—who actually was dead. It had taken all the self-control Jerrow could muster to complete his assignment and return, angry and sullen, to the canal hotel. He lost his self-control when he opened the door to find Rita in one of his clean shirts, her hair still wet from the shampooing and shower.

Jerrow moved toward her and found his arms around her kissing her still damp hair, her tear-filled eyes. They had made love that night, ignoring all the rules, letting their pent-up emotions spill out, their loneliness and fear exposed. Jerrow had never forgotten the look of her in the morning, tousled hair splayed on the pillow, yellow in the morning sun, the curve of her breasts under the sheet. She had woken up and smiled at him and they had made love again, slowly, rhythmically. That was ten years ago. That morning they had gone their separate ways and Jerrow had not even been in the same room with her, except for a very few times since.

When three years ago, he met Michelle and they courted with passion, Jerrow had still kept his Washington D. C. apartment, but increasingly spent more time at Michelle's loft in Baltimore. Jerrow did not know if that night with Rita was just two people in the right place at the right time or more than that. For ten years, Jerrow told himself that it was the tension and stress of the mission that had made him get involved, "to break-down."

Now, as he looked into the dark window, his reflection staring back at him as the jet began its descent into Buffalo airport, he wasn't so sure. Perhaps his reluctance to wholly commit to Michelle, something which was beginning to sour their relationship, had more to do with vestigial feelings for Rita than his claim that his job wouldn't allow for a normal relationship, which, by itself, was certainly true. One thing was sure, Jerrow felt a deeper connection to Rita, one quite different from connections with other female agents.

"First things first," he told himself. "The microdot. Then the debriefing. Then...."

Chapter Nine

The shower curtain was thrown open behind her so suddenly and a hand clamped over her mouth and another around her waist pinioning her arms, she had no time to react, except to let the bar of soap drop from her hand with a clang onto the bottom of the bathtub. While the man began dragging her out of the tub, one part of Rita's mind was registering everything that was happening as if it were all taking place in slow motion.

Once out of the tub, the shower water continuing to pound with steam now pouring through the space created by the open curtain, water splashing on the floor being soaked up by the bathroom rug and the bare hairy feet of her adductor, Rita was faced with a handsome man who had something in his hand. A washcloth. As the man behind removed his hand the one in front inserted the washcloth into her mouth, effectively gagging her.

When two fingers were inserted to their full length into her anus by the man behind, Rita gave an involuntary start. She noted her jar of face cream open on the counter and realized the cream on the fingers inside her was the cause of the stinging sensation. The blond man facing her did not look over Rita's wet naked body with lust in his eyes. The blue eyes were ice cold and looked straight into hers. Rape was not the motivation. This was not the sleazy desk clerk and one of his buddies. The hunters had caught their prey.

The man facing her leaned forward and whispered in her ear. "We know who you are and what you've got. You know who we are and what we want. My friend and I are experts at this. If you do not tell us what we want to know in the next ten seconds, he will begin to lift you up off the floor using his fingers as the focal point. Trust me when I say it is the least unpleasant thing we are prepared to do." The man behind her began to demonstrate and Rita couldn't avoid wincing. The blond put up his hand for the "unpleasantness" to stop and looked into Rita's watering eyes. "I would regret to have him do that and more to so clever and beautiful an adversary. Do you understand?"

Rita nodded her head. The man rolled up his sleeves and walked to the shower and turned off the water. The bathroom air was heavy with moisture even as the steam began to subside. Behind her she could feel the other man's erect penis rubbing against her buttocks.

When the blond turned back to her, she knew the ten seconds were up. She looked straight into his cold blue eyes and shook her head. Immediately the man behind began to demonstrate his strength lifting her so she could barely touch the floor with her tips of her toes. The pain was intense. It was difficult to tell if Rita was still shaking her head "No" or in agony. Again the blond brought the pain to an end by raising his hand. Rita's heels had barely reached the floor when he pulled her arms from the man behind and yanked her forward doubling her over at the waist.

With one arm around her waist the man behind inserted two fingers into her vagina spreading her legs to get better leverage and vigorously began to probe, obviously looking for some kind of a packet. She knew he would put his whole hand in there if necessary. When he had finished he began on her anus. In spite of her determination, Rita's eyes began to tear from the pain, and she released an occasional muffled involuntary sob. Through it all a possible escape plan came to her.

The brutal cavity searches seemed to go on forever, but only lasted a couple of minutes. The blond man gave her arms up to the hairy man behind who pulled them rigid behind her back. As the hairy man pushed his penis against her left thigh, he began to roughly massage her left nipple between his forefinger and thumb. Rita started at this move, and then lucidly put in place her plan, slowly gyrating her hips against the hairy man's penis. As he grew hard and breathed heavier, she knew that she had him.

The blond seemed not to notice. He looked straight into her eyes.

"Well?" he said. Rita tilted her head in the direction of the bedroom. Her plan would work better if she now seemed compliant.

"We're going to remove your gag, if you yell we will put it back and hurt you like you've never been hurt before. Understand?" said the blond.

Rita nodded.

In the bedroom, Rita's gag was removed and she was pushed onto the bed. When she sat up she nodded in the direction of the clothes at the bed feet. The blond picked up the bra looking at Rita. She shook her head and he dropped the bra back on the bed and picked up the panties. Rita nodded.

Rita watched as the man felt the crotch seams of the panties until he found what he was looking for—an irregular stitch over a section of the seam which was slightly lumpier than the rest.

For Rita, her main problem was the leader, the handsome blond man with the cold blue eyes. The man was a professional who could not be easily manipulated like the other man. He was also clearly focused on one goal—to recover the stolen information. While he would do whatever was necessary to Rita to get it, he would not torture her with pleasure, and when he was satisfied he had what he wanted he would kill her swiftly and cleanly and probably with regret.

As for the aroused thug, he would be pleasured by giving her pain. Rita knew a sadist when she saw one. He was the weak link. Full of himself and his so-called masculine superiority. Trusting in brutality to get what he wanted. Someone Rita knew she could easily outwit and dispatch if she was given an opportunity, something that seemed unlikely given the blond man.

Rita had promised not to scream, a promise she would be a fool to break under the circumstances, but she had not promised not to escape and the way to do that was to enhance the evident dissension between the two Russian agents. The more she could make them focus on each other the less they would pay attention to her. She just might make it into the hotel hallway. If it didn't work, then there was her back-up plan. Not her first choice, but that was why it was a back-up plan. That and its consequences.

Alexei gently and meticulously began to tear at the seam of the panties. A microchip was there. Whether or not it was the right microchip remained to be discovered. "It could be the chip we've come for, it is a good hiding place, but not that good," he thought, "it could be a decoy. We won't be able to stop yet." He realized this with more reluctance than he wanted.

Damp haired, still naked, chilled in the air-conditioned air and in pain, Rita sat on the edge of the bed. With the leader focused on the microchip, and only an eager leering Mikanovich standing guard watching her, Rita knew her opportunity had arrived.

She glanced at Mikanovich, a coy look on her face, a shy smile on her lips and, in spite of the pain, she sat straighter perking her breasts. The look on his face was clear, he wanted to touch them. He wanted to touch her. To fuck her and hurt her. She could see his mind estimating the chances while his colleague, back turned, tore at her briefs. Her eyes, her posture egged him on. Rita knew she would only have a second's warning. Suddenly a change came to Mikanovich's eyes. He had made a decision. As his right hand reached for her left breast Rita grabbed its wrist yanking him forward causing his head to impact the headboard. Rita's other hand shot upward grasping his balls and squeezing, hard. Mikanovich screamed. Rita brought her head up to meet his chin bringing him more pain and making it easy for her to knock him to the floor as she got off the bed and lunged for the door.

It had been a good plan, well executed. It would have worked smoothly if Alexei hadn't double locked the door and put the chain on. She got the chain off and had turned the door knob before Alexei's hand grasped at her shoulder. It was a fleeting grasp. Rita's heel forcefully snapped back into Alexei's knee causing him to stumble, his right hand sliding off Rita's slippery bare shoulder. She yanked open the door inadvertently onto Alexei's ankle and her own knee. The hallway's seedy, filthy carpet, her pathway to freedom, was arrayed before her. Rita half stumbled and half plunged into the shadows cast by the dim lighting, past the ice machine and into the stairwell.

Seven floors. She could scream, but that would take breath and she needed all the breath she could muster to make the lobby. Downward she dove. As she reached the fifth floor landing she heard someone on the stairs above her. Ignoring the pain of her bruised knee she propelled herself downward. The slap of bare feet tramping after her. At the third floor landing, her whole body now hurting in sympathy with her knee, her breath coming in short gasps, Rita sensed rather than knew the pounding feet were getting closer. Could she make the lobby? Rita pushed harder.

On the second floor landing, the red glow of the exit sign now visible, her knee buckled. Narrowly she avoided spiraling headfirst down the stairs. Her pursuer was continuing to narrow the gap. She could now hear his hard breathing. Less than a landing separated them. On her feet once more Rita found the strength to fling herself forward. Downward. The lobby was surely in reach! Then, there it was. The door into the lobby. The panic bar was in her hand. Rita pushed. Staggered forward with the movement of the swinging door. The lobby came into view. She saw a quizzical look on the face of the sleazy clerk behind reception followed by a leer as he realized she was naked.

Then the man dropped from view and the lobby ceiling appeared as an arm went around her neck changing her emerging scream into a gurgle. As she began to choke, Alexei dragged her back into the stairwell. The door closed behind them

As he pulled Rita up the stairs, Alexei correctly assessed that the desk clerk would say and do nothing, expecting monetary compensation when the fun and games were over. Momentarily, Rita lost conscious-ness from the lack of oxygen, but Alexei was adept at allowing just enough of an open airway to sustain life. Finally they were back in the bedroom, the door once again double-locked, chain on, Rita now freed from the choke-hold sucked in oxygen as they dragged her to the sunrise bed her heels getting carpet burn.

Bending forward, with a modicum of respect in his tone, Alexei whispered in her ear, "Nice try."

Rita didn't have time to appreciate the compliment. With the return of oxygen her brain was struggling with "what do I do now"? Her thinking was brought up short when a gingerly standing Mikanovich punched her in the abdomen doubling her over. If Alexei hadn't let her slip coughing and barely conscious to the floor she would have choked herself on his arm. It seemed that the torture was about to begin.

Through watering eyes Rita could see Mikanovich's bare foot swing back to continue the beating. It didn't connect. Instead, Mikanovich went backwards onto the floor his head just missing the bedside table. Alexei had caught the swinging foot and toppled his partner to the ground. "Enough," he said, "for now."

Stepping out of the reach of the no longer gasping Rita, he said, "Get on the bed."

Doing as she was told, Rita's mind began planning again. Her only hope was that the desk clerk would find the courage and sense of civic duty to call the police. She pictured the clerk's leering face. "No hope there," she thought. What was to come next seemed obvious. Alexei would not be happy with what seemed so easy a triumph getting the microchip from her panties. Looming in the background was the clear threat of Mikanovich who, if possible, would glean even more pleasure making sure the microchip was the real one. Torture that would no doubt include not just punches to the outside of Rita's body.

Her not very cheery thought process was halted by Alexei asking in a soft voice, "Where is the real microchip?"

Making eye contact she answered, "There was only one, and you have it." Certainly he would not believe her, indeed, he couldn't afford to believe her.

Mikanovich moved up to the edge of the bed, a look of anticipation on his face, Alexei kept eye contact and in the same soft voice, "We both know you are far too intelligent an agent for that to be true. You also know I don't have much time before your team arrives. It would be very regretful for me to turn you over to *him*." He nodded in Mikanovich's direction.

Rita believed Alexei when he said he would have regret in her torture, but she knew it would happen nonetheless. It was time for plan Z. Still holding Alexei's eyes in her own she opened her mouth as wide as she could and closed it with the force needed to break the capsule in a back molar.

The poison trickled into her throat, and the last thing Rita heard was Alexi scream as he dived toward her. In vain, he forced open her mouth as her body slumped into his arms.

Alexei gently pushed Rita's body back toward the bedhead. Angry, he turned toward the still immobile, shocked Mikanovich. When he spoke you could freeze vodka on the tone.

"We have a great deal to do and very little time. For a change, do your job."

Within thirty minutes the two Russians had destroyed Rita's overnight bag, purse and most of her clothes, looking for another microchip. Alexei had left to Mikanovich a further search of Rita's body. Finally, he believed they had found what they were looking for, another microchip in the bra strap and a third one embedded in the strap of the overnight bag. While pleased, Alexei still found it difficult to believe that one of the three microchips they had found could be the real one. Naturally enough, he was certain that the first chip the American agent had given up as quickly as she did was not the real one.

His portable scanner indicated there was a substantial amount of data on all three chips. The data had been encrypted, so until it was downloaded and de-encrypted they wouldn't know if the chips were what they were looking for. There was always a chance they were all red herrings. Alexei was certain the American agent was capable of withstanding far more torture. It was possible that she had killed herself in the hope that the real chip wasn't found and if it were she wouldn't be able to tell them which of them was real.

As for Alexei's associate, Mikanovich said it was the fear of torture in her genitals that had made the woman give in quickly. He believed that all Western women, as opposed to Russian women, made terrible agents for this reason.

"They all care so much for their genitals and are, therefore, too easily tortured."

Alexei knew better and did not even grace Mikanovich's stupidity with a comment. To Alexei, an agent was an agent, man or woman, Russian or American. Clearly, she had not been afraid of death, even an unpleasant one. As for Mikanovich, if he stayed in the field long enough his stupidity and brutality would surely kill him.

"Yet, still," Alexei thought, "I've seen many tough agents disintegrate in the face of torture, yet never back away from death."

The Russians had run out of time. While he wasn't completely convinced all the microchips had been found, Alexei knew they had to leave or risk being caught. Dressing Rita's body in the dress and shoes they had saved for the purpose, they went out into the hallway, stumbling along as though a little drunk, Rita's eyes staring wide between them.

The hallway was empty and everything went smoothly until they reached the second floor landing. There was a man with a waste basket full of ice at his feet staring silently at the Coke machine. He turned to the surprised looking threesome.

"Just my lucky day. Yessir. My lucky night I suppose I should say. Ha! Ha! Just a little play on words there. Yessir. Ma'am!" he looked directly into Rita's unblinking eyes and nodded his head. After all the "yessirs" it would have been discourteous not to recognize the presence of a lady.

Rita did not respond. Alexei opened his mouth, but was not fast enough. Undaunted by the obvious aloofness of the black-haired woman with the funny eyes, the gregarious man ploughed on.

"Say, fellas, got any change. I got this great bottle in my room but the little lady wants Coke. Gotta have Coke. Won't drink alcohol unless she has Coke in it. Don't know what it is with women that they always want to ruin good liquor with Coke. No offense meant, ma'am."

Rita took none. The man stopped talking and it wasn't just to breathe. His newfound friends were leaving.

Moving forward to the next flight of stairs, Alexei said in his best British accent, "Dreadfully sorry, old boy, don't have a farthing. Cheerio. Good luck with the fluff," and the crisis was over.

The man could only mumble a surprised "Yeah, sure. Thanks, anyway," uncertain what "fluff" had to do with anything.

Alexei was grateful that the hotel had a rear entrance, though he would not have expected the American agent to stay there otherwise. He made Mikanovich stand by the rear door pretending to neck with his female companion while he went and got the car. Alexei already knew where he was taking Rita's body.

They had not wanted to leave the body in the hotel room because they didn't want the CIA to know that Rita was dead. If they found the body in the hotel room it would be easy for them to cover up the death. On the other hand, Alexei reasoned that by leaving the body in the trunk of a car in the overnight parking area of the airport, it could be days before it was found. Once found there would be a great deal of publicity and it would be hard for the CIA to access it. By then the

Russians would be long gone and the identity of the secret SVR mole with them. There was, of course, another reason to dump the body at the airport. If the microchips proved to be false, the body would be readily available. It all certainly seemed like a good idea to Alexei at the time.

Buffalo airport is not especially crowded at ten fifteen p.m. There were seventeen cars in the long-term lot, over half of them hatchbacks. Alexei picked the charcoal grey Camry with the out of state license plates. This could mean the body, when found, might be out of the state too, adding even more confusion. An artist in the profession can open a locked trunk in less than two seconds. It took Mikanovich twenty-three.

At ten twenty-five the two Russians were waiting for the results of the encrypted data of the downloaded chips to come in from the Washington Embassy. If the results were positive, then they would catch the late night to New York City. If negative, then back to the body. As they waited, the passengers came through the airport from the delayed Boston flight. They didn't even notice David Stone as he ambled past them.

Chapter Ten

The CIA Lear jet taxied to a stop at five minutes after eleven Buffalo time and Jerrow, Gardiner and Pasquale walked up to the car rental, picked up the papers and walked to where the car was waiting without paying any attention to the two men two rental agents down franticly trying to get the counter clerk to hurry up. Their car found, Jerrow and his team climbed in and headed out of the airport. A map of Buffalo had been left on the front seat, ignored. While Gardiner took care of the car Pasquale looked up the address of the Broadway, Jerrow programmed the GPS.

They were lucky. It only took thirty-nine minutes to arrive at the hotel. Jerrow went in and walked alone to the front desk and Gardiner stayed in the shadows while Pasquale took the car to the rear door. Jerrow would get Rita out of there and the four of them would go back to the jet and safety.

The night clerk was very reluctant to ring the good looking woman's phone at eleven fifty-eight at night, but the twenty dollars given him by Jerrow seemed to cover his out-of-pocket expenses. When there was no answer, Jerrow flashed an identity card, mumbled something about being a police officer and demanded the room number. Jerrow signaled to a large man—with a brush cut and looking like a Marine, the night clerk noticed for the first time in the doorway, the man began to move forward. The night clerk decided of his own volition to provide the information asked for free of charge. It was not his problem that two men had already gone up to that room a couple of hours before and for all he knew were still there having a good time. Room 716 was a busy place. When all the men had gone he wouldn't mind visiting 716 himself. He had seen for himself how much pleasure a body like hers could give a man.

With Gardiner in tow—the large man—Jerrow found the door to seven sixteen locked. He opened it with the spare key given him by the night clerk.

It was obvious immediately. A small child would have known. The room was more than in disarray and clearly empty. There was no doubt that Rita had been in the room. The fragrance of her perfume still lingered, faintly, in the air. Brutally, Jerrow suppressed a pain which he felt creeping up from somewhere deep inside. He reinforced it with action.

Striding firmly into the room, Jerrow walked up to the night table where there were bits and pieces which could easily have once been Rita's purse. On the floor enough of her face stared sullenly back at him from an open passport. Jerrow was unable to suppress a sad smile.

It had been Russians, Jerrow was sure. He had seen rooms like this before. Moreover, he was himself an expert at tearing apart hotel rooms and personal effects like this. The expertly torn clothing, along the seams, the meticulously shredded overnight case were not unfamiliar sights. It took no more than a glance to realize that in another time, another place, it could have been Jerrow's hands which had done this. The scene was not entirely without hope, however. Rita could still be alive. She might also be dead. Jerrow was willing to acknowledge to himself that the latter was more likely than the former.

He sent Gardiner downstairs to squeeze the night clerk. That would not be too difficult for a man of Gardiner's size and abilities. He'd have the night clerk believing that his entire future survival would depend on the quality of the answers Gardiner was given. Indeed, the night clerk would be right to believe that.

It did not take Jerrow long to find what he was looking for—torn black panties—they were on the carpet under the emptied and cut-up overnight bag, half under the bed with the sunrise painting. He had already noted the slit overnight bag strap and the bra strap. They had found the three microchips. Rita was gone. Mission failure loomed.

While he had no proof, Jerrow felt he was not more than an hour and a half behind Rita and the Russians. It was too long. A person could be anyplace within a sixty-mile radius in that time and moving further away at the minimum rate of a mile every minute. There was nothing Jerrow could do—for the second time he was impotent to help Rita when she needed him. He did not ponder this truth for long.

He separated a pillowcase from its pillow on the sunrise bed and dumped everything from Rita's purse in it along with her passport, black panties, and shredded bra. Jerrow also noted the face cream jar open on the bathroom counter. The cream inside had deep finger sized wedges scooped out. He put the top on the jar, pocketed it and walked into the bedroom again.

For a moment he stood surveying the room. Seeing nothing. Images of Rita threatened to overwhelm him. He knew images would be all he'd have now. Those and images of revenge which he'd have to learn to control when the time came, but not now. Not at this moment. Not here.

Slowly, Jerrow turned his back on the devastated sunrise and immaculate sunset beds, and left, careful to wipe his finger prints off the door knob, his pillowcase bundle dangling from his left hand.

Without knowing it, Jerrow chose to leave the hotel by the same exit as Alexei and Mikanovich. Looking a little like a burglar with his loot in a pillowcase, Jerrow stepped out the rear exit of the hotel. The parking lights on a car in the left-hand corner of the parking lot flashed briefly. Jerrow knew it would be Pasquale, who had been left with the task of covering the outside rear exits, just in case. He waved him forward. Jerrow tossed his load into the trunk.

For his part, the night clerk was beginning to seriously question his ogling of the single women who occasionally stayed in the hotel. Long ago, he had abandoned his fantasy about an early morning visit to Room 716. The good-looking woman with the short black hair, firm breasts and inviting ass who had registered three or four hours before, and he had briefly seen naked confirming all he had imagined, was not worth all this trouble.

While he had not exactly believed the story the two men, who had paid him fifty dollars for her room number, had told him, he did not see it as any more than some kind of a lovers' quarrel. Well, if he was to be honest with himself—a stance with which he was not overly familiar—he knew that he was taking a chance, the two men could easily have been from the mob. Of course, in that case they would have gotten the information out of him one way or the other.

The night clerk knew he was a sleaze. Rightly or wrongly, he had no intention of changing, assuming such change was possible. In the case of the two "guys from the mob," which was how he thought of the two Russians, now the police were involved, he still felt that he had got the best of the deal—fifty dollars for some babe with phony black hair and another twenty from the skinny cop. His current plight, however, could change his way of thinking.

"This man can, and will, do whatever he wants to me. If I walk away with my life—and my seventy dollars, I'll be lucky," he thought as Gardiner held what looked and felt like a cannon to the night clerk's crotch.

"Tell me again," Gardiner said while increasing the pressure of the barrel against the clerk's shrinking testicles.

For the third time the night clerk told his story, obsequiously, and with no embellishment. From the description the petrified man gave,

Gardiner realized that the clerk thought the two men were mob. He did not enlighten him. Gardiner simply told the clerk to empty his pockets and when a fifty dollar bill appeared he asked:

"Is your life worth fifty dollars?" The clerk, who knew better, was not sure of the right answer. The question had a double meaning. The man remained silent, the gun still pressed tightly against his crotch. Changing his mind the clerk opted for evasion, familiar territory.

"It was given to me by the two men," he pointed at the bill, "for the information I gave them," he added hastily.

"Well," said the man, "it did not buy your silence did it?" The clerk said nothing—he thought perhaps more money would be coming his way—he tried to anticipate the next question and placed a dollar figure on the price of his silence.

"I am not buying your silence," Gardiner said, as though reading the clerk's mind, "you are," and he pocketed the fifty dollars. The clerk's mouth opened, but no sound came out.

"If you tell anyone of this, I shall find out, and you will be maimed for life, not killed, maimed. The fifty dollars you have just given me is an investment in your own silence. Because you have given me the money I accept your word that you will say nothing. I will be back in four weeks for fifty more. Will you have it?"

The clerk nodded. Gardiner hit him across the face with the flat of his hand. The clerk's head hit the wall almost concussing him.

"Capiche?" Gardiner asked again as blood trickled from the clerk's split lips.

"Yes," he said barely able to look Gardiner in the face. Gardiner brought the barrel of the gun up hitting the clerk so hard in the diaphragm that he slumped forward and wretched all over the registration counter.

In a cheery voice Gardiner said, "Good. Catch you later," and walked out the hotel's front door into a waiting car. The lucky clerk still had Jerrow's twenty for all his trouble. And the secret of what he had witnessed.

Chapter Eleven

Alexei Petrovsky should have known. There was no excuse he could make to himself. It was obvious. In his mind's eye Alexei could see Rita standing in the shower naked, droplets running down her short black hair like rain onto her breasts and shoulders.

One final deception by the American agent had come to haunt him after her death. Alexei now knew there were no more microchips. He had screwed up. Rita had deceived him one final time. She had used a microdot to convey the information and used the three microchips as decoys. "Brilliant," he thought, thinking of Rita, then "Stupid," thinking of himself. Emotionalism at the sudden suicide of the American agent had led to a mistake, a mistake which, if it did not eventually cost him his life, could certainly cost him the mission. He should never have trusted Mikanovich with the body search, but it was a job he wanted to avoid and they had a lot to search and very little time. It was reasonable to have given the easier job to Mikanovich. After all there was not much to search on a naked body. Was it inexperience that Mikanovich missed it or was he finding too much pleasure in re-searching Rita's body even without any life in it.

At least Alexei was now certain exactly where the microdot was and all he had to do was go and pluck it off the body.

When he had gotten the call that all three microchips were false, Alexei had bounded out of the airport to the parking garage, Mikanovich trailing him. As they watched the car with Rita's body in it drive out of the airport parking lot, the man behind the wheel patently ignoring their waves, he did the only thing he could. Memorize the license plate number. Something a little more useful than Mikanovich's confused epithets. Alexei was not pleased with himself. Putting the body in a out of country car trunk seemed brilliant at the time. When it was found, there would be all kinds of jurisdictional problems, not just between US authorities but between Canadian ones as well. "Very clever," he thought to himself, "and stupid." By the time he and Mikanovich had dealt with a tired, if not incompetent, car rental agent and found their rental, Alexei was in a rage.

His rage, however, was currently under control as General Zukarov's rage was holding centre stage. In fact, it had just delivered one of the longest soliloquies ever given in the Russian language. Certainly far superior in length, if not in content, to anything written by the English upstart, William Shakespeare—an author privately admired and read at length by Alexei. The General seemed to have run out of invective and was in the period of transition from vilification to exhortation which seems to overcome all commanders when their plans are thwarted by the vagaries of luck and the occasional incompetence of their subordinates.

"You must leave immediately," Zukarov said to Alexei who was sitting in the Buffalo Hertz car rental lot trying to do just that.

"I agree, my General," said Alexei, with no hint of sarcasm in his voice. Alexei had wanted to leave twenty minutes ago.

"I would hate for you to fail again, Colonel," stated the General, a hint of menace in his voice.

"Fuck you," thought Alexei, "I've failed before and I'm still around. Failure goes with the job."

He knew that somewhere in a back closet in Yasenevo, the headquarters for the SVR in Moscow, there was an underpaid statistician who could tell you the ratio of success to failure among field agents in the SVR. Alexei was confident that his record showed him solidly within the success curve. Of course, most agents communicated their failures through death. Their own.

Alexei Petrovsky was not in the business for the success curve or to bring fleeting moments of titillation to some backroom drudge of a statistician. He was in the business for the same reason a marathon runner is in a race, to beat himself, to better his last time, to reach a new threshold of personal endurance. Alexei intended to recover the microdot, not so much because Mother Russia wanted it recovered, but because of the personal challenge. When all was said and done, Alexei Petrovsky found fulfilment out on the fringe of a mission, with little more than his own instincts between its success and his death.

"General, I realize you feel I and Mikanovich have let you down, indeed, Mother Russia down, but we need to get after the man with the body as soon as possible." The General having vented his spleen, in fact several spleens, was mellowing.

"Resources?"

Alexei was waiting for this moment. Having had the clarity of mind to note the license number of the car as it drove away with Rita's body in its trunk Alexei now needed to locate the address of the car owner. He now seized the opportunity to inform the good General that prior to calling him he had requested the Russian Consulate in Toronto to get the name and address of the Ontario driver and send someone to watch the man's home. He needed Zukarov to call and ensure that the request had been filled with dispatch. He made his other requests and waited for Zukarov's response.

"All will be taken care of right away. In addition, I will arrange for one of our top SVR agents from the Ottawa Embassy to supplement your team first thing in the morning. You will meet him at Toronto's airport. The details will be sent to you Colonel."

Immediately Alexei began to argue vehemently with Zukarov that every hour wasted was an hour lost in recovering the microdot. Even worse, with each hour that passed they were an hour closer to the time when the body would be discovered. If it hadn't already been. Once discovered, the body would be lost to them and the mission would end in failure. Perhaps Zukarov was used to failure, but he was not. Of course, this last thought was something Alexei kept to himself, it was not the kind of thing he felt comfortable sharing with his superior officer.

For his part, Zukarov pointed out that Alexei and Mikanovich needed papers and special identification and that these could only be safely manufactured at the Embassy in Ottawa. Zukarov's argument continued that since the body wasn't found in the airport parking garage it was not very likely it would be in the middle of the night. He reasoned that even North Americans did not spend a lot of time in the trunks of their cars at three in the morning. No mention was made of flat tires.

In a moment of supportiveness Zukarov assured Alexei that there would be no hitches—the trio could be at the body by nine a.m. "That," thought Alexei, "was if nothing else went wrong."

And with those words Zukarov hung up and immediately called the Russian Embassy in Ottawa and the Consulate in Toronto. Having given his instructions, he went back to attending to the many papers and file folders on the large mahogany desk he was using on the third floor of the Russian Embassy in Washington where he was staying while meeting with the CIA Director to discuss ways in which the two intelligence services could "work together."

*　*　*　*　*

"Well?" asked Mikanovich as Alexei squealed out of the parking lot.

"He looks like a hairy pig," thought Alexei of Mikanovich as he said out loud. "We have to hurry."

"Where are we going?"

"Toronto," came the terse reply.

Alexei's anger hadn't been helped by the car in which they had dumped Rita's body disappearing down the exit ramp, or by his conversation with General Zukarov. Then there was another focus for his anger.

Mikanovich had used Russian at the airport car rental counter and the girl who waited on them recognized the language and responded but with a Kyiv accent and a look of distaste. Alexei had seen the distaste cross her face and reside in her eyes. Mikanovich had only noticed her beautiful face and ample breasts.

The pig's mistake meant only one thing: the CIA would pick up their trail. Alexei knew that Rita's compatriots would certainly question airport staff first thing in the morning, including the car rental counter personnel, in their desperate search for what they must know would be her body and what it contained.

Anger wasn't useful to Alexei and it was time to let it go. Time to calm himself. Like the professional of his craft that he was, he began shutting down his emotional responses like so many switches on a control panel. His mind took over. While the odds were against them, there was still a possibility that the mission could be saved and the mole left unrevealed.

Mikanovich's use of Russian with the woman at the car rental agency meant the car was traceable. They had to ditch the car and get another. Canada would be an ideal ditching place.

The man at the gas station where Alexei and Mikanovich bought a map of Ontario directed them to the Lewiston/Queenston Bridge —"fastest way to Canada," the gas station attendant had said, having never gone there himself.

"Where are you headed?" he'd asked.

"North Bay," Alexei had replied, seeing a small map of the northern Ontario town on the back cover of his road map.

"Oh, yeah," said the man, obviously not knowing where it was and, therefore, losing interest.

"Going skiing, huh?" he still managed. Alexei nodded absently, knowing as little as the American about North Bay in August. The only skiing taking place there would be on water.

As he drove to the bridge to Canada, Alexei phoned the Embassy in Ottawa getting assurance that the orders given by General Zukarov had already been complied with. A resident SVR officer would meet them at Pearson airport in Toronto at 7:00 a.m. and the Toronto Consulate had already gotten an address to go with the license number of the car and dispatched a man to the address. Finally, Alexei was told to memorize a phone number and code should he have an emergency.

* * * * *

Crossing the border at Lewiston had been easy. Alexei's and Mikanovich's story about visiting relatives in Kingston, believed. Their fluency in American dialects made it equally believable that they were natives of upstate New York. Travelling along Highway 405 Alexei and Mikanovich passed the spot where Rita's body lay. A car was parked on the soft shoulder, a woman standing near the embankment edge staring downward. Sitting at the wheel of the powerful Chrysler Alexei decided he liked Canada. Canadians had less paranoia than Americans and besides they used kilometres, something he understood better than miles.

As they drove, Alexei's cell rang. It was the Toronto Consulate calling to give him the name and address of David Stone and to tell him they had sent a man to watch his house. When told, Mikanovich checked the map and urged Alexei to go straight to Stoney Creek, the small city next to Hamilton where it was assumed the owner of the car had taken the body.

Reluctantly, Alexei disagreed. "Zukarov's orders. We're going to Toronto. This David Stone will be watched." They were driving along the QEW to Toronto airport as they passed over the Garden City Skyway Bridge over the Welland Canal. Twenty minutes later they passed three highway exits for Stoney Creek. Alexei's anger returned, this time directed at General Zukarov.

They made record time getting to Pearson International Airport arriving there in under seventy-five minutes. Once at Pearson, they parked the car with Hertz and rented a room at the Sheraton while they waited for the early morning flight from Ottawa. It was one twenty-five a.m. By six they would have already rented another car at a different agency and be ready to leave for Stoney Creek once their colleague arrived on the seven o'clock flight.

The airport was the perfect place to confuse the hunters. Leaving the Hertz car at Pearson would ensure that confusion if their trail were picked up and they were followed as a result of Mikanovich's stupidity. While the CIA checked airplane flights, Alexei and Mikanovich would be driving in the warm August sun of Southern Ontario to Stoney Creek where they would pay a courtesy call on David Stone.

Chapter Twelve

Relocating the body did have its difficult moments. Even at twelve-thirty in the morning the highway still had traffic on it. The risk of exposure was great during the last twenty minutes of their search. David had walked along the lip of the embankment shining the fading light of his flashlight to the bottom while Mary drove at a snail's pace on the soft shoulder beside him. To say they looked suspicious was an understatement, but they had an excuse ready at hand. Scrupulously they avoided thinking about what might happen if the same OPP constable should stop to assist or investigate their behaviour and recognize David or the car. Such thoughts were dismissed by a simple decision that it would not happen because he would be off shift. Obviously, time would tell.

If the OPP did come along and wanted an explanation, David and Mary intended to explain how they had been driving along the highway earlier in the evening with the three children in the back and how one of them, the two-year-old, had thrown the fourteen-year-old's summer school science project out the window. At the time, everyone thought it had been scrap paper and the two-year-old had been appropriately chastised, the car window closed and the family had harmoniously gone on its way. Only when they arrived home did they realize that the "scrap paper" had been Cindy's—their fourteen-year-old—science project which was due on the upcoming Monday morning. David and Mary were convinced that there was no cop in the world who could resist such a plausible, heart-tugging story. It was fortunate that they did not have to test their belief.

Finding the body was one thing, putting it back in the trunk of the car, another. Until she looked over the embankment and saw the unblinking eyes in the rigid white face staring up at her, the enormity of it all had not hit Mary. It had been an abstraction. The body merely the subject of a macabre conversation. She puked. David was lucky he saw it coming and moved out of the way.

In accordance with the rest of his evening, he wasn't that lucky. He lost his footing and slid, stumbled and tripped down the hill, finally rolling, unhurt, to lie next to Rita's body.

David tried to scramble away, only to find himself pinned between the inflexible and immovable corpse and the incline of the embankment. Mary was so focused on her husband's macabre predicament that she did not see the car pull off the highway a couple of hundred feet down the shoulder and start to back toward her. It was only as the red brake lights hit her face that she realized a motorist had stopped. Below, David saw his wife suddenly bathed in a red glow and he felt a stillness settle over his body.

"Hello, there. You alright?" asked a heavy set man as he climbed out of his American made compact.

"Oh, yes," said Mary, suddenly calm, moving away from the lip of the embankment. "Must have been something I ate," she said, unashamedly pointing to the recent contents of her stomach liberally colouring the grass verge.

"You sure?" the man persisted, declining the generous offer to look.

"Oh, yes, quite. Thank you so much," and Mary got into her car and started the engine. She gave the man a wave and a smile for his trouble, locked the door and fastened her seat belt. He heaved himself into his small car and succeeded in making a little gravel fly proving his masculinity as he pulled from the shoulder onto the road. Mary switched on the headlights and her left blinker as a large truck roared past blocking her view of the rapidly disappearing motorist.

She switched off the lights and turned off the engine and walked back to the edge of the embankment in time to see David crawling up it on his stomach. He had obviously heard her coming and had his face pressed into the grass and was lying perfectly still like some unusually shaped log.

When Mary said at the top of her lungs "OK, David, let's get a move on," she startled him and he began to roll down the hill again. This time he landed on top of the body. It was a position from which he quickly removed himself. Mary gasped in horror.

It took only five minutes to get the body up the incline, the three of them only slipping once, ending up in a tangle at the bottom of the embankment. David brought the car to the very edge to shorten the distance the corpse had to be lifted before disappearing once again into the trunk. The deed done, David and Mary ran to their respective sides of the car and David drove away, gravel flying.

Only after they had safely left several kilometres behind the place where the body once lay, the two of them sitting in pale-faced silence, Mary asked a very logical question, "Where are we going?"

"What?"

"Where are we going?"

"I don't know," David said. "I guess I was so focused on recovering the body, I didn't take time to think about what we're going to do with it."

Silence reigned. Then. "How about the Welland Canal? We could dump the body in the Welland Canal. They're always fishing bodies out of there." David smiled, pleased with his idea. He pointed out the car window to reveal the twinkling lights of a large bridge just up ahead. It was the Queen E Garden City Skyway Bridge over the Welland Canal. The canal, running strictly through Canadian territory, joined Lake Erie with Lake Ontario and allowed for the passage of ships, lakers and ocean-going, around Niagara Falls up to the Lakehead or out to the North Atlantic through the St. Lawrence Seaway.

David had spent many childhood years in the Garden City, St. Catharines, and enjoyed many a family picnic along the canal in summers and smelt fishing with his father when the fish ran in the spring.

"What will we use?"

"What?"

"That's right, 'what'?"

"I don't understand."

"What will we weigh the body down with? I'm sure I read somewhere that bodies fill up with gases as they decompose and that makes them float to the surface if they're in water."

"You're right, but what do we care if it floats?"

"Well, we might be seen driving away and it might not even sink in the first place. Besides, gangland killers always weigh the bodies down." There were times when Mary could be irritatingly right.

David realized he was still too edgy, he really had to calm himself down. Once beside the canal, he and Mary looked over the dark oily water just past the Port Weller Lock. David was sweating profusely and he could feel the exhaustion from all the adrenalin claiming him.

"What will we use to weigh it down with?" The thought came clearly. A practical problem to solve. Something David was good at. It was time for him to do his best to cast aside the emotional shock and start using his brain. Up to now, Mary had done most of the work and it was about time that he helped out.

"How about the flat tire," he announced, facing Mary. "It's heavy enough to sink the body and keep it down." A smile crossed his lips. A smile which Mary returned. David got out of the car and opened the trunk, Mary a few steps behind him. David was bending over to lift out the body when the man spoke.

"Excuse me."

Crash. A loud groan. "Ohhh, shit. Shit, shit, shit." Rubbing his head David flung himself out from under the trunk lid and towards the voice. Mary squealed.

"Are you alright?" The shadowy figure asked.

Rage almost escaped David's mouth. "Alright? I'm sick of stupid interfering people asking me if I'm alright. I'll be a lot more alright if you weren't asking me asinine questions and scaring my wife half to death. Of course we're alright." Grasping self-control David kept his mouth shut and tried to smile disarmingly. Mary smiled in agreement.

"You can't park here," said the man pointing at a dimly lighted "restricted area" sign on a nearby post. "Besides, what are you doing?"

"Doing?" the question clanged around David's head searching for an answer. David was sure the man would see the panic in his eyes as his face contorted while his mind frantically threw up useless answers to the question. It had to be minutes before the right answer came. Surely the man would notice and become suspicious. The man seemed oblivious. Time stood still. It was the same experience as when one sees an accident, the vehicles relentlessly sliding toward each other.

In point of fact, the answer came in seconds: "We were getting lawn chairs out of the trunk so we could sit by the canal and watch the ships go by," David heard himself say. Mary nodded enthusiastic agreement.

His listener was not so impressed. "What nuts sit by the canal in the middle of the night?" he thought. Then he remembered that in his days working at the Canal he'd seen it all. "More likely getting out a blanket for a little clandestine roll in the hay," he thought.

"Well, you can't do it here, so move on."

Relief was not David's first emotion. Anger was. The "you can't talk to me like that," kind of anger. He expressed it by slamming the trunk and stomping to the driver's door. Mary smiled at the man and followed more sedately. Only when he was sitting behind the wheel did the relief come to David. Along with the shakes. Barely able, he turned the key in the ignition and roared away. It was three-o-six. He was getting a full first-hand course in dealing with a serious personal crisis. Up to now, he wouldn't give himself a passing grade.

Around Jordan Station was where sufficient calmness returned for them to deal with real questions once again. The first one was "Now what?" David pulled off the highway, combed his hair and put on his suit coat still on the back seat to hide the grease and grass stained clothing, and nodded at the Prudhomme's Tim Horton's. Mary shook her head and opted to stay in the car. David's brain welcomed the caffeine gladly, but his stomach wasn't so sure. With the car parked in the shadows, they sat in silence for a short while. David looked around while he drank his coffee. Orchards and vineyards stretched away to one side. As a teenager, he and his friends had picked strawberries and other fruit in the summers to make money. An idea pressed itself upon him. Scalding his mouth he downed the coffee, the unusual experience of hope tentatively muscling its way to the forefront. "The vineyards and orchards," he said excitedly.

The land from Niagara Falls to Hamilton was Ontario's fruit growing region. When the glaciers had retreated a few million years ago they had carved out an escarpment of hundreds of kilometres. At one end the Niagara River flowed over it making the famous Falls. The alluvial soil left behind between the escarpment and Lake Ontario and the hot summers made for excellent fruit growing, producing strawberries, peaches, cherries, plums, apricots and grapes. Lots and lots of grapes. Vineyards abounded, with some of the wines winning international awards, beating out the French, Italians and Californians.

It was three-thirty when David and Mary pulled down the track running off old Highway 8 in Vineland and parked next to the carefully labelled rows of grapes. It was not far from one of the wineries they had visited the previous weekend. With the engine dead the only sound was that of the crickets and the distant barking of a farm dog. The plan was simple, as were all plans hatched by the genius and the exhausted. The difference, of course, was that the plans of the exhausted were very often flawed.

It was not the flaw which was going to sink David's plan. It was the four. The four feet of the farm dog.

Rita's body was hanging out of the trunk when the bells went off in Mary's head. The barking of the dog was getting louder. There was also a distant light that wasn't there before. The large outside flood lights people often have around their homes. Or in their farmyard.

Mary poked David and put her fingers to her lips. Standing perfectly still they both thought they could hear the crashing sound of the farm dog as it hurtled its way toward them. Squinting, they could see the jiggling motion of an electric lantern as the farmer followed his dog.

Adrenal glands are marvelous things. Aided by caffeine and the last vestiges of adrenalin, David stuffed Rita's increasingly abused body, none too decorously, into the trunk and ran for the car door behind Mary. As the engine roared and the lights came on, the farm dog, teeth bared, came flying out of the darkness where the beam ended.

David floored the gas pedal. The car surged forward, meeting the dog in mid-stride. In reaction David slammed the car into reverse weaving at speed down the rutted track toward Highway 8. Behind him he heard the muffled blast of the farmer's shotgun as he tried to revenge his fatally injured best friend.

Guilt. It hadn't played much part in the evening's potpourri of emotion so far. Now it dominated as David sped well in excess of posted limits down Highway 8 towards Grimsby. He had not meant to run over the dog. In panic he had not put the car into reverse, but into drive. Remorse overcame him and tears streaked down his face. He was not crying for the dog, or for the dead woman. The tears were for himself. Mary sat pale-faced in shock next to him.

It was almost four a.m. The kids would have come home long ago and their hastily written message to them would be wearing kind of thin. Their mother and David rarely went out for four hour dinners, especially late at night. At least not since they were married and no longer courting.

As David and Mary were rapidly approaching home a new idea came to them. It was not any better than the ones already rejected, but desperation and the late hour made it more attractive. It was then that they ran out of gas.

CHAPTER 13

Due to a certainty, wrongly, that he was being followed, it had taken the SVR agent from the Toronto Consulate an hour and a half to reach the street on which the Stones house stood. He was very fortunate, and appropriately grateful, for the fact that not only was all-night parking allowed, but he was actually able to find a place to park just one house down from where the Stones lived. A fact that would help unravel the whole mission.

It was a little after midnight. He got out of his car and walked up the street and around the corner onto the cross street. In this fashion he was able to walk around the entire block and approach the Stones' house from the other direction. It was definitely his lucky day. The Stones house was on the dark patch between street lights and he simply went up their driveway, his rubber-soled shoes noiseless on the asphalt, and through a well-oiled gate into their back yard, as though he did it every night at that same time.

The man was able to position himself so as to have cover in the darkness of night and be close to the first floor and basement windows.

He would, however, have to find another hiding place when dawn came, he could hardly pass himself off as a large tomato plant or a Pee Gee Hydrangea. Because of the high fence on one side and the clipped cedars on the other, the yard was dark and gave him the freedom to move around, if he was careful. The balmy air that caused David Stone to sweat earlier would keep the Russian warm throughout the night.

"There will be no cramped muscles tonight," he thought. "No sleep, either."

* * * * *

Michael Graves hated with a passion coming home to an empty house, especially at night. Michael, Mary's son from her first marriage, was seventeen. Sixteen months older than his sister Sara. Michael returned home in his mother's small Japanese car from his job at the movie house where he worked. He moved through the house putting on lights as he went until he reached the kitchen where he added the refrigerator light to the brightness.

Dumping his gym bag with his dress clothes inside on the kitchen table, he made himself a couple of sandwiches, read the note left for him and Sara on the fridge door, poured himself a full-pint mug of Pepsi, with ice, put the Red Sox baseball cap on his head and light switched his way downstairs to the family room, where he proceeded to watch the last portion of David Letterman, ready for a PVR'd John Stewart's *The Daily Show.*

Before sitting down he made sure the baseball bat he kept around for such times as this was at hand. It was where he'd left it, under the couch along with an assortment of dirty dishes, half-eaten bags of potato chips, sunflower seeds and unshelled peanuts—all hastily deposited there so the owner would not get caught eating them—an apparent crime in Michael's eyes though in no one else's. The other reason things were deposited under the couch was a very practical one —to avoid having to take them on the apparently arduous journey upstairs to the kitchen from whence they had come.

For years Mary and then together with David had lectured the kids on keeping the family room clean. Like most parents they had not succeeded. They were not highly motivated to succeed in this endeavour, however, which made failure easier to live with. It never ceased to amaze them how adolescents always had the strength and skill to carry glasses and plates heavily laden with drink and food down into the family room but possessed neither when the same glasses and plates were empty and needing to be carried back to the kitchen.

All this bothered David far more than Mary, who tended to be of the opinion that a house should have a definite lived-in look. David, an only child with a neatnik for a mother, used to go through agony bordering on the apoplectic when they first all lived together. Mary, Michael and Sara were all grateful and amazed at how far David had come since those occasionally tense times.

Michael, intent on his food and David Letterman, did not see the face looking in on him through the outside window. He was missing his one real-life opportunity to do something with his baseball bat. Here was a situation he had prepared himself for ever since he had first stayed home alone and he missed it all for another poor Letterman interview. Then again, baseball had never been Michael's game.

* * * * *

When the car pulled into the driveway the Russian could not see it because of the fence. It was fortunate, because if the fence had not been there he would have stood out clear as day in the headlights, looking like some guilty, surprised animal caught at night in the glare of light. Sara thought it strange that David's car was not in the driveway; it was, after all, one twenty-five in the morning and David should have been home hours ago. She thanked her ride—the father of the two children she had been babysitting—and walked up the front steps, getting herself admitted through the front door by continuously ringing the bell until her baseball-bat-toting brother emerged out of the basement family room to open it. Of course, Sara had a key, but it was more pleasurable to make her brother have to leave his TV show and snack to answer the door.

There were the familiar grudging remarks between them about people not carrying keys and people not leaving doors unlocked with occasional phrases such as "moron" and "jerk" thrown in.

This typical game playing between siblings had another side. It wasn't all about who could torment who the most. Both held secrets about the other and in spite of periodic temptations and threats to reveal them, all the secrets were kept. For his part, Michael was well-aware of the navel ring Sara had acquired. With a teenager's certainty she knew her Mom and David would not approve and she needed her secret kept. She could still wear a bikini and do the beach scene, sans navel ring, on the occasions the family vacationed together. This secret hadn't come to the fore because Michael was a voyeur, but because he had somewhat innocently overheard Sara talking on her cell phone one night behind her half-open bedroom door. Sara and a friend were comparing notes on their new acquisitions.

When he confronted Sara a couple of days later in some kind of attempt to blackmail her, she revealed that she knew where he kept his marijuana stash in his bedroom and should feel free to tell Mom and David about her secrets. For her part, Sara had been keeping Michael's secret for use at just such a moment. All this was four months ago. A deal had been quickly struck and so far had been kept.

For now, the not-very-serious sparring ended with Sara asking "where's Mom? Where's David?" Sara was not satisfied with the note —dinner didn't take until two in the morning, and besides, David had just gotten back from Boston. Michael, a little more blasé, as was his approach to such matters in front of his sister, mumbled something about "running out of gas" or "running into friends" and "maybe David was hungry."

Still dissatisfied, but having no recourse, Sara put on the kettle for tea and went to change into her favourite, dated old sweatshirt—former property of a previous boyfriend. Michael found the new hiding place for the butter tarts, took two, filled a clean glass with Pepsi and followed her upstairs. It was time for bed. Besides, he had to be at the cinema by twelve thirty for the Saturday matinee.

Michael stepped expertly over his bow and arrows in the upstairs hallway near his room without breaking stride. It was obvious that they would be there forever if left up to him. He knew all too well the extent of his mother's threshold in such matters and he knew he had time yet before the real lectures began.

Sara came out of her room, also stepping over the "junk," but seizing the opportunity to mumble "jerk," under her breath and cast a look of disgust in the direction of her brother's three-quarter closed bedroom door.

Unlike her brother, Sara had nowhere to go in particular in the morning, or afternoon for that matter. She was staying up to do some taping on the PVR—a mock Beatles concert that was coming on the pay-tv channel at three a.m. Going downstairs and into the kitchen, Sara made her tea, took some cherry yogurt out of the fridge and went downstairs to watch videos and wait for her concert to begin.

Lying on the same couch her brother had lain on earlier, she pulled a blanket over herself against the chill. Also, like her brother before her, Sara did not see the face at the window watching her every move.

Chapter 14

Joel Jerrow sat in the lounge chair, eating his Chinese food and drinking his green Chinese tea, while Gardiner and Pasquale did the same on the beds. If the night manager at the Buffalo Holiday Inn thought that the three men were planning a ménage à trois he did not indicate it. Perhaps he thought they were union negotiators, who always kept strange hours and tended to sleep together in one room. The three men had been watching Alan Arkin and Carl Reiner in *The Russians Are Coming, The Russians Are Coming* on late night Buffalo television and were in need of the distraction in spite of the irony.

Only a few hours had passed since Jerrow and his Langley team had arrived at the two-star Buffalo hotel to bring their fellow agent home to safety. It was not out of any desire to avoid the happy ending of the movie that Jerrow got up and turned off the television just as the child fell, hanging from the church steeple. He had spent more time thinking of Rita than seeing the movie. When he wasn't seeing Rita's face and feeling her touch he was thinking. Now, he had made a decision.

"I'm going out to get some air and call Langley and ask for an emergency APB to be put out on Rita. We've got to find the body"—this was the first time Rita had been spoken of as a body. It hurt, but it had to be said. "We know from the shredded clothing and bags the Russians got the false microchips but we don't know about the real one. It was somewhere on or in her body and we have got to find it." Whether the "it" was the microchip or Rita's body was left unclear. Jerrow had not told them that it was a microdot they sought. Until that moment he had kept the secret to himself fearing an accidental leak reaching the mole.

"We may be too late," he continued, "but it's the only chance we've got. Questions?"

There were none.

Gardiner got up, put his cardboard take-out carton on the desk and walked toward the bathroom. He had on only his underwear.

"Pasquale and I will share a bed," he said, stopping at the bathroom door. "You need a bed to yourself. It's three a.m. now, how about a wake-up call at eight?"

"Six," came Jerrow's quick reply and he nodded appreciation for the offer to sleep alone. God knew he needed the sleep. Somewhere his brain noted that "eight" was an unusual suggestion given the situation. Although he knew it should be eight when they got up because they all desperately needed the sleep. "Gardiner should know better," the thought flitted by.

"Never mind not getting what you want," he told himself, "in this business you're not likely to get what you need either." The couple of hours sleep he might get if the person he needed at Langley was immediately available wouldn't even dent his exhaustion. Out of necessity he would make it enough.

Jerrow was glad to have Gardiner along. He was supremely confident that the experienced agent would stick it out to the end. Indeed, he was counting on it. He had worked with Gardiner before and knew just how far the six-foot-two, two hundred twenty-five pound agent could go. It was a long way. Jerrow hoped it wouldn't be too far. Or too much. It had been some time since they had worked together —"a good four or five years," Jerrow thought. The man seemed different somehow, "and well he might," Jerrow commented to himself. Yet, while Jerrow couldn't quite put his finger on it there was a definite remoteness about Gardiner that he did not remember being there in the old days. Something had happened to Gardiner over the years Jerrow felt, something that went far beyond professional maturity, beyond the coldness that agents develop in time to protect themselves, not just from emotional entanglements while on missions but from their own corked-in feelings—feelings that once turned lose could ruin a man's career if they didn't kill him first.

In the "profession" you learned to always be on guard, to always save a private corner of yourself, to only have the emotions you deliberately chose to have, to only say exactly what it was you needed to say to ensure the success of your mission. Jerrow remembered the last time he had broken that rule of the trade. It was only a few days ago in a telephone conversation with a woman with whom he had once shared passion, and perhaps would have again. A woman who was now dead.

"Still, we all change," Jerrow thought. "I'm sure I'm not the same man I was five years ago either." He was pleased it had been Gardiner who had passed the trust test to be a member of his very small team.

As for Pasquale, he was a different kettle of fish. He was green and Jerrow had no real sense of his perseverance and resilience. Pasquale was along precisely because he was green, and knew of no options to loyalty. While many years senior to Pasquale, Jerrow recognized in the near-rookie agent the potential he thought he had read in the man's file before he had agreed to accept him. Because of the mole, Jerrow had been given one alternative to Pasquale, no one. This had not stopped Jerrow from scrutinizing the file and asking a lot of questions. The thought train stopped as the phone rang at the other end of the line.

He was lucky. His chief was immediately available. "She must be very nervous," he thought.

Jerrow asked for the emergency APB. It would be done.

Jerrow let himself into the room to be greeted with silence. No light had been left on for him and he needed none. He knew where every piece of furniture, lamp, ashtray, and chair was. Likewise, Jerrow knew how many steps it was to the far wall and the exact location of every switch and doorknob. He knew also, that neither Gardiner nor Pasquale would move anything. Their lives depended on the knowledge as much as his did.

Jerrow went to the bathroom and then to bed. It was three forty-five a.m. He could not sleep—his mind was still working things out, still processing and still trying not to succumb to grief and the even more dangerous, guilt. Jerrow knew that in the next twenty-four hours his mission could be as dead as Rita. "Poor, poor, Rita". He clamped down that train of thinking. It went nowhere but to dusty death.

Jerrow was counting on the faint hope that the Russians had settled for the false microchips and ignored the embedded microdot. As for Rita's body, the Russians had done what he would have done—taken it away to confuse things. If his intuition was correct, however, it was only a matter of time before they returned, recovered Rita's body from wherever they had dumped it and cut it to pieces if necessary. Of course, he could be wrong and the Russians had worked it all out and gone home, taking their prize and Jerrow's mission with them.

Still not able to sleep, Jerrow got up and poured himself a glass of cold Chinese tea and stared out the window at the Youngman Highway, the traffic still moving on it. As the sky began to lighten in anticipation of dawn, Jerrow finally closed his eyes and fell almost instantly asleep. He was surprised, momentarily, by the wake-up call which Gardiner took, out of a sound sleep, as though he had been fully awake. Through the window, dawn was imminent.

They had a great deal to do and probably an even greater amount of waiting. They did not have an abundance of hope for success. After all, Jerrow was banking on the possibility that the Russians had dumped Rita's body, leaving the microdot and its camouflage behind. It was a safe assumption that if that were so, then the Russians would have by now discovered their mistake and would return for the body making for an uneven race between the SVR and the CIA to get to it first. For Jerrow there was a secondary benefit. If the SVR agents did return, he and his team could follow them to Rita and the microdot. Of course, if the Russians had discovered the microdot what Jerrow did now wouldn't matter a tittle.

Breakfast acquired at a drive-thru, Jerrow and his team's first item was the airport to question all service staff and check on outgoing flights the previous night and check incoming flights.

Pasquale did not bother to find a parking spot. He pulled up to the 'Arrivals' doors and nodded as he and Gardiner got out and Jerrow walked around the car and got behind the wheel and drove away. Gardiner headed for the 'Arrivals' board while Pasquale went in search of the 'Departures' lounge.

Pasquale had little trouble. Buffalo does not have a big airport. Pasquale had drawn the job of finding out if anyone could remember the two Russian agents on the chance they had left by air. It was a long shot; the night staff were at home in bed or had left on the plane they were helping to board and the day workers would have no knowledge. He might get to see the night records and get lucky with a name, a destination. With more luck he might even convince someone to check the computer for a specific name on the previous night's arrivals list.

Representing himself as a state police officer from Texas, hoping to gain some advantage from the romance associated with the Texas Rangers and putting his Southern drawl to good use, Pasquale began his task with about as much enthusiasm as a lazy monarch butterfly approaches flying to Mexico from Point Pelee.

While Pasquale worked the Departures, Gardiner had stayed on the lower level to work the Arrivals' workers and car rentals. After thirty minutes he came to Pasquale waving his notebook and said he decided his time would be better spent visiting the homes of staff on duty the previous night but not working until much later or were on their day off. "This is not a large airport and I figure you can take care of the car rentals. Visiting off-duty staff will take time and could give us the info we need." With that he went back down to the car rental area, rented a car and left the airport. Pasquale looked forward to the day when he could make independent decisions that differed with a leader's instructions. Nevertheless, Gardiner's idea made sense.

Jerrow had assigned himself the job of going to the hotel where Rita had stayed. The hotel with the frightened, sleazy night clerk. There was a chance, extraordinarily slim, that the Russians might return to the hotel in search of the microdot. Jerrow walked right into the hotel and registered for a room on the seventh floor. He'd like seven sixteen he told the day clerk since that was his lucky number and he expected to win the New York State Lottery with it. He was told that seven sixteen was taken but the desk clerk believed the party was leaving today and would the gentleman like to wait or would he prefer another room. The information told him that the hotel hadn't yet discovered the condition of Room 716. Jerrow said he'd wait for his lucky room. Having provided a reason for his hanging about he went into the coffee shop taking a table from which he could see the rear exits from the hotel as well as the lobby. It was eight-thirty a.m. It was going to be a long day.

In the meantime, besides waiting for the unlikely-to-appear SVR agents, Jerrow's job was to wait for his cell phone to ring. He waited for Gardiner and Pasquale to phone with information from the airport and for Langley to phone to tell him where to go to identify and claim a body. It was going to be a long day indeed and in spite of the exhaustion setting in he could not sleep, always a danger for those who get bored sitting and waiting. Especially on hot, lazy, summer days following a night of only a couple hours sleep.

Chapter 15

Running out of gas with a dead woman's body in the trunk of your car is not substantially different than running out of gas with a trunk load of groceries or returnable bottles or even an empty one. The car won't go and the problem remains the same—finding gasoline.

David's and Mary's luck had held, however. There was an all-night gas station less than a kilometre away and it only took David twenty minutes to return with a can of gas—a kind motorist had given him a ride one way. Meanwhile, Mary had had the dubious pleasure of guarding the car and, of course, the body.

It was four forty-three according to David's digital, when the tired, frazzled couple made it to the freight yard. Their nerves frayed at both ends, their senses of humour definitely on the wane, various parts of their bodies developing involuntary ticks and twitches bordering on muscle spasms.

Hamilton, Ontario calls itself Steel Town. Where there is steel, there is coal. The furnaces of AralorMittal Dofasco and US Steel burn millions of tons of coal a year, requiring the use of coal-laden lakers entering Hamilton Harbour and then transferred to hundreds of hopper cars for delivery to the harbour side mills and to the US Steel Mill at Nanticoke on Lake Erie.

Their coal delivered, and dumped, the coal cars often sit several days or even weeks in a siding of the relatively small freight yards off Lawrence Road waiting for a laker load to come in.

Without a great deal of ceremony, it was into the bottom of one of these empty coal cars that Mary and David had determined to dump Rita's last remains. It was a stupid idea and they would have done well to have stuck with their original ideas of the Welland Canal or the vineyards around Jordan.

It is not easy hauling a dead weight, in the form of a body not yet in rigor, into a coal car, especially in the dark and the body is wearing a dress and nothing else. It is hard, sweaty and dirty work. Work, which in this case at least, was accompanied with many epithets not suitable for virgin ears—there were none present—and which undoubtedly brought about many more chargeable offenses of defiling a corpse to add to those already committed.

By the time the deed was done both Mary and David were exhausted, both had back muscles threatening to spasm along with their civility. As he climbed down from the coal car looking more like a chimney sweep than a clinical psychologist, David had taken one last look at the body that had consumed so much of his attention in the last few hours. He was saddened but relieved when he saw that Rita's dead eyes were no longer staring at the night sky but into the endless blackness of the coal car bottom. The only light was a sparkle from the moon reflecting its light off something in her hair.

Suffering from adrenergic hangovers brought on by the constant fear-induced high over the last few hours, coupled with natural fatigue, David and Mary drove home in silence. Their earlier pledge to place an anonymous call to the police unconsciously repressed rather than forgotten. The process of rationalizing for not making the call was already well under way.

As they drove home, David and Mary had forgotten that Sara was staying up to tape a concert. They knew from past experience that while Sara could easily go to bed at ten and sleep twelve hours, it was not unusual that she could stay up half the night if something drew her. That Sara could be awake dawned on them at the same moment and they both started talking about how Sara could well be awake and it would not be easy to explain their coal- and sweat-stained clothes and coal dust-blackened skin to their usually inquisitive and eagle-eyed daughter.

The disheveled, exhausted and grimy parents need not have worried. Sara had either fallen asleep on the rec room couch or was too engrossed in the TV program they could hear playing downstairs.

Mary and David decided that after five a.m. it was more likely their daughter had fallen asleep. They would go and wake her and send her to bed, but only after cleaning themselves up and putting on sleep and lounge wear. With luck, Sara would be too drowsy to pepper them with a flood of "where have you been? Why are you so late? What did you do?" questions which would have been forth coming were she fully awake. As they went downstairs to the family room ten minutes later to send their daughter to bed, Mary and David did not see the man watching through the basement window.

Chapter 16

Mikanovich stood, watching. He always enjoyed standing in the Arrivals section of large airports. The women were always looking their best, eagerly awaiting the arrival of some returning traveler who they could impress with their good looks. He never noticed the children, the middle-aged or the seniors, just the girls and women between the ages of 16 and occasionally 45. He also ignored Alexei, whom he knew was glaring at him from time to time as he seemingly casually paced near the area where the passengers from the Ottawa plane would come into the airport.

Mikanovich had requested a mission with Alexei Petrovsky, for he knew that if he survived, it would be a real plus on his record when the time came. Petrovsky had a good, if somewhat rebellious, reputation. If he was not the best field agent the SVR had, then he was well on his way. Mikanovich, however, was not really interested in Petrovsky's future, only his own, and his own demanded that he get through this mission in one piece and move on.

Field experience, he had been told, was imperative if he were to climb to the heights he desired. No one was motivated to tell Mikanovich that he did not really have what it takes. Even the vast Russian bureaucracy had its standards.

It was true that, if all went well, Mikanovich could count on a cushy job with the FSB in Dzerzhinsky Square in two years, with a pass to use the special government employees' store. He definitely did not want to be in the SVR in Yasenevo. He had little to worry about, if General Zukarov had any influence at all. It had not occurred to Mikanovich that he could just as easily wind up shuffling papers in a kerosene-heated portable in the barren, dark wastes of Novaya Zemelya, tracking subversive polar bears and decoding messages from prowling American submarines. His special pass would be of little use to him when the spring supply ship docked. Moscow was Mikanovich's goal—that was where the power was, the prestige, the women and his father with all the contacts.

Mikanovich was a Muscovite by upbringing, having spent most of his school years in boarding school in the capital, though he had been born and spent some childhood years in the Ukraine where his father had once been the Commissar responsible for agricultural production in the vast farming areas west of Dnepropetrovsk. Mikanovich's father had not been especially efficient at his job, but given the generally poor quality of the agricultural Commissars, he had stood out among his peers. While other areas were doing no better than two per cent production increases, Mikanovich's father's area was getting three.

Mikanovich got his general social ignorance from his father, along with his lack of human sensitivity and his abusive attitude toward women. Mikanovich's father had the pleasure of preparing many a poor peasant girl for one of the most important duties of womanhood—fulfilling the physical needs of men. Not that Mikanovich's father was a committed paedophile. He paid equal attention to married buxom farm labourers, using his position and power to ensure that a little extra food went to them and their families when production quotas were down and inadequate for Russia's needs—an annual event. There was, however, little doubt in anyone's mind that the father preferred his female partners to be young and virginal, a preference he had somehow passed on to his son.

Mikanovich's mother had done her fair share of personality forming by using her power and prestige as the Commissar's wife to lord it over all and sundry, except for the wife of the District KBG Chief who was clearly a person to be feared. The District Chief's wife did to Mikanovich's mother what she did to all those over whom she had power. As the Soviet Union was collapsing and Ukraine asserted its independence, Mikanovich's father had been astute enough to see the writing on the wall and had supported Yeltsin. He was rewarded for his astuteness by getting a highly placed job in the now Russian Department of Agriculture.

Ever interested in power and status, Mikanovich noticed quickly that there was a definite deference in the way his father treated the KGB men. It did not take Mikanovich long to decide he wanted to be in the FSB or the SVR—the still powerful and newly renamed First and Second Directorates of the KGB. He began to court the favour of his father's good friend, the Moscow SVR Chief.

Not afraid of hard work when he could see the personal gain and with the kind of contacts that made it easy for him to attain solid academic standing, Mikanovich soon stood out among his peers. Through his father's political contacts and with the glowing support of the Moscow SVR Chief, he got himself admitted to Moscow University and then to ABP—Academy of Foreign Intelligence, the SVR training centre.

Piotr Mikanovich was on his way. He seemed to fit in. He ensured that he was ideologically correct with just the right amount of cynicism. He ingratiated himself, he believed, to the right people by being very good at saying the right things at the right time. Mikanovich prided himself on always having the proper opinion, knowing which egos to flatter. His peers disliked him, didn't trust him, but they counted for little. No one had any doubts that Mikanovich was a climber and he would make it a long way up the ladder before he got out of his league, the place where the really big decisions were made and where, sometimes, the greater good was actually considered more important than personal ambition.

For now, Mikanovich knew, he had not reached that place. He was still an up-and-comer—not in Alexei Petrovsky's league, of course, but then Alexei would always be a field agent, living on raw nerve and intuition, possessing a professional integrity which to Mikanovich was a weakness. Once again he looked over in Alexei's direction. His current superior was still pacing.

Alexei realized he was pacing and forced himself to stop and lean nonchalantly against a wall from where he could still see the arrivals doors through which the Ottawa man would come. He had not wanted the man from Ottawa in on his mission. As for the papers, they could be left in a dead drop or handed off on a busy street or men's room. Being a man who preferred to work alone in the field, Alexei was already saddled with the fuck-up Mikanovich. Leaving out the line about Mikanovich, he had said as much to General Zukarov on the telephone. The General looked at things differently and he had the authority in this case to impose his will.

Part of the argument went that since the operation had now moved to Canada there should be an agent stationed in Canada on the mission. When Alexei had pointed to the Toronto man who had been sent on ahead, Zukarov dismissed him as a joke. In fact, he dismissed him as "another Mikanovich".

"It's time to let go of all this useless shit," Alexei told himself. "Accept reality and move on."

As he had been thinking against the wall and prior to that, pacing, Alexei had been watching the increasingly large number of greeters. Unlike Mikanovich, whose observations amounted to ogling at the women, Alexei was looking for anything odd or out of place. He had

had considerable experience at airports and was quite adept at recognizing the opposition. Sometimes, it was a matter of survival.

At first he had thought the clean cut, mustachioed, man in the dark blue suit and red tie was just another company representative sent to the airport to pick up a returning vice president or important customer from out of town. But there was something about him that seemed to set him apart. Alexei began to put his finger on it.

The man wasn't eager enough. He obviously was not a rising star in some company eager to please by demonstrating how well he could deliver a vice president from the airport. Likewise, the man wasn't a dead star either. A man by-passed and pigeon-holed some time ago destined to drive back and forth to airports forever, or thirty-five years, whichever came first. The man was not languid enough for that to be his reality. Certainly, and here was the key, the man was far too interested in everything that was going on. Like Alexei, he had positioned himself so that he could easily survey the entire arrivals area where the Ottawa flight passengers would enter the airport terminal.

At this moment Alexei knew the other reason why the Ottawa man should not have been involved. Quickly he eliminated the possibility that the Canadians could know anything about the mission. He was equally convinced that the Americans could not know they were in Toronto and even if they had some men scattered around the airport the Ottawa flight was an unlikely candidate for surveillance. Besides, the Americans would be watching Departures, not Arrivals, though Alexei was confident that they weren't watching anybody.

"This is a very tight, sensitive mission for the Americans," he reminded himself again. "They don't have their usual resources in cannon fodder."

The man with the moustache, blue suit and red tie was not American. That left the RCMP or CSIS, which meant the man from Ottawa, the so-important man from Ottawa, had been tagged boarding the plane and CSIS or the RCMP were doing a standard surveillance.

Alexei went into action. Moving into position directly in front, but ten feet back, of the doors through which the Ottawa agent would pass, he glanced at the flight monitor. The Ottawa flight was in. He had fingered the Canadian man just in time.

Minutes later some passengers began emerging, mostly government employees and businessmen coming in to Toronto for the weekend. Alexei saw the SVR man as he approached the exit. Before Alexei could make a signal the man displayed the sign that they could not meet because he had been tagged.

As Alexei continued to look expectantly for the person he was waiting for, the Ottawa agent moved passed him and out of the airport to the lines of limos, buses and taxis. Out of the corner of his eye Alexei noticed that the moustache had gone out behind him.

"Gottcha," he thought. He also thought he might like this new member of the mission team, at least he was smart enough to know that he'd been tagged and that there was a possibility of a pick up waiting for him on arrival in Toronto. The signal between them had not been anything complicated. The man from the plane carried his briefcase in his right hand, a signal that he'd been identified and was possibly being watched. Alexei's signal was simply to stand directly in front of the doors, three metres back. Consensual validation.

"Well?" asked Mikanovich. Not sure why Alexei had brought him to one of the airport coffee shops.

"You didn't see him, did you?" It was a statement, not a question.

"Who?"

"CSIS, RCMP."

"No."

"They fooled you Mikanovich. They sent a man so you wouldn't notice."

"I'm sorry comrade. I was selfish and short-sighted, overly confident of success, perhaps. It won't happen again." Mikanovich looked appropriately penitent. Indeed, he felt penitent—one more slip-up could ruin his career, and remove forever from his grasp the cushy job in Moscow.

"Now what? The famous plan B?" He didn't stay penitent long, exchanging it quickly for flippancy.

Alexei nodded and sipped his coffee. It was going to be a long day. So much for the best-laid plans of mice and men and Zukarov. There were not going to be any 9 a.m. wake-ups in the Stone household that morning. Now the chances of police being parked in front of the Stones' house had just expanded exponentially.

CHAPTER 17

Superintendent Michel Labelle liked the RCMP. At the age of fifty-three he could look back over a thirty-year career with pride and some distinction. Now head of CID for the RCMP in Hamilton/Niagara area of southern Ontario, the Superintendent was based in Hamilton. A city of a little over five hundred thousand, Hamilton was located almost in the centre of what is known locally as the "golden horseshoe"—the fertile, heavily populated, industrialized crescent of land around the shores of the western end of Lake Ontario from Niagara Falls to Toronto.

Labelle was not a Hamiltonian by birth, indeed, he was not even from Ontario, having grown up in the Eastern Townships of Quebec. A francophone, with Polish roots several generations back, despite being forced to speak English in the heavily predominant Anglophone areas of Southern Ontario, Labelle still preferred his Quebecois French.

Three of his office's undercover agents had just cracked a car repair scam throughout the Niagara Region and Labelle was feeling good. While it was not as exciting as some of the big drug busts or even the basic police work that the force did in most of Canada's provinces, Labelle enjoyed his Hamilton posting.

Since he had been widowed three years earlier, Superintendent Labelle made it a habit to stop by the HWY 8 office in Stoney Creek around nine a.m. on Saturday mornings. Usually there was very little for him to do, but then, he had very little to do himself: his son was a student at the University of British Columbia and his daughter was in Regina at the RCMP training centre following in her father's footsteps.

This particular Saturday started off as no exception in Labelle's routine. Besides the constable on duty, there was virtually no activity. The teletype, of course, was active, rattling and chattering away like an undisciplined rhesus monkey.

As was his habit, Labelle took the sheets, along with a Tim Horton's coffee and a couple of donuts, into his office. Sipping his extra-large coffee, he read the teletype reports and found, in the midst of the administrative directives and the update on two runaways from a Penitentiary in Quebec, that there was a high priority U. S.-based APB out on a thirty-five year old woman, five feet six inches tall, weight one hundred and twenty-eight pounds, brown eyes, unknown hair colour or length, small mole...

He wondered what could be so special about so common a woman, though he knew that such teletype descriptions gave no insight into the personality of the person. For all Labelle knew she could be a raging maniac, though most likely she was just a missing housewife, a woman who couldn't stand the pace of suburban motherhood and had given it all up for a new life in a new town. Reading on, Labelle came across an informational item from CSIS on the fact that "a suspected SVR agent, resident with the Russian Embassy in Ottawa, was sighted boarding a six thirty a.m. flight for Toronto, ultimate destination unknown." The item ended with a request that RCMP HQ in Toronto assist CSIS in an attempt to identify the alleged agent at Pearson International and learn his destination. A description of the SVR man followed.

Labelle was always fascinated by the occasional teletype tidbits which allowed him a brief window into the world of espionage and counter-espionage. The subject fascinated him. He had often contemplated requesting assignment to counter-espionage work, and when CSIS—Canadian Security and Intelligence Service—was created in the early eighties he came very close to making application. In the early days its membership was almost entirely made up of former RCMP men. Indeed, to this day this is one of the many criticisms launched against it.

Labelle had never applied for a transfer, always being successfully seduced away by some exciting case in CID—Criminal Investigations Division. In reality, he had even been seduced by an ordinary, run-of-the-mill criminal investigation. When push came to shove the spy business was an interest with Labelle, not a passion. Still, on a relatively quiet Saturday morning, Boston Cream oozing out of his second donut, the coffee hot, and good, he let his mind roam free and speculate as to the destination of the Russian agent.

"Probably going to a Blue Jays game," he thought, "nobody would travel that far to see the Argonauts." The Toronto Argonauts were that city's generally ineffective entry into the Canadian Football League. The League began its play in June and it all ended in an East verses West confrontation in mid-November called the Grey Cup.

"Then again," Labelle thought, "he could be up to something." The RCMP Superintendent quickly became bored with the useless speculation, especially since it wasn't his problem. He read through the rest of the teletype material, finished his coffee, washed his sticky fingers and went out to do his weekly shopping. The constable giving him a casual salute in farewell.

From past experience, the constable knew that the Superintendent would be back around noon, having completed his grocery shopping and other errands. This visit, however, would be a very brief one as Labelle would have fresh, hot bread in the car and would be eager to go home, where he would eat it cut thick, with lots of butter and slices of well-aged cheddar on the side. A Molson would wash the whole down. In the meantime, the constable could rest easy.

Chapter 18

David Stone did not sleep well. He envied Mary her ability to sleep no matter what catastrophe befell the family or the world. By eight o'clock he was up, cooking himself a big breakfast. He always ate when he was overtired and dealing with a crisis. Such overeating did not seem to affect his generally wiry body—David burned off the extra calories in nervous energy. The eating was a necessary survival technique he'd learned when working in the group home business with emotionally disturbed and delinquent adolescents. A job he had enjoyed for six years before he burned himself out. Many days would go by where little sleep was possible as one crisis followed another. David would eat in the lulls, ensuring energy for the next upheaval.

In the cold light of day David could not believe what he and Mary had done. In the same light, when his ability to use rational thought returned, he could not see any alternative either. He had to fight the urge to rush out and buy a morning paper so he could search it for some clue as to the body's identity. He realized that even if the body had been found, neither the *Globe and Mail*, which came out at midnight, nor the *Hamilton Spectator*, would hardly have the news. Perhaps a missing person story. He tried the radio newscasts. Nothing. No one had found a body, anywhere. There was a missing person, but she was six. Besides, David's missing person was American. David was left with his unbelief, his fear and his thoughts.

* * * * *

Former RCMP Staff Sgt., now CSIS agent, Wilson was no neophyte. He had been out at airports before. Today was not the first time he'd waited at Pearson International for a SVR agent to turn himself loose in Toronto. Successfully, he thought, he followed the Ottawa Embassy Russian from the airport to the Consulate and began to settle himself in for the long haul.

It had come as no surprise that the SVR man had gone to the Consulate. He would hardly take a room at the King Edward. Equally certain, it was not likely that he was visiting friends in Cabbagetown—one of the many Toronto neighbourhoods—and it was a known fact that his parents lived in St. Petersburg. Where else would he go?

"Nowhere with me on his arse," thought Wilson. Smug as he was, Wilson urgently needed to pass on the fact that he had identified—not by name, of course—at least one, possibly two, foreign—presumably Russian—agents at the airport. The definite was a tall blond, the uncertain was a dark, swarthy guy covered in hair. The decision to telephone in the information was Wilson's only mistake. Believing he had at least five minutes to not give the Consulate his undivided attention, Wilson crossed the street and moved behind a shade tree and made a phone call. He was wrong.

Barely had Wilson moved toward the corner and the shade tree, than a large boned, well-dressed, dark complexioned woman—not unattractive—came out of the front door of the Consulate and swished down the street in the opposite direction and disappeared down the steps to the subway. While Wilson got a twinge of something amiss, his party came on the line and distracted him.

With one eye on the receding woman and another on the Consulate door he reported his observations at the airport to his local RCMP contact. The men would be checked out and a telex would be sent. Wilson was asked to stay in place but to be careful because the identified Ottawa agent, Uri Prokanin, the head SVR man in Canada, was well-known for his disguises. While he had known the other information this was the first he had known about the disguises.

The RCMP inspector continued to share more information but there was no one listening. Wilson was bounding down the street to the subway. He was too late. The platform was empty, an eastbound train disappearing into its tunnel. Wilson had lost his man. Cursing under his breath he slowly left the station. Something was on and he had come that close to getting a piece of it. From the shadows Uri Prokanin watched him go. A faint smile passed over his reddened lips.

*****

No one had asked Uri Prokanin to go to Toronto. Uri's instructions had been clear, "send, immediately, a top representative to join two international field agents in Toronto to assist in an important and urgent undertaking. Take them necessary identification papers to act as police and have the Toronto Consulate prepare backup passports." But he was left the option by the directive and he did not hesitate to seize the opportunity.

Prokanin had felt stagnated in Ottawa where he had been stuck for nine weeks controlling a clandestine operation in the PMO—Prime Minister's Office. It had not panned out as the admin assistant had been transferred over to the office of the Minister of Employment where the most secret information she was able to obtain was the design of the new Employment Insurance application form. Uri was very pleased to go into action and was looking forward to working with Alexei Petrovsky.

First Prokanin had to re-establish contact, which meant using his newly acquired cell phone. He knew Alexei would be waiting for a call and had called his hotel room and arranged for a relieved though agitated Alexei to pick him up at the northern end of the subway line at the Downsview Station. Uri then took the westbound train from the Bloor Street Consulate to the St. George Station where he went north.

His rendezvous with Alexei arranged, Uri had another problem—he was still dressed as a woman. Everything he owned was in the handbag over his shoulder, and it did not exactly contain a three-piece suit. If the arrangements he had made panned out, he would not have the problem for long.

A regular member of the consulate staff would, ten minutes after Uri had left, get into his car, briefcase in hand and drive north where he would eventually meet up with the car containing Alexei, Mikanovich and Prokanin—still dressed as a woman. The briefcase contained his recently discarded dress pants, suit jacket, and wrinkled shirt. There would be no tie, no socks and no soft leather dress shoes; these things, along with Kleenex and cold cream, Uri had in his handbag. The transformation from woman to man would take place at 120 kilometres per hour in the back seat of Alexei's car somewhere near the Toronto/Mississauga line as the three men headed southwest to Stoney Creek.

*   *   *   *   *

Mary was grateful. Of all the gifts she had been born with she placed her ability to sleep near the top of the list. In fact, if it had not been for the increasingly frequent comings and goings of David in their bedroom, she might have slept until noon. As it was, ten thirty came and she was awake. One of David's gifts—Mary thought of it more as a curse—was to be able to glean pleasure, not to mention information, from hard-nosed analytical conversations first thing in the morning. Such conversations immediately upon waking were definitely not one of Mary's strong points. Even fully awake, Mary tended to see such verbal interchanges as just "so much analytical crap." In reality an opinion not far from the truth.

Such divergence of view did not seem to deter David from these pursuits and this particular Saturday morning was no exception and certainly more understandable. All was overshadowed by David's fear of what could happen if they did the wrong thing—a fear Mary shared.

David had had an opportunity to refine and consolidate what he wanted to say during the two and a half hours that had passed between his getting out of bed and Mary's bleary-eyed emergence from the bedroom. When she entered the kitchen she found what she expected. David travelling at one hundred and eighty kilometres per hour and that was when he stood still, which did not often occur. David was a pacer.

It is not easy to stay up half the night collecting a strange body from a ditch at the side of the highway and after a few misadventures dump it into an empty coal car some fifteen kilometres away, and then get up the next morning, analyze your actions and attempt to make a decision to make it all go away and be better.

With a large mug of freshly brewed coffee in hand, Mary braced herself and sat down blank faced on one of the kitchen stools armed with her lighter and cigarettes and listened to David go over the main points of his thinking and the pro and con arguments he had discovered over calling the police.

While she agreed with David that what had happened to them was horrendous and terrifying, she desperately needed to not dwell on it but rather to cling to a more simple reality.

They had done what they'd done. It could not be undone. Surely the best way to begin to put it all behind them was calling the police with an anonymous tip. Clearly it was the right thing to do, as there might well be a grieving relative somewhere who would like to find the body and be satisfied it was "accorded a proper burial" as she had heard them say in the movies.

Mary was confident that this is what they would do, but she knew David had to get there in his own way—he was much better than she was at letting it all hang out. Right now he needed to safely navigate the tempest he caused for himself in his teapot.

Mary had a second cup of coffee, a third cigarette. She did manage to say, when David asked what she thought, that the police wouldn't be able to get telephone records and trace an anonymous call to them. David definitively said she was wrong. Any calls would have to be made from a phone booth preferably using gloved hands. Neither of them had any idea where one could find a phone booth—as they had apparently gone the way of the Dodo bird. Further discussion was brought to a halt when Michael entered the room.

.

CHAPTER 19

At two minutes after nine Jerrow was helped in his struggle to stay awake. There was a flurry of activity in the hotel lobby—a gesticulating housekeeper, a panicked reception clerk disappearing through a door behind the reception desk followed by a fifty-something manager-type rushing to the elevator with the housekeeper and reception clerk in tow. Jerrow understood that the condition of Room 716 had been discovered. It was also when he realized he had not put the "Do Not Disturb" sign on the door, thereby inviting the housekeeper to enter after knocking. He was less in control of his emotions than he had thought.

It wasn't until fifteen minutes later that a police car arrived, followed twenty minutes after that by a forensic van. It soon became obvious that no one was going to get room 716 until very late in the day, if at all. If the Russians were planning to come back and check the room one final time they would be out of luck.

He had had only a report from Pasquale to say he was still checking the airport and that Gardiner had gotten the names and addresses of evening staff and rented a car to go and visit their homes. The latter was good thinking. "Should have thought of that myself," Jerrow had muttered to himself. Another mistake—caused by what, emotions or exhaustion, perhaps both. He needed to check himself.

As there was nothing from Gardiner, and no call from Langley and now no chance of catching the Russians at the hotel, Jerrow decided to seize the opportunity to go back to the Holiday Inn. He knew he had an inner exhaustion that was untapped, and once unleashed, would cause him to sleep twelve and fifteen hours a day for a week. This was not the time, however. Jerrow was clear—he could not afford to send his body signals that it could do anything more than add to its dwindling reserves of energy. His body received the message loud and clear when he stepped into the ice cold shower, only climbing out when he noticed a bluish tinge appearing around his finger tips and his feet became the colour of alabaster. By the time he stepped out of the shower his whole being was focused on the cold, and thoughts of Rita had been driven deeper along with his capillaries.

The phone calls he had been waiting for had still not materialized. None from Langley, and nothing more from Pasquale and only silence from Gardiner. With the air conditioner on freezing, Jerrow had resorted to pacing the room while watching a replay of the Toronto Blue Jays wallop one of America's best. He started when the phone rang and glanced at the clock. It was ten twelve.

"Pasquale," said the voice through the phone when Jerrow picked it up saying, "Yes."

"Something?" Jerrow asked.

"Not sure," said Pasquale.

"Must be something or you wouldn't call," said Jerrow keeping the frustration out of his voice, hoping to sound supportive. Pasquale was young and needed encouragement to trust his instincts and intuition. Jerrow recognized immediately the ephemeral uncertainties of intuition in Pasquale's "Not sure."

"Well, I might have seen them," Pasquale said tentatively.

"When?"

"Well, I don't know for sure it was them," came the still tentative answer to Jerrow's cold, authoritative "when?"

"Listen to me Pasquale, cut out the shit and tell me what it is your intuition is telling you. You might be wrong and all it means is that we've wasted time. You might be right and get yourself a fucking medal. Tell me from the top." Thus ended Jerrow's attempt to coax the information out of Pasquale in a gentle, supportive manner.

Pasquale told his tale. When they had arrived the previous evening and were walking to the car rental booth he had noticed two men rush through the exit. Then a few minutes later while Jerrow was renting a car the same men rushed up and asked for a car at one of the adjoining rental agencies. The tall blond one wanted a Lincoln or Cadillac but settled for a Chrysler. He was highly agitated and in a furious hurry. Both he and his stocky, dark complexioned, hairy friend had been running. When Pasquale had seen them earlier leaving the arrivals area in a great hurry he had not thought much about it. It was only when the girl at the rental desk asked the men if they were going to use a credit card and Pasquale thought the dark hairy one answered "Da." Soon after, the men left on the run and the girl had looked after them with distaste and returned to her paperwork. At the time Pasquale dismissed it as nerves on his part.

Pasquale had noticed the girl on duty again at the Hertz desk apparently having the kind of schedule that called for working until midnight and then starting up again at seven a.m. When asked if she remembered the men, the look of distaste appeared again on her face as she said: "Russians," the distaste turning to disgust bordering on loathing in her voice.

"Russians?" asked Pasquale, "they didn't seem like Russians to me."

"Russians," said the girl, "believe me. I'm Ukrainian and I know Russians when I hear them. The dark smarmy one tried to flirt and I recognized his accent and when I asked about credit cards he said yes in Russian."

Pasquale did not report that the girl looked disappointed when he suddenly looked at his watch and said, "Oh, my God, I've got to make a phone call."

On the other hand Jerrow was not disappointed at all. He was beside himself with relief.

"It had to be them, he told himself." He ordered Pasquale to get all the information he could on the rental car and the name and bank information of the renter and then check the airlines for the pair's names and city of departure. He next called Gardiner on his cell to come back to the Holiday Inn. There was no answer so he left a message. Phone calls over, Jerrow returned to his baseball game and his pacing.

"The Yankees may be losing on television in Toronto but they're about to win on the ground here in Buffalo," he told himself. Jerrow could feel his body bracing itself for the hunt. He liked the feeling. He suppressed the desire for revenge.

* * * * *

Twenty minutes passed before Gardiner called Jerrow back.

"Fantastic," he said with the appropriate amount of enthusiasm, in response to Jerrow's information, "this knocking on doors was beginning to get to me. Besides, half the people aren't home."

"I'm not interested in your mithering," came Jerrow's good-natured reply. "Get your ass back here. It looks as if we are a step closer to catching up with those god-damned Russians."

"And the microdot," he thought to himself.

Gardiner told Jerrow he was on the opposite side of Buffalo, in Lackawanna, and a long way from the Holiday Inn, so it would take him some time to get back.

* * * * *

The cell rang again before Jerrow could put it down. "Pasquale, what have you got?"

Pasquale reported he had the make, colour and license plate number of the Russian's rental car and had learned that they had come on a flight from New York early Friday evening. Not much. Maybe enough.

"They could be anywhere," said Pasquale.

"No, they couldn't be in Nome, Alaska," said Jerrow a smile on his face. "They must have been waiting at the airport for confirmation on the validity of some microchips Rita was carrying. They learned the chips were false and needed to get back to the body," he continued, "so it can't be that far away. Tell me again what happened at the car rental counter."

Pasquale told it again for the second time. Jerrow instinctively knew there was a piece of information there which was eluding him. Some fact that he was overlooking. He would have Pasquale keep repeating the story over and over again until the clue showed itself.

"Say that again," he ordered.

"They were out of breath?"

"Yes, that's it they were out of breath. That's the clue. Or at least a part of the clue."

"I don't get it," said Pasquale "they had been running and were out of breath."

"Say again!"

"What? They had been running and..."

"That's it," said Jerrow jubilantly. "That's mother fucking it."

"I don't understand."

"Let me enlighten you," said Jerrow, obviously pleased with himself.

"Before, you said they rushed, almost ran, out of the terminal and then a few minutes later ran in out of breath to the car rental counter."

"That's right, but...?"

"Patience, Pasquale, patience. Where do you suppose they were rushing to?"

"I don't know."

"Guess."

"Let me see, a bus or limo service to downtown, a taxi."

"Good guess, but not right. Think about it. Were there limos and taxis about, perhaps even a bus?"

"Well yes, there were, I saw the drivers in their uniforms, the flashing cab lights through the airport window."

"Well then, you can scratch that one," said Jerrow triumphantly,

"Think again."

"I don't know."

"What else was beyond those doors?"

"A road, private cars, a parking garage, a..."

"That's it," said Jerrow, "you've got it."

"The parking garage?"

"Where would you hide a body you had taken from a hotel room thinking you were no more than an hour ahead of the opposition?"

"I, I, well, I suppose it would depend."

"You cannot afford for it to depend Pasquale. You don't have all day to decide. How about an airport parking garage? How's about that for a place to hide a body? What do you find in parking garages?"

"Asphalt, painted lines, cars..."

"That's it, Pasquale! Cars. And cars have trunks. The god-damned Russians put Rita's body in the trunk of a car in the parking garage at Buffalo airport. When they discovered they still needed it, the car was gone and I'll bet they know whose car it was and they're on their way right now to recover the body." Jerrow had tired of the lesson.

Jerrow knew he was right. It all hung together. It was the kind of thing he could see himself doing. There were two reasons: if the microchips proved to be false the body was handy and if not, when the body was found the murder would be confused by the gangland nature of the place where the body was dumped. It all made good sense, except it had gone wrong and they now wanted the body back which meant they hadn't found the microdot, which meant they had left the microdot on Rita's once beautiful face.

What he needed now, Jerrow realized, was some fast police work. "Get over to the airport parking authority and use your charm and false papers to convince the parking authority people to give you access to their records. Find out how many long-term cars left last night. I'll join you as soon as I can"

It was a long shot, the body could have been dumped in anyone's trunk, but Jerrow was willing to bet it was in the trunk of a car parked in the long-term parking lot whose owner could possibly be away for several days. It had been a good idea, but it hadn't worked out. The owner had returned from his long trip and taken the body home. The Russians must have been lucky, Jerrow thought, the owner could have opened the trunk and found the gift they had left. Apparently the owner of the car had just driven away with his bags on the back seat.

With Pasquale using his charm at the airport and Gardiner disentangling himself from Lackawanna, Jerrow called Langley to arrange to have the car the Russians had rented put on the wire as stolen, identifying Western New York, in particular the Buffalo/Niagara area, as the expected location of the car. This decision came back to haunt Jerrow later. He checked out of the hotel and drove to the airport to meet Pasquale.

Chapter 20

There is no doubt, parents are definitely weird. Or so it seems to an adolescent, even one going into his last year of high school in a couple of weeks. Michael was no exception. He was sure his parents were "weird." He had gotten up, showered and washed his hair and dressed himself for work. He knew something strange was happening, some great mysterious event which only older adults seem to find anything worthwhile in, when he entered the kitchen and all talking ceased. Not that this was a new experience for Michael, he could not remember a time when his parents kept talking when he entered a room, unless, of course, they were using the conversation as a tool to communicate to him a particular parental perspective or directive. These latter thoughts were throwbacks to the paranoid year he had at fifteen. He still occasionally had relapses.

Michael was convinced something was happening when he asked, innocently, what was wrong and was overwhelmed with "nothings" and "why do you asks!?" Always the first signs of parental deception. Michael decided not to pursue it. Since he'd grown older and wiser he had learned that the vast majority of things which were perceived as horrible in the world of his parents were generally a bore. He was convinced that for now his stash remained undiscovered, otherwise they would be all over him.

Michael made himself a sandwich of pimento loaf and said his goodbyes, reminding his parents that he would not be home until late as he was going out after work. They seemed genuinely glad to see him go and his mother had put a little more into the goodbye hug and kiss than usual. "Parents are weird."

As he got into his mother's Toyota and pulled out of the driveway, the seventeen-year-old did not notice the man sitting in a parked car watching him. Eagerly he pushed the button that replaced the CBC station with a rock station, jacking up the volume to ear-splitting level, scattering excess decibels along the street as he opened the windows and let the warm humidity of late summer into the car. Michael did not notice the car follow him down the street.

For the Russian, following Michael was the best thing that would happen to him that day. He did not know it, but his day had just peaked.

* * * * *

On every street in the world is a busybody, and the street where the Stones lived was no exception. It's common knowledge that busybodies have their upside and their downside. Geraldine Schultz, the official busybody on the Stones' street, lived next door to them.

It took every ounce of self-control the Stones possessed not to respond with what would have been perceived as an inexplicable vehemence when Mrs. Schultz called up one day to complement Mary on the new nightgown she wore the night before. She made no mention of whether or not she had seen David remove it as the evening had progressed.

David in particular found it difficult to not simulate terribly suggestive actions in front of the windows facing the Schultzs', occasionally waving coyly or smiling knowingly at the window which was the busybody's favourite for her voyeurism. David was careful, he only did this while wearing his bikini style underwear, never in the nude.

This particular day, however, was Mrs. Schultz's day to be helpful. She had spent a good part of the morning worrying away at the fact that right in front of her house there was a strange man just sitting in his car. In fact, this had intrigued her to such an extent that she had ceased, temporarily, to ponder how to find out what the Stones had been up to until the very wee hours of the morning. It was unclear when Mrs. Schultz slept.

Mrs. Schultz had spotted the man when making her morning rounds from window to window dutifully keeping herself abreast of all the neighbourhood's comings and goings.

The major problem Mrs. Schultz faced was her indecision over whether the man was a police officer keeping an eye on the Stones, who she definitely did not like, or was a "pervert" eagerly awaiting his chance or perhaps even a man who was sizing up the street for a rash of break-ins.

In the end, Mrs. Schultz decided that the man was not clean-cut enough to be a police officer and, therefore, had to be a representative of the criminal element. She called the police.

Ten minutes later, the man drove away. Mrs. Schultz, who noticed Michael backing out his driveway, she missed very little, did not perceive that the man might be following Michael. When the police arrived eight minutes later, Mrs. Schultz gave them a real ear full, along with the license number of the man's car.

*   *   *   *   *

Something very strange happened to David Stone's bowels. While deep down inside he expected to be arrested any minute, it was, nevertheless, a considerable shock to hear the front doorbell, look out the window and see a police car in the driveway and a uniformed officer on the front stoop.

David stood transfixed. Mary, sensing something wrong, asked what the matter was. David stepped back from the curtained window and said, "It's the police." Mary turned pale, the laugh lines around her eyes somehow darkened and her hand went to her open mouth.

The doorbell rang again. David found his clinical skills and calmly—so he believed—answered the door.

"Sorry to bother you, sir, but we've had a complaint from a neighbour," the constable said with a perfectly straight and even friendly face, nodding in the direction of Mrs. Schultz's. David wasn't certain but he thought he noticed a slight roll to the constable's eyes.

"So this is how it happens," David irrationally thought, "a neighbour complains that you keep her awake late at night hiding dead bodies."

"Oh?" he said blandly, looking the constable straight in the eye with his best psychologist's stare, his tone indicating what he thought of the veracity of that particular neighbour's complaints.

"Yes," the officer said, surrendering eye contact. "Did you happen to notice anything strange?"

Mary, who had come up behind her husband to protect him, squeezed his waist a little too hard.

"Strange?" David asked, softening his expression, hoping Mary wasn't looking nervous and afraid.

"Yes, your neighbour," another nod in Mrs. Schultz's direction, no eye rolling, "reported a strange man parked outside her house all morning."

David looked in the direction of the empty parking spot left by the man's car and then back at the constable.

"She said he drove away fifteen minutes ago," the officer blushed, remembering the lecture he had received on police tardiness, from Mrs. Schultz.

"No, I'm sorry, constable, we did not see a thing. Did we dear?"

"Oh, no," Mary said innocently.

"Well, sorry to have bothered you. Thank you very much," and miraculously the constable walked off their front porch and down the driveway and into the police car.

David closed the door carefully and turned to make a beeline for the downstairs bathroom. Mary beat him to it.

*   *   *   *   *

Alexei Petrovsky was shocked. This feeling was swept aside by his anger, as the car he and the other two Russians were riding in glided by the Stones' house with a police car in its driveway.

As rapidly as the anger had replaced the shock, calm asserted itself. Calm made of steel. Alexei drove around the block and came down a side street to see the police car backing out of the Stones' driveway. Alexei came around again on the cross street further up and saw the police car parked on the street a couple of houses down from the Stones. It was going to be a long day. Alexei decided they would return in half an hour.

*   *   *   *   *

Jerrow jumped when the phone rang. He had been deep in thought as he and Pasquale waited for the parking authority computer to do its thing. It was Langley.

"This may be something, or it may be nothing," a woman's voice said. "CSIS reports that Prokanin is on the move. He left Ottawa this morning and they lost him at the Toronto Consulate when he came out dressed as a woman."

Scrambling around in dusty corners of his mind in search of Prokanin's identity, Jerrow said nothing. A man's dossier began to flit across his mind. He'd found Prokanin.

"The CSIS man at the Toronto airport observed what he believed to be two Russian agents obviously waiting for Prokanin's flight" the voice went on. "They did not contact him, however. The Canadian agent believes he had been fingered."

"Here it comes," thought Jerrow.

"The two men match the description of your missing Russians."

"Right, thank you." Jerrow finally spoke, and hung up.

Immediately Jerrow got long distance, Pearson International Airport, Hertz car rental. If the Russians he wanted were there then the chances were they had ditched the car. Hertz confirmed the presence of the New York state licensed Fifth Avenue, but had no record of renting "the tall, polite, good looking blond man" another car.

"Naturally," thought Jerrow.

The mystery was, why Canada? It made no sense—field agents avoided crossing international boundaries unnecessarily like the plague. Then Jerrow smiled, the light went on and it suddenly all made very good sense. He should have thought of it before. From now on he would have more respect for whoever was running the Russian mission on the ground. The car trunk in which they had dumped the body must have been from Ontario. A great plan if they no longer needed it and really wanted to confuse the issue, but now…

At that moment Pasquale stood over him with a long list of license numbers. Jerrow looked at Pasquale's list of overnight cars parked at Buffalo airport which had left between nine and eleven Friday night. There were four with Ontario license plate registrations. The license numbers meant nothing to him. He had no idea if Ontario numbers reflected geographic locations. Jerrow picked up his cell and called Langley. He'd need help with the license numbers.

Now however, Jerrow had some of the answers he needed and the hunt was on again, though already the scent was getting cold. The fact that the Russians were waiting for a colleague from Ottawa could mean two things: they needed fresh documents or they needed help locating the car with Rita's body. He told Pasquale to drive to the border while he would see what he could do with the other rental agencies at the Toronto airport, though he knew it was unlikely the Russians were still around, they might return to the airport to flee the country. Besides, until he got the names and addresses of the mystery car's owner he may as well get across the border. He called Gardiner again and his phone was answered. He briefly explained to him what had happened and told him to get over the border and wait for instructions. Gardiner said he wasn't far from the Peace Bridge, which was not close to where Pasquale and Jerrow would cross, but did put him on a main Ontario Highway, something his map called the QEW.

"Get over and wait," was all Jerrow told him.

Briefly, Jerrow paused for Rita. If the Russians were in Canada, Rita's body could be anywhere and the only way he could find it and bring it home was through them.

Briefly revenge came to the foreground. He brutally suppressed it, for now at least. With his brown eyes like flint, Jerrow told himself, "with any luck only one of those cars will come from Toronto." He was wrong. It was eleven thirty.

* * * * *

"The plot thickens," Michel Labelle told himself when he read the printout from Ottawa regarding the loss of the Russian agent in Toronto.

"Poor bugger," he shook his head as he thought of Wilson, though he did not know his name. Labelle had lost a few tails in his time and he did not envy Wilson, whom he knew would not only be racked with guilt and feelings of incompetency, but would also have to face the icy temper of a superior officer.

Labelle had a feeling about "this one." His intuition told him that there were going to be a few more printouts about the Russians before the day was out. As he got up and left the RCMP office for his fresh bread, cheese and beer, he decided he'd drop back about four in the afternoon "just in case." Because he had a rotten sense of humour, he did not notify the duty man of his intention to return. "Keep him on his toes."

* * * * *

Mrs. Schultz took her dog for a walk. It was a poorly trained Heinz fifty-seven that daily half strangled itself on its backyard chain attempting to attack the squirrels which used the telephone cable line as a pathway. Obviously, the dog had a plan for scaling the telephone poles and racing along the cable, otherwise, why waste its energy. At the times when the squirrels playfully came and sat unnervingly just out of chain range the dog's plan became clear, break the chain through a well-timed combination of running leaps and neck muscle flexing.

It was fortunate for the Russian, who had followed Michael to the cinema where he worked, that Mrs. Schultz was not at home when he returned. Gone also were the police, who had successfully interviewed one other neighbour of the Stones who, like Mrs. Schultz, had noticed the man apparently watching the houses on the Stone/Schultz side of the street.

The police had also learned, through a license check, that the car driven by the man was not reported stolen. Interestingly enough, from a police perspective, the car was registered to a member of the diplomatic corps stationed at the Russian Consulate in Toronto.

It all seemed harmless enough, they thought—Russian diplomats are not normally known for making a habit of performing break-and-enters, especially in the homes of average middle-class Canadians. Nevertheless, they decided they had better report it to the RCMP anyway—there being a certain amount of unease caused in the minds of the local constabulary when encountering unusual behaviour by foreign diplomats, especially those from nations with which Canada had difficult relations.

Oblivious of all this activity he had caused, the Russian, pleased with himself to the point of smugness, parked his car a couple of doors down from Mrs. Schultz's and waited. The creeping fatigue that he had felt earlier was now held at bay by his sense of accomplishment. He did not have to wait long—at one seventeen Alexei Petrovsky arrived. The consulate Russian's life would never be the same.

CHAPTER 21

The tenor of David's and Mary's conversation changed dramatically after the police had left and the two had relieved the sudden pressure on their bowels the police visit had caused. It was as if, for the first time, the couple fully realized the implications of what they had done. They had actually committed a crime. They had jeopardized their own professional reputations and credibility in the community and even more importantly, exposed their children to an unknown amount of embarrassment, ridicule and only God knew what else.

That was not all. Not only had they committed a crime, but they had assisted someone else with their crime. The woman must have been murdered. Why else would she have been dumped in a car trunk? Slowly, but inexorably, it began to occur to David and Mary that someone else might know of their involvement. After all, all that someone else would need was the license number of David's car. This was a whole new aspect that hadn't occurred to them before.

In Ontario anyone with half a brain can, in time, have anyone else identified through their car license plate number. It was public information. It would undoubtedly take a few days, or so they thought, but if the person or persons who dumped the body in the car trunk had taken the license number down then they could locate David, and with him, his family.

The shock of this truth hit like a ton of bricks. Quickly, the couple reasoned that whoever had put the body in the trunk would have expected the owner of the car to report the fact to the police. The story would then, through the natural course of events, be picked up by the media and be given considerable public exposure. When there was no mention in the media, David and Mary reasoned, then the killer or more likely, killers, would come looking to find out what happened.

Just as this realization was sinking in, permeating all their thinking, the doorbell rang once again. White-faced, David opened the door to find three men standing in front of it with a fourth man coming up the walkway, the early afternoon sunlight highlighting the auburn strands in his brown hair.

One of the men pulled out some identification and said they were police officers and wanted to talk with David and his family about a very serious matter. They wanted to come in.

David was caught off guard. He found himself teetering on the brink of making a confession right there and then. Then, surging out of nowhere came the urge to slam the door and deny entry. The tall blond man who seemed to be the leader, waited patiently, non-threateningly, for an answer.

"Well, what exactly is it all about?" David heard himself say without backing away from the door. A part of his brain noting there was something familiar about the man. Perhaps he had seen him somewhere before.

"It is a matter of the commission of a serious crime in which we have reason to believe you were made an innocent victim," answered Alexei reasonably.

The fourth man had reached the porch and one of the other men turned to speak with him. They were speaking in hushed tones and

David caught the words "...not more than an hour ago, to a movie house where he works." The other man nodded and turned his back, once again facing David.

"I see," he said letting the professional clinical psychologist come to the surface. "And exactly what is the nature of this crime?" he stayed in the doorway.

"If we may," said Alexei, "we would like to look in the trunk of your car?"

"Why should I allow you to do that?"

"Because, Mr. Stone, we have reason to believe that the body of a woman was placed there last night at Buffalo airport."

"You must be mistaken, I looked in my trunk last night and there was no body. I think you have picked on the wrong Camry, or the wrong Stone. Though I was at Buffalo airport last night." Maybe that was where he had seen the man. At Buffalo airport waving frantically as he looked through his rear view mirror. Although, it had just been a fleeting glance. As he scanned the trio of men accompanying the blond he became more certain when he saw a somewhat squat, heavier-set man next to him. The two of them could have been the pair in the parking garage. Of course, if he were correct, that wouldn't invalidate the man's claim. David's suspicions were not mollified by this thought.

There was a slight hesitation, then Alexei said "Mr. Stone, I know that there was a body in the trunk of your car. The Buffalo police have already arrested one of the men who put it there and expect to arrest two others in the next twenty-four hours. The arrested man gave the license number and a description of your car to the Buffalo police. There is no mistake.

"Now, if you have done something with the body that would be understandable under the circumstances and we may be able to overlook the various crimes involved. However, this is a very serious matter and if you make it necessary we will arrest you and lay charges. The choice is yours," Alexei allowed a tinge of frustrated anger to creep into his voice.

"Come in," David said resignedly. His suspicion could be misplaced, but he would still be on guard. Then again, this was a chance to come clean and bring an end to it all. The head cop seemed to be reasonable and clearly suggested he would be full of understanding.

"Thank you, Mr. Stone," came the police-tone reply.

David put his arm around Mary and moved into the living room, while the four men came into the entry way and had a hushed conversation with some gesticulating. The tall blond man came forward and was obviously about to speak. David beat him to it.

"You said your name was?" he asked.

"Brown," answered Alexei, "Chief Inspector Brown. Your son, Mr. Stone, is he at work?"

"Yes," David found himself answering before he thought.

"Why do you ask?" questioned Mary.

"And your daughter, Mrs. Stone, she is home?"

"Perhaps you could answer my wife's question first," came David's icy reply.

Alexei ignored David and turned and nodded to Prokanin and the man from the consulate. They returned the nod, the consulate man saluted without even moving his hands, noticed David. It was as if the superior/inferior demarcation line was military rather than civilian police. He looked at Mary who was clearly not happy with how things were developing. The two men left.

"Michael," whispered Mary to David. David nodded.

"No, not your son, Mrs. Stone. My men are following up another lead in this case. My questions were to determine who was in the house"

The couple stood close together. They did not believe him.

"Please," said Alexei, "sit down," and he began to sit himself.

"We'll stand," was David's chilled reply. "And I think we'd better see your identification again."

"Alright," and Alexei remained on his feet as he handed over his document identifying him as a Chief Inspector with the Ontario Provincial Police.

David and Mary studied the I.D. but were faced with the reality that, like most average citizens, they would not be able to distinguish between actual or false police identification if their lives depended on it, which, in this case was a distinct possibility. The need for such skills had never occurred in their lives. Dissatisfied that his demand had told him nothing, David handed the document back, saying nothing, his face a blank.

Alexei took it graciously and returned David's stare with an open face and said softly, "Now, please tell us about the body."

David felt Mary's fingers tighten around his and he looked into her eyes and understood that she felt something was not right. He knew she would not be able to tell him any specifics even if they could have had an open conversation. Mary's intuition did not easily lend itself to rational explanation. However, David had never known it to be wrong and he was not prepared to abandon his faith in it now.

"I think," he replied," that we would like to call our lawyer. I'm sure you have no objections," and he walked to the small telephone table and took out a personal telephone directory and turned it to the "G" section where next to the printed word "lawyer" was a name and a phone number.

David placed the open book on the couch arm and picked up the phone.

To this point the only movement had been an obvious tensing of Mikanovich's leg muscles as he had had to struggle with himself not to get up from the black Boston rocker in which he had seated himself. The muscles tensing did not escape David's attention as he put his whole being into what he called "clinical mode."

"That man wants to stop me," he thought. The tall Chief Inspector, on the other hand, had neither moved nor batted an eye.

Only when David began dialing the number was there a reaction—Alexei, after what seemed to be one swift and smooth motion, pointed what looked to David like an enormous gun at Mary.

"Please put down the phone, Mr. Stone. While I would greatly regret doing so please be assured that I would not hesitate to use my gun."

This had all happened so quickly that the swarthy man on the rocker had barely stood up and was still fumbling for what could only be his gun.

David's finger froze in the process of pushing the sixth digit of the phone number. He then became aware of two quite distinct feelings. One was an almost heart-breaking fear for the safety of his woman—the kind of bottomless fear from which he felt he could never return should he surrender to it. The second, equally strong feeling was a rage so deep and so violent that he knew it would be his road back should anything happen to Mary.

David put down the phone and walked calmly between the pointed gun and his wife. Alexei stepped back in order to maintain the same distance between himself and the possible target should one or both attempt to wrest the gun from him. Having found the spot he wanted Alexei, inclined his head towards the stairs. Mikanovich returned his gun with more skill than he had displayed in pulling it out and moved to the stairs.

"Please, Mr. and Mrs. Stone, sit down," Alexei said in the same calm police voice, "as you can see, we are not from the police, but we mean you no harm."

"We'll stand," answered Mary, as she moved next to her husband. She could hear Mikanovich stumble as he tripped over something in the upstairs hallway.

* * * * *

Mikanovich had not been very happy. Since Prokanin had arrived he had been relegated to third place. There had been a rapport between Alexei and Prokanin which he knew could never exist between himself and either of the two men. It was not that Mikanovich wanted to have rapport with the Alexeis and Prokanins of this world, he didn't. What made Mikanovich unhappy, indeed angry, was the way in which the two men flaunted their superiority and he was impotent to do anything about it. In the Ukraine, and later in Moscow, when he felt impotent Mikanovich had found a way to relieve himself of those feelings of impotency by demonstrating to himself his manhood. No such opportunity seemed to present itself as he began to check out the upstairs of the Stones' house. For the time being he contented himself with the thought that the day would come when he would be able to have some power and the two field agents—"puppets"—would dance on the strings that he would pull.

It was in this frame of mind that Mikanovich opened a door to discover that it was a bedroom and there, asleep, angel-like, in a brass double bed was an attractive young woman, "sixteen or seventeen," he guessed.

Chapter 22

Prokanin and the man from the consulate, whom he had learned was called Talinsky, sat in the parking lot facing the side and main doors of the movie house. They had no choice. It is very difficult to walk into a six-cinema movie house in the middle of the day and abduct one of the workers without the theatre management getting upset. The exercise is made even more difficult if the abductee is almost seventeen years old, weighs one hundred and eighty pounds, is six foot one and plays on his high school's football team.

The two men were not uncomfortable with the wait. It had really been their preferred option from the beginning. Their task was to ascertain whether Michael was still there and, having done so, to make sure that he did not leave and return home. Their instructions in that regard were clear, the method of prevention left to the imagination, hopefully laced with common sense and humanity.

Both problems—that of ensuring Michael was indeed at work, and that of stopping him—were solved together. The car he had driven was still parked near the rear of the parking lot where Talinsky had last seen it. It was easy to flatten the right front and rear tires. Now there was nothing for the two Russians to do but sit and eat their German sausages from the nearby Denniger's deli, and be bored.

The movie house was located in its own building in the corner of a parking lot of a large shopping centre and in the rear of a popular supermarket. This location made it easy for the two men to sit in their car—many men did the same thing while their women went shopping. The location also provided occasional relief to the boredom as, from time to time, an interesting person walked past, many of them attractive women enjoying the warmth of the August sun and exposing as much flesh to its rays as was appropriate to the circumstances.

* * * * *

The telephone did not startle Jerrow when it broke his reverie. Though his mind had been far away thinking of Rita, the noise did not even cause a flicker of an eyelid.

"Jerrow," he said simply.

"We have names and addresses for you," the voice said.

Jerrow pulled the necessary accoutrements from his jacket pocket and began scribbling rapidly.

As Jerrow hung up, Pasquale was meticulously following the airport signs off the Queen E onto Highway 427, "el Camino real," he said to Jerrow who smiled and understood the Spanish—"the Royal Highway." All Provincial roads in Ontario have a crown above the highway number and some older roads still have the old label: "King's Highway," notwithstanding the fact that Canada has had a Queen for over sixty years.

For his part, Jerrow wondered if they would get anything at the airport or from the CSIS man Wilson whom he had arranged to meet there. To Jerrow it was a long shot, but it was the only shot he had. He called Gardiner who answered on the first ring.

* * * * *

For the third time that day, Alexei was not happy. His police cover had not worked with the Stones. He now had to fall back on his secondary plan. The problem with most secondary plans in these circumstances was that in order for them to be effective they had to not only achieve the desired goal—get the information required—but they also had to be plausible unto themselves while adequately explaining away the reason for the revealed untruth of the primary plan. Alexei's plan depended on the mafia.

Alexei had two other problems that he had to deal with as well. One was the apparent stubbornness of the Stones and the anxiety he shared with them about the amount of time Mikanovich was taking upstairs.

"The truth, Mr. and Mrs. Stone, is that we represent a certain group in society which does not always work completely inside the law. Frankly, if I may speak frankly?" There being only nervous, blank stares in response, Alexei pressed on, "Frankly, the dead woman in the trunk of your car was killed by a faction within our organization and while we have taken certain steps to ensure that this faction will not behave so abhorrently in the future, we are here out of a concern for the grieving husband, children and parents of the dead woman. They so badly want to be able to bury their wife, mother, daughter. In our culture such things are extremely important. Please be assured that to recover the body and return it to the family for burial is our only reason for being here.

"Please just tell me what you have done with the body and we will leave right away. No harm will come to you, you have my promise."

Before David or Mary could respond to this highly suggestive, sincere sounding statement by Alexei all three of them had their attention diverted to the ceiling, where a loud thump, as though someone had stamped or fallen on the floor hard, was heard.

* * * * *

Mikanovich moved quietly to the bed, glancing around the room as he went. On the floor he found what he wanted, a pair of cast off pantyhose and briefs. He understood that his task was to get the Stones' daughter and escort her downstairs. He determined that the how was up to him.

Carefully, he moved to the head of the bed. As he stared at her, Sara murmured and rolled onto her back. She stayed asleep.

The briefs in his left hand, Mikanovich looked down at the still-sleeping girl. He was getting aroused, as he stealthily moved into position. The girl stirred, but did not wake up. As he moved closer, he saw her with a mixture of fantasy and reality. She had dark brown shoulder length hair and from the length of her body under the bed clothes Mikanovich correctly guessed she was five five and weighed about one hundred and fifteen pounds.

He could see the top of her night dress and the mound of her breasts under the covers. He slowly pulled them back.

With the covers down he saw her breasts through the cotton night dress, the nipples poking it as the change in air caused them to become erect. As he pulled the bed clothes further he could see the dark swatch of pubic hair through the nylon panties.

The cool air was now hitting the girl's thighs and she was waking up. In half sleep she tried to pull up the covers and found she couldn't reach them. Suddenly, Sara came instantly awake, fear in her eyes, her mouth opening.

She did not scream, there was a pause of perhaps two seconds while realization sank into her sleep-clogged brain. There was an ugly man in her room standing over her holding her tights and briefs. Those two seconds to full realization were all Mikanovich needed. Adeptly, he stuffed the briefs into Sara's open mouth. Now she could only whimper. Mikanovich noted that the girl's eyes were green. He was partial to green eyes.

Before Sara could react he grabbed her right wrist in his right hand and yanked her forward twisting her round causing the short nightgown to ride up above her waist. Sara began to squirm and wriggle but Mikanovich was too strong and he grabbed the left wrist pulling it toward the right behind her back so that he could grasp both wrists in one hand. This accomplished, he climbed on the bed behind her pushing her down pinioning her legs with his body. With his free hand, still holding the tights, he pushed her face into her pillow and leaned forward to speak in her ear.

"I won't hurt you if you stop moving," he said in slightly accented English. "Otherwise you will suffocate." Sara, already beginning to gasp for air, stopped and Mikanovich reduced the pressure on the back of her head so that she could breathe. The girl stayed still, so Mikanovich released his hand entirely and began to tie Sara's wrists with the tights.

Having finished he relaxed his grip. Sensing this was her chance, Sara tried to roll away from him throwing him off balance, causing him to fall sideways off the bed onto the floor, where only his training prevented him from landing too hard and badly injuring himself. As it was he would have a black eye from landing on one of Sara's block-heel shoes.

Recovering quickly, Mikanovich grabbed one of Sara's ankles as she went for the other side of the bed knocking her against the wall and dazing her. The noise meant that Mikanovich did not hear the muffled sound of a silenced gunshot or the sound of his approaching death.

Chapter 23

The thump of Mikanovich hitting the floor while his eye blackened had brought the eyes of David, Mary and Alexei to the living room ceiling. It was at this particular moment that Alexei lost control not only of the people he was leading and of the people he was holding captive at gun point, but also of his life.

Alexei was a professional, one of the best his country could produce. Spy against spy, professional against professional, Alexei could come out on top more times than not. But here, in Stoney Creek, he was with amateurs, indeed, less than amateurs. Ordinary citizens.

In some strange way, the Stones were the people for whom Alexei did what he did. It was the belief that he was making the world safe for the "average" man that sometimes kept Alexei going. No ideologue, Alexei had never been the committed communist his father was. Firmly he believed that Russia was in a struggle to maintain its position in the world, sometimes more aggressively than it needed to be, against the so-called Western democracies and the equally deceitful Chinese.

Alexei had no love for America. On the contrary, he found the United States disgusting, without genuine convictions or morals—though he thoroughly enjoyed the vast array of material goods available to the "average" man. As for Canadians, he hadn't thought much about them, other than they seemed to be a smaller lap dog to American wishes than the British.

In so far as the average Westerner was concerned, however, Alexei had no issues. He saw the ordinary European, Canadian, American as no different, substantially, than the ordinary Russian. Such people were, if anything, victims of their governments, cultures, societies, merely trying to get by, survive, and get ahead.

Universally, Alexei believed that the ordinary citizen, in any country, only wanted good things for himself, his family, his friends and sometimes, his community. The ordinary citizen was not a player in the great international game of espionage. He was not even an onlooker of this usually silent, though sometimes deadly, war. In Alexei's mind, the day-to-day life of the ordinary citizen did not reach such supposedly esoteric plains.

Perhaps it was out of these convictions that Alexei made his mistake. Certainly, he was angry at Mikanovich, who, if he were doing what Alexei suspected, he would kill when the mission was over. However angry he was, his judgment would not be coloured by it. Alexei had experienced out-of-control missions in the past and it had been his judgment which had given him the power to regain control. Perhaps it was that his conditioned response was not instantaneous when it came to killing an ordinary citizen, however.

Whatever the case, he hesitated when Mary Stone ran to the stairs to save her child. When he fired the silenced pistol, the bullet shattered the newel post, injuring Mary with a one inch splinter lodging itself a good half inch into her right cheek.

Alexei was not able to get off a second well-directed shot at the running woman as David dove at his extended gun arm causing the bullet to go through the hall closet door, through Mary's favourite summer jacket, through the plaster to its final resting place in the wood lath beneath.

As David rammed into him, Alexei fell over backward, the corner of the sideboard smashing into his wrist knocking the gun from his hand. Momentarily the pain and loss of balance delayed his response. Before Alexei could stop him, David went for the stairs after his wife, but he never made it. Alexei's off-balanced kick sent David sprawling on the foyer floor at the bottom of the steps, a heavy object jamming into his kidneys.

Alexei, the professional, knew David was on top of the gun before realization came to David. In fact David rolled off the gun not just because of the pain from his fall but to escape Alexei. David wasn't fast enough. Alexei grabbed him, spinning him around and throwing him against a door to wind him while he reached for the gun. It was a good strategy, but it failed. David hit the door with force, again pained in the kidneys, this time by a doorknob, but the door had a weak latch—David had been going to repair it for several months—and the door flew open and David went none too quietly careening down the basement stairs hitting the bottom with a soft "Ooooff".

Alexei adeptly lifted the gun off the floor and with it in hand rushed to the top of the basement steps. He could see nothing. The basement was dark and the sunlight streaming through the small front door window framed Alexei at the top. Instinctively he moved out of the light, squatted and slowly put one eye across the doorframe and squinted down the stairs. He thought he could see some lump at the bottom of the stairs.

Keeping his eyes on the lump, he stood and listened. There was no sound in the house except for a muffled kind of thumping upstairs as though someone was kicking a large pillow with their heel. Nothing came from the basement.

Having checked his gun and confident that Mikanovich could deal with a teenage girl and a hysterical mother, Alexei moved silently onto the top step. Slowly, step by step, Alexei eased his way down the stairs, gun at the ready hoping that the lump at the bottom was still breathing.

* * * * *

Mary went upstairs in panic. Between the bottom step and the upper landing something happened to her. She arrived in the upstairs hallway with a one inch splinter from the shattered newel post in her right cheek and consumed with a white rage. The kind of rage which was unidirectional, with only one focus, one purpose and it consumed her entire being. As she approached her daughter's bedroom door she saw the means to do what she had to do.

With a resolute smoothness, that belied the whiteness of her rage, Mary swung open Sara's door standing back a little as she did so. The man's buttocks confronted her, as Mikanovich was leaning over Sara who was now lying dazed on the floor.

The shaft disappeared a good eight inches up the anus, into the bowel, severing the rectal artery and penetrating the bladder. Mikanovich gave a jerk, projected by the force and the intensity of the pain, pitched forward over Sara's left leg and onto his face and stomach. The fall gave the arrow an opportunity to slice off a piece of his prostate and cut the vas deferens and urethra in half. Had he survived, Mikanovich's sex life would have been significantly changed. Since he was dead, it didn't matter. The agony of the method was written in the contortions of his face. An odour of feces mixed with that of urine as Mikanovich's bowels and bladder emptied.

Mary dropped the bow in the doorway and ran to her daughter, pulling the panties from her mouth, tearing at the pantyhose bonds, tears streaming down her face. The two women held each other and cried. Reassured each other and cried some more, each giving to and drawing on the strength they shared. They did not hear the man come up the stairs and down the hallway.

* * * * *

Naturally, Mrs. Schultz had noted the strange, though obviously brand new car in the Stones' driveway. Almost resentful at the Stones for having company while she was not at home and, therefore, not able to watch, she settled herself down with a can of pop and box of chocolates to watch for further developments.

For Geraldine Schultz it looked like a triple "A"- rated day. On her way home Mrs. Schultz thought she had seen the strange man. She had been waddling down the street, periodically being towed by her dog until she yanked him back in place—undoubtedly part of the dog's training program for strengthening his neck muscles—all four feet usually leaving the ground as the rotund, powerful woman asserted herself. It was just following one of these exercises when she noticed him. She was sure it was the man she had called the police about earlier. This time he had a companion with him and she did not get a clear view but she was certain it was the man and the same car.

Even more amazing, Mrs. Schultz had seen the two men come down what she thought was the Stones' front walk. She could not be certain because of the distance between herself and that end of the street. It occurred to her that it could have been her own front walk but she quickly repressed such thinking. Ever eagle-eyed, Mrs. Schultz observed the two men get into their car and then drive up the street and past her and Pookie.

Installed once more at her favourite watch station, when the soft sound of two silenced gunshots came from the Stones' house and through her open window, Mrs. Schultz was almost beside herself with excitement. She was not positive that they were gunshots, of course, but a noise, any noise, from next door could be a harbinger of better things to come. She ate four more chocolates. As she thought about the noise she began to convince herself that they had to be gunshots she had heard—her experience of such things being somewhat limited to the movies and television. Certainly gunshots were more exciting than David Stone doing some hammering in the family's seemingly never ending rounds of renovation.

"Still," she told herself "I must remain open to the possibility of gunshots." Mrs. Schultz did not wish to be too precipitous in calling the police again. She decided to wait on developments.

Chapter 24

When he fell down the basement stairs, David was lucky. Michael had not done as instructed and his sleeping bag and tent were still at the bottom of the stairs where he had tossed them after the previous weekend camp-out with his friends. They broke David's fall. Only winded and slightly bruised from his various falls, David had seen Alexei outlined at the top of the stairs and then suddenly disappear. It was at that moment that he had rolled off the tent and sleeping bag and out of sight.

David's only thought was to get upstairs and save his wife and daughter. Forcing himself not to go charging up the stairs "a foolhardy act which would only get me killed or seriously hurt," David tried to concentrate on what else he could do. If he were lucky, the man with the gun would come down after him. The alternative was for the two men to stand at the top of the stairs with Mary and Sara at gunpoint and simply tell him to come up or else. While he suppressed the thoughts of panic and consequences, he did allow his anger to surface and spur him on.

Basements, and David's was no exception, are full of useful things, such as tools, lumber, and dark and dingy corners. David knew he had very little time. He went into the furnace room, nothing, in his work area he looked almost frantically around and then saw what he wanted.

It was fortunate he did not have any time to think, for if he had, he would have realized the hopelessness of his situation and the utter naïveté of the plan that he was now formulating for dealing with it.

*   *   *   *   *

It wasn't until he was halfway down that Alexei realized that the lump at the bottom of the stairs wasn't a body, but some sort of cloth. He immediately squatted, balancing carefully on the balls of his feet, ready to spring up and forward. Nothing happened. Suddenly he realized that he didn't know if Canadians usually kept guns in their house the way he had been taught Americans do. He knew he would soon find out. He stood erect again and continued to descend the stairs.

On the one hand, Alexei knew that David Stone would be a piece of cake. What chance does the ordinary citizen have against the professional? But, unlike the professional, David Stone would be unpredictable, undisciplined, and irrational and it was these elements that made him dangerous to Alexei.

The Russian agent realized that he very much did not want to be here in this house, interfering in the lives of these innocent people. The Stones did not deserve what had befallen them. Certainly, Alexei did not want to be going down the basement stairs stalking a man with whom he had no quarrel and for whom he had nothing but sympathy.

As for Mikanovich, Alexei had no doubt that the pig had opted for some aggressive, physical, hands-on approach to waking the Stones' daughter and getting her to come downstairs. Instead of pursuing an innocent David Stone down basement stairs, Alexei would much prefer rushing up stairs and terminating the pig's life, not because he was a fool, not because his behaviour was now endangering the mission, but because he had no respect for the sanctity of this family, no realization that they could be in Kharkov or Moscow or Smolensk. Then Alexei realized Mikanovich would have behaved exactly the same in Kharkov, Moscow or Smolensk. Mikanovich would never see Russia again, but that was for later. Only once Alexei had the microdot.

Casting aside, for the time being, such thoughts, the Russian squatted on the third step before the bottom, removed his tie and threw it down the stairs. It floated safely to the open basement floor beyond the bottom stair, unmolested. Alexei followed it, landing on his haunches for a second, long enough to establish that no one was there and then rolled over to the side of the couch which he had seen as he scanned the room. There was no sign of David Stone.

Alexei did not expect to find David in the recreation room, but he had to eliminate sections of the basement one at a time. As he searched he kept himself ready to pivot and shoot at anything that moved to climb the stairs—a stunt he half expected the Canadian to pull. As an ordinary citizen he had to be most worried about his wife and daughter whom he had to fear were now both under Mikanovich's control.

Nothing happened. No dash for the stairs. No one in the recreation room. Alexei noted in the back of his mind that he did not expect Mikanovich to come charging downstairs to his aid. It would make killing him more of a pleasure—"no, wrong word"—justifiable was better.

Alexei now reached the room farthest from the stairs. If the man were to rush the stairs, this would be the time. Police-style, Alexei kicked open the door. Nothing. It was a storage room. There was broken summer furniture, a camp stove, and assorted cans of paints and varnishes on shelves, but no man.

Alexei then, for the first time, noticed a similar door at the other end of the recreation room, on the same wall as the stairs, but at the other side of the house. Silently he walked to the door, again police-style, he kicked it in, this time squatting as he did so. Nothing. It was an old fruit cellar and he could see the results of Mary's summer canning along the shelves.

Thoughts of home flashed across his mind as he saw the jars of jam, fruit and pickles. A room came into view and a woman stirring a pot on a stove. His mind went on relentlessly moving back to images of Ilyich and Galina, his best friend and the woman they had both loved.

Galina canned whenever she could get the fresh fruits and vegetables. Galina was his—Ilyich had, once, been a second choice, a way to ensure occasional and rare contact with Alexei. That had been twelve years ago. Now the relationship between Galina and Ilyich had taken on its own life, its own importance. Galina had given her love to Ilyich and their children and Alexei was now the outsider, the interloper, always welcome, always loved, but always on the outside.

Snapping back to the present, Alexei shook such thoughts from his mind, throwing aside the pain that they brought—a reminder of his aloneness. He moved to the laundry area under the stairs. There was no one. With a smile he approached the half size door which closed out a storage space under the stairs.

"This," he thought, "is where I would expect a frightened, ordinary citizen to hide." He squatted down, pointed the gun at the door and jerked the door open in one fluid movement. Nothing.

Alexei turned around. All that was left were the two doors off the laundry room. Alexei opted for the rational approach.

"Mr. Stone, please be reasonable. I have no wish to hurt you. Please, come out with your hands up and together you and I will put an end to whatever is happening upstairs." Nothing.

"Mr. Stone, I share your concern for your wife and daughter and any possible inappropriate behaviour on the part of my colleague and I assure you he will be severely dealt with. Please come out and together we will ensure he does no harm. I give you my solemn word." Nothing.

Alexei prepared himself to throw open the door. Gun pointed, he threw back the door, once again squatting as he did so. The full force of a bare two hundred watt light bulb blinded him as David switched it on when the door flew back.

Involuntarily, Alexei moved his left hand to shade his eyes, as he did so he saw the rifle pointing at him. Too late, he moved his right hand, the one holding the gun, to a proper firing position. The pellet penetrated his neck, stinging him and causing him to stagger backwards—more because of the psychological expectation than any force of impact.

Alexei had expected to be shot. When he heard the bang of the air rifle and felt the pellet penetrate his neck, his mind expected a bullet and reacted accordingly. This reaction was what David, the clinician, was counting on. It gave him the edge he needed.

Unhesitatingly, David brought the edge of a large pipe wrench down on Alexei's wrist, breaking it and causing the gun to clatter to the cement floor. Alexei staggered back further from the impact, his mind rapidly regaining control, assessing, judging. Too late. The pipe wrench swung upward so hard that it shattered Alexei's lower jaw, driving his lower teeth into the uppers with such force that several of his teeth fractured and splinted. Blood trickled from Alexei's mouth as he fell to his knees. The pipe wrench swung one more time and unconsciousness removed the excruciating pain from Alexei's mind.

The Russian fell, face first onto the hard, cool cement floor while the sickened ordinary citizen, David Stone, rushed to the laundry sink and puked.

* * * * *

By the time David reached Sara's bedroom the two women were beginning to laugh. They jumped as he entered the room and he saw guilt cross over Mary's face as she realized she had left him downstairs to his fate. The look passed quickly. They rushed to each other's arms, Sara joining in. The grisly remains of Mikanovich lay as a silent witness.

David and Mary exchanged looks and knew that it would be later that each would tell their tale. First things first and that was to leave.

Quickly. Without anything passing between them but looks, both knew what to do.

"Hurry, we have to get Michael," said David.

"Come along sweetheart," Mary took Sara by the hand.

David threw a cover over Mikanovich's body, and went back to the basement to retrieve Alexei's gun. Glancing at the Russian's inert body on the basement floor, David shuddered. A conscientious objector during the Vietnam War, he now believed he had killed a man. He felt no regrets, only a distant remorse.

His family had been threatened—no man could remain non-violent in the face of that. He instantly knew that to be true. He went upstairs to tell Mary and Sara that it was safe. After one intense hug, the three hurried through the front door.

Alexei's rental car was parked in the driveway, blocking them in. On a whim, David tried the driver's door. It opened. Even better, the keys were in the ignition. David had not fancied searching through the pockets of the dead men left in the house. The three Stones got into the rental car and drove away. Not slowly.

*   *   *   *   *

Mrs. Schultz was beside herself. She could not understand what was happening at the Stones' house. She reaffirmed for herself her dislike of them, in no way understanding that like all next-door busybodies she resented her neighbours because she did not understand them and because they did not inform her, in detail, of their every move and activity. Mrs. Schultz "harrumphed" to herself and opened another can of pop and a box of chocolate digestives, even going so far as to share one with Pookie. It was a quarter to three.

Chapter 25

The litany of names and numbers over, Gardiner hung up. Besides David Stone's name there were names of two men and one woman. The latter lived in Dunneville, Ontario, a small town on Lake Erie where the Grand River enters the Lake, and the two men in St. Catharines and Milton, respectively.

"Poor old Jerrow," he thought, "no Torontonians."

Gardiner's job, as Jerrow had assigned it to him, was to begin with the town closest to Buffalo and then go to the one furthest away from Toronto. After consulting a map it was obvious he was going to St. Catharines and Dunneville and check out the cars and their owners while Jerrow and Pasquale would do the reverse starting from Toronto.

The operative assumption had been that the cars and their owners would come from communities within a fifty mile/eighty kilometre, radius of Buffalo with, if they were lucky, an oddball in Toronto. They were not lucky. Gardiner shrugged, pulled out of the lay-by and went on his way.

* * * * *

Jerrow made out better than he'd expected. Within twenty minutes of his arrival at Toronto airport he had several pieces of valuable information. Pasquale had been lucky and had a fairly positive identification of the second Russian—stocky, hirsute, olive-skinned—who had rented a Chrysler from Budget. Coincidentally, a rental which had taken place at about the same time by the blond Russian, whom Jerrow now believed to be Alexei Petrovsky, was returning the Fifth Avenue at Hertz.

There may have been a number of men answering Mikanovich's description renting cars at the airport, but he had been the only one who had been easily remembered by a counter girl. Evidently he had looked at her in a "creepy way." The short of it was that Jerrow had a description and a license number of a car.

"Point for our side," he had said to Pasquale.

Sergeant Wilson was able to provide the consensual validation Jerrow needed of the description of the two Russians. He had had plenty of time to memorize their appearance while waiting for the emergence of the still-lost Prokanin. The sergeant also had another piece of news, which at first Jerrow was ready to dismiss without paying it much attention. It seemed that the Hamilton-Wentworth Regional Police—the local police for the Regional Municipality of Hamilton-Wentworth, which, among other communities included the large City of Hamilton and the smaller City of Stoney Creek—reported the presence of a car from the Russian Consulate in Toronto parked for an excessive amount of time with a man in it, in a residential neighbourhood in Stoney Creek.

At the time, the report meant nothing to Jerrow, though Wilson speculated that there might be some connection between this and the presence of Prokanin and the other Russians. According to the police, the description they had did not match either Prokanin or that of Jerrow's two Russians.

It was only when Jerrow remembered a third piece of information that he really came alive. Langley's list. There was Stoney Creek again. Jerrow's mind raced. He looked at his watch, but it told him nothing. Wilson was talking on in the background. Jerrow was not listening, only mumbling replies which he couldn't remember the moment they left his mouth.

"Tell me where these places are," Jerrow interrupted Wilson shoving a list of towns under Wilson's slightly out of joint nose.

Wilson scanned the list, took Jerrow over to a map of Ontario on the wall and pointed out the locations of Milton, Stoney Creek, St. Catharines and Dunneville.

Gardiner would be going to the latter two, Jerrow quickly reasoned, and for now it still made sense to cover those bases. Tracing a highway route to Milton and Stoney Creek, he realized that it was six of one and half a dozen of the other which was easier to get to from Toronto. But the evidence such as it was pointed to Stoney Creek and the car belonging to a David Stone. It was still a long shot, but Jerrow was beginning to get used to having only that kind of shot.

"Get the name of the street the consulate car was on," he ordered Wilson.

"It's in the report," he answered coolly. "Why?" He was not about to let this American take over, giving him orders. This was CSIS and RCMP business now and Wilson was going to make sure that everyone understood the jurisdictional issues. Besides, he had his own personal score to settle with the Russians—a matter of a little face-saving.

Jerrow's mind snapped back, his eyes cleared and refocused on the here and now. He understood that he had been back in the forefront of the chase—he had the scent now, more solidly than he'd had it before. In his mind he was already forty miles away in Stoney Creek.

"Sorry," he apologized to Wilson. "It's been a long chase and at no time was the outcome clear."

Wilson's only reply was a nod. Like the good agent and former police officer he was, he gave nothing away.

Pasquale said nothing. He decided that his silent observation was going to be one of the learning experiences he would have that day.

Jerrow had a choice. To spend the next several hours cajoling and convincing the Canadian and going through channels or he could go for a believable "truth" and make rash promises about shared information that he might not be able to keep. The problem, as usual, was time. He looked at his watch. Two-o-five. Gardiner could be close to St. Catharines now. Jerrow could call him and tell him to go to Stoney Creek.

First and foremost, however, Jerrow had to deal with a stubborn Canadian who was not going to be easily side-tracked. He made a decision.

"It's a long story sergeant, and before I tell you, I need a quick conference with my colleague here."

Once outside he told Pasquale to call Gardiner and tell him to go to the Stoney Creek address first because they had learned that it was an address of special interest to the Russians and the most likely site of Rita's body.

Pasquale nodded, taking the proffered list of owners' addresses from Jerrow's hand. Gardiner's phone went unanswered. Knowing nothing about southern Ontario, Pasquale assumed Gardiner was out of cell range.

"Now, Mr. Jerrow?" Wilson, taking charge, asked Jerrow on his return.

Jerrow had his tale ready. Within half an hour the three men were racing to Stoney Creek in a borrowed RCMP unmarked police car, a red light flashing in the front grillwork to tell the Ontario Provincial Police that this was official business. The time was two thirty-five.

Chapter 26

At two twenty, a man pulled his car into the Stones driveway and walked boldly up the front porch steps and rang the doorbell. There was no answer. It was then he noticed that the inside front door was ajar.

Looking as if the door had been answered, he smiled, nodded and went into the front hallway. His gun was in his hand the minute he was sure he could no longer be seen from the street.

All the time screwing an illegal silencer into the muzzle of his gun, the burly man stood in the main entryway listening to the noises of the house sending all his senses into the far corners. There was a smell of death about the place. A faint hint of cordite in the air. He started up the stairs, the long barrel of the gun pointing at the floor as it hung loosely in his left hand. Fragments of splintered newel post snapped as he stepped on them, announcing his approach. He saw the bullet hole in the closet door and moved on without breaking stride.

Without realizing it, the man reached a conclusion—it was the kind of conclusion one demonstrates by action rather than by formal announcement. He had concluded that there was no one alive in the house. He was wrong, and it was not to be the first time that day.

In the old-fashioned bedroom with the brass bed he found part of his answer, dead from an arrow, under a bedspread on the bedroom floor. Looking down at the body surrounded by various multi-coloured bodily fluids, the man did not know who the dead man was, not by name, but there was no doubt in his mind that the body was that of a Russian SVR agent.

The press card identifying him as a photographer for *Izvestia* proved his point, if he discounted the one saying he was a member of the OPP. The man pocketed all the Russian's papers and wallet, shrugging off the fact that there was no weapon. The Russian might not have bothered with one.

The arrow was a puzzle. Not that it was there or where it came from —he had stepped over the bow to enter the room. Where were the others, was the puzzle. Where was the archer? Who was the archer? Did the evidence mean that he had to consider another group? The British? CSIS? The Chinese? In the master bedroom he found David's blood-stained clothes on the hardwood floor.

Next, the man went downstairs, scanning quickly, and then into the basement. The silenced gun still hanging limply by his side, he stepped off the bottom stair, onto the sleeping bag and tent into the family room, turning the corner. He was ill-prepared for what happened.

Fully expecting to see more death, the stench of it was in the copper tinged air of drying blood, he was almost upended. Frightened, momentarily, by a hand that gripped tightly his ankle. As he yanked himself free, the gun now firmly grasped pointing downward, the trigger pressed, the hammer sliding back, he saw the battered, bloodied face of Alexei, too weak to stand without help or to maintain his grip on the ankle.

The once handsome Alexei could not speak clearly through the broken jaw and smashed teeth. The right wrist was obviously useless. The chin and lips had patches of encrusted blood. The pupils, however, were clear in the blood-shot sea and the man knew he was looking at a professional. A professional who had been injured doing his job, not like the fool upstairs.

Having unscrewed the silencer, the man dropped it into his pocket and returned the gun to its back holster, never taking his eyes from Alexei's. He smiled. It was neither a smile of friendship nor enmity, but a smile of superiority. The smile was a message to Alexei that the man with the put-away gun would not have let this happen to him.

Alexei was unmoved. He had seen that smile many times before on other faces, and he could not think of any face on which he'd seen it that was not now frozen stiff in death. Alexei knew that a feeling of superiority on the part of a professional was a sign of weakness, a loss of humility. It was usually a crippling, death-bringing sign.

Alexei looked away from the man with the shadow of death behind him and succeeded in pulling himself up into to sitting position. He was not interested in the man's fleeting feelings of superiority—that was between him and his God.

Ignoring the incapacitated Russian, the man looked in all the rooms and by the blood on the floor knew the battle had been lost and won at the furnace room door. His sense of superiority was heightened when he saw the cast-aside air rifle. He felt smug. He knew he should have known better. Smug can kill. But not him. Not today.

Out of mockery rather than pity, he picked up the discarded air rifle and dropped it at Alexei's feet. Alexei got the double message. He picked up the rifle in his uninjured left hand and began to use it as a staff to pull himself to his feet. Alexei had been mocked before—to react was a waste of energy. Besides, he needed all his energy now if he was ever to see home again.

Back on the first floor, the man went through each room and found the clue he was looking for, an open telephone book on the arm of the couch next to the telephone table. Without hesitation he held the book down with one hand while he tore the top page out cleanly with the other. Slipping the page into the left-hand pocket of his sport coat, he replaced the book as he had found it on the couch arm, only closing it.

Without another thought for the struggling Russian now on the bottom step of the basement stairs, the man left the way he had come, self-assuredly, boldly, out the front door, locking it tightly behind him. Walking down the porch steps as though he had just had a nice visit with his friends, he smiled once in the direction of the house and got into his car.

Not knowing the direction of his final destination, he started the car with its Statue of Liberty-embossed license plate and drove away in the direction from which he had come. The man did not notice Mrs. Schultz peeking at him through a corner of her dining room window. She was busy copying down the license number. It was turning out to be better than a triple-"A" day.

* * * * *

It was two-forty when Superintendent Michel Labelle arrived at the office. It was an hour and twenty minutes earlier than he had planned because of the phone call. Labelle had spoken to a Sergeant Wilson and agreed to meet him at the Stones' house at three-fifteen. That could put Labelle there well ahead of Wilson and he was asked not to do anything but observe the house discreetly.

Labelle had gone to the office to pick up an official car, a walkie-talkie and a tear gas gun. While not a lover of violence, Labelle had been a cop too long not to be smart enough to take precautions knowing all too well that they could prove their value. Wilson had not entrusted a great deal of information to Labelle over the telephone and had certainly not asked that Labelle take any unusual precautions. As he left his office, Labelle was feeling vindicated as his instincts of that morning had proven to be true. Here he was involved in possible espionage.

* * * * *

Ten after three was significant to the Stones. It was around that time that they had assessed the situation and had come up with a plan to get their son out of the cinema where he was still working.

In less than eleven hours the Stones had disposed of one body and left two more, one killed and another for dead by their own hands, lying in their home. There was no thought of calling the police for they believed firmly that by the time explanations had been made and believed Michael would be dead, killed by the two Mafiosi who clearly went after him at the movie theatre.

Besides, what could they explain? They knew nothing. They had no answers. The so-called Inspector Brown had said as much. Besides, who else goes around dumping bodies in trunks of cars and threatening innocent families? It was a well-established fact that Hamilton was a centre for some of the mafia families controlling Southern Ontario and Western New York.

There were, of course, terrorists, but that was even more frightening to contemplate than the syndicate, and terrorists did not act with quite as much cold-blooded rationality—if that word could be used to describe the four men who had invaded their lives.

In the end there was no time. No time to think. No time to talk. Only time to act. They told Sara the little they knew, greatly shortening the story about the woman's body, telling her only that they had left it at the side of the road.

Sara turned sheet white and seemed on the verge of hysteria. Then, obviously inheriting her mother's steel-like inner strength, passed to the other side of hysterics saying simply "OK." Indicating by that one word that she would now be fine, that she was in command of herself —she understood. It was also the "OK" which wanted to get on with whatever had to be got on with to make sure that Michael was able to join them. There would be plenty of time for hysteria later, or no time at all.

All of that had been half an hour before. Since then there had been some hard work done. A clear and concise plan developed.

The Stones had easily spotted the two Mafiosi parked strategically to observe all the entrances and exits of the movie house. They also noticed the two flat tires on Mary's car—the one Michael had driven earlier to work.

Quickly, the Stones decided that they could not walk into the movie house and out again with Michael. Nor could they warn him, for there was nothing he could do except get nervous. Whatever they did, the Stones knew they had to distract the two men while someone went inside and got Michael out. Mistakenly, David and Mary assumed that neither of the two men had seen Sara. She had been asleep upstairs when they arrived at the house. On this erroneous assumption, a decision was made that Sara could be seen by the two gangsters. The Stones did not know about the man who had been watching through their family room windows in the early morning hours. A man who was now watching the cinema exits through car windows.

Both David and Mary were still enraged, the white heat of their deep-seated anger permeated every thought, every decision. Sara too shared these feelings—and for good reason. All three saw no difference in what had happened to each of them from what they believed would happen to Michael if the two men succeeded in taking him. There was neither pity nor mercy in any of the thoughts the Stones had for the two men sitting so relaxed in their car, smoking and enjoying the warm August sunshine.

One of the plans being considered was simple. David and Mary could walk up to either side of the car and fire the captured pistols point blank into the heads of the two men. Easy to say. Difficult to do. David and Mary quickly realized that in spite of their anger, their desperation, they could not carry that off. It was simply just a little too cold-blooded. If the men threatened them directly, then yes. But to casually walk up to the car and open fire repulsed them. Gladly they would have paid someone else to do it and maybe even watched from a distance, but then, there was no time for such elaborate arrangements. Whatever they did, Mary, David and Sara had to do it now.

If the men had to be incapacitated, and the Stones were thoroughly convinced that this was the case, then they had to find a more indirect way of accomplishing the task. Whether incapacitation meant death to the men did not matter to the Stones. Together they formulated a plan. Each—David, Mary and Sara—contributed in their own way. It was certainly not a foolproof plan by any means, what plan ever is? It was a plan that they could live with, or die with, if it came down to that, though while knowing it was dangerous they didn't consider that they could die. Dying simply wasn't an option.

CHAPTER 27

For Prokanin, the afternoon was passing without incident. He and Talinsky had enjoyed themselves to the extent that the boring nature of their immediate task allowed. There had been the good German sausages from a famous local deli called Denninger's and then light conversation and the warm sun. Also, there was the occasional woman or girl showing a nice proportion of her supple body as she too enjoyed the sun while going about her business. When the attractive sixteen- or seventeen-year-old girl, music blaring from her iPhone, approached them the two men were wholly relaxed.

"Excuse me," she spoke, almost too softly to be heard over her music.

"What?" asked Prokanin who was on the passenger side where the girl stood.

The girl smiled and moved a little closer, raising her voice as she did so.

"I said, 'excuse me'," she smiled disarmingly.

Prokanin smiled back and Talinsky leaned forward and to his right wishing to be included in this unexpected conversation with the attractive teenager.

"Why, what did you do?" asked Prokanin in an older man's abortive attempt at flirting with a young girl.

"Nothing!" came the response, along with the smile, and a barely hidden "Oh brother" look in the green eyes. The whole, of course, accompanied by loud music.

Talinsky began to look hard at the girl. He had seen her somewhere before. The where was right there on the cusp of his memory, but it would not come forward and reveal itself.

Prokanin, embarrassed by the failure of his flirt and being genuinely uninterested in teenage girls, resorted to straight conversation.

"What can we do for you?" he asked warmly. Talinsky did not smile, he kept working hard, but the memory would not come. Something told him it was important that he remember, but the block remained firmly in place.

"Well," answered the girl a trifle coyly, "I was just wondering if you could tell me what time it is. You see I have to meet my friends at three and I've lost track of time in the mall," she inclined her head in the direction of the shopping centre, "and I'm afraid that I've missed them."

Prokanin, his guard down, was charmed, and did not hear or feel the scrape at the rear of the car. Talinsky missed it as well. He could feel recognition rising out of his subconscious as a result of his concentration. In a minute he would know who the girl was, or at least where he had seen her before and why it was important.

"It is only two minutes after," Talinsky heard Prokanin say.

"Thank you so much," the girl smiled her smile and turned away toward the movie house, replacing the earphones and moving her body in time with the now inaudible music, ensuring that the men's full attention went with her.

It was in the profile of the turn that recognition came to Talinsky. Recognition was reinforced by the walk. He had watched this girl just the night before through a basement window. Recognition came too late.

As the girl entered the movie house and Talinsky pushed on his door and Prokanin shook his head at the innocence of youth, their car's gas tank exploded.

The impact of the explosion threw Prokanin's head against the dashboard breaking his nose and dazing him. He reached for the door and realized the frame had buckled, the door would never open again. As he turned to his left to scramble out the driver's side the seat burst into flame and Prokanin had enough presence of mind to bite down on his poison pill before he died a far more painful death of fire.

For the merest instant, Talinsky thought he would survive. The thought barely registered. The explosion threw wide the door he was opening, shearing off the hinges and propelling him out of the car. There was no relatively soft dashboard for Talinsky. The force of the blast careened him against the car parked in the next spot. The impact broke his neck. Fire engulfed the car. People began to run in its direction. Some moved away, discreetly.

The Stone family, or those of it in the parking lot, had implemented their plan like a military operation. On the surface it had been a simple plan. Execution was a different matter, and fortunately their lack of knowledge kept them ignorant of its unreliability.

Sara's task had been that of distraction. She was to ask the men if they had the time. Not going too close and being ever ready to run. It had been Sara who suggested the music as the noise would further distract the men and cover up any sounds made by David and Mary. Mary and Sara had gone into the nearby Canadian Tire store and purchased a new iPhone for Sara. Needless to say, she had been pleased with her new acquisition.

Mary's role had been that of defender. She was to fire one of the guns, obtained courtesy of the Russian invaders, at anything but Sara and David. Mary was to stand two cars back and to Sara's side in case the men attempted to grab her. Mary felt confident with a bow, but she detested and felt totally unsure of herself with a gun.

David had had his difficult part to play as well. Removing one of his socks, he soaked it in gasoline from his own gas tank by lowering the sock into the tank fastened to the end of his belt by an elastic band Mary had found in her handbag.

Waiting until Sara had distracted the two Russians, David boldly walked toward the back of their car from the opposite side to Sara, where he had squatted down as though about to tie a shoelace. The success of the plan had depended on a well-known psychological phenomenon of North American society, people's passionate desire not to get involved. David rightly assumed that any passers-by who noticed him obviously interfering with the back of a car which clearly did not belong to him would choose not to get involved. Anyone who even began to get a sense that something was amiss would quickly suppress such thoughts with heavy-handed rationalization.

While Sara and her loud music had distracted the two Russians, David slowly and carefully removed the gas cap, dropping half the gasoline-soaked sock into the opening. From the corner of his right eye he saw Mary standing casually, her hand in her handbag, presumably on the gun she was to use in an emergency. David did not have sufficient faith in the North American aversion to involvement that he was willing to chance people ignoring a woman standing in a parking lot waving a gun around. Alexei's gun lay at David's feet on the asphalt of the parking lot.

Mary's cigarette lighter had not worked. David began to feel panic welling up inside. He began to taste the bile from his stomach as the lighter failed time after time. Finally, just as the panic had been about to gain an upper hand, it had caught as the movie house door opened to Sara's pull. The sock burst into flame. Grabbing the gun David crawled on his hands and knees, like some overgrown ten-month-old trying out for the Olympics, to the rear of the car parked behind the Russians where Mary was now standing her vigil.

As the movie house door closed behind Sara, Mary squatted next to David, just in time. The explosion wracked the Russian Consulate car and even on the ground where they were David and Mary could feel the intensity of the heat. Pieces of the car, some large, flew by overhead. After a few seconds David and Mary summoned up their courage, stood up and walked casually to where their own car was parked—the one rented by the now dead Mikanovich the day before at Pearson International Airport.

People began to run in the direction of the burning car. David and Mary disinterestedly got into their car and David drove up to just past the front entrance of the cinema. Sara, a confused but obedient Michael in tow, came out with some of the other movie house staff. The two teenagers got into the car. A crowd was rapidly beginning to gather around the now flame-engulfed car, fearful of getting too close in case of a further explosion.

Vainly, someone was trying to get the engine to turn over in the car in front of the burning wreck. A man stupidly risking his life to save an insured automobile. Finally he succeeded, managing in his rush to do a few hundred dollars-worth of damage to his own car and a similar amount to the one parallel parked across the way.

As David pulled away from in front of the cinema he noticed the ghastly figure of Prokanin encased in flame, the body seeming to dance as terrible heat contorted the long-dead body distorting it out of all human recognition.

A yellow fire truck, red lights flashing, siren wailing could be heard in the distance as the Stones left the mall and headed up a side road to Barton Street. At the intersection, David had to stop to let the screaming yellow monster pass.

The Stones needed time to think. Their future plans had stopped at blowing up the car and getting their son and themselves away. Surprisingly enough David found himself thinking of food, he pointed the car in the direction of a local roadhouse he frequented and which he knew would provide the ambience and the food he needed. The shock of having committed another two murders had not set in. The human mind being the wonderful thing it is had devised for David some excellent coping mechanisms. For now.

Michael's confusion was not significantly alleviated by the fact that both his mother and sister attempted to tell him what was going on at the same time.

It was three thirteen. By their own count David and Mary Stone, ordinary citizens, had personally killed four men and disposed of the body of an unknown woman, all in barely eleven hours. The life of the ordinary citizens from Stoney Creek had certainly taken a turn.

Chapter 28

Alexei Petrovsky was tough. He possessed more than his share of pertinacity when it came to survival. It took him ten minutes to make his way from the bottom of the basement steps to the back door of the Stones' house. Unlike the cock-sure prick, Alexei in his current condition did not possess either the mindset or the stamina to be bold. He preferred the back door.

On a hook, in the kitchen, as he stumbled by, he saw the spare key to David's Camry which was now the only car in the driveway. Alexei also saw a seven hundred and fifty millilitre bottle of Pepsi Cola on the kitchen counter along with an old fedora that David used as a gardening hat in the summer heat, hanging on a hook near the back door.

Stealing himself against the pain of his broken and oozing teeth, Alexei took the time to run cold tap water over his head and face to remove the dried blood and in a failing attempt to lessen the headache which was making him nauseous. Jamming the bottle against the counter wall Alexei succeeded in uncapping the Pepsi bottle with his left hand. Painfully, he managed to get half the contents of the bottle into his stomach. He badly needed the energy that both the sugar and the caffeine would provide and the warm pop might just settle his stomach.

The gash on the back of his head had stopped bleeding, as had his broken jaw and mangled gums. Alexei knew he had suffered a terrible concussion that explained his weakness. Indeed, it was probably only the severe pain that was keeping him awake.

Leaving the air rifle on the kitchen floor, Alexei stumbled down the back porch steps, the fedora on his head, half-filled Pepsi bottle in hand. On the whole he looked like some drunk leaving a party at four a.m. He was only thirteen hours early.

Alexei had known pain before, worse than this. His body had the scars to prove it. It had been pain so bad that he had relied on the below- zero temperatures of Siberian tundra to keep it in check. Using the bitter winds and skin-tearing ice spicules as a bloody but natural anesthesia.

Back in the present, in the muggy mid-afternoon heat of the Southern Ontario summer, he fumbled with the locked door of the Camry. The heat causing perspiration to flow freely down his face and its salt delivering more pain. For what seemed the longest time, but was only two minutes, Alexei could not understand why the key would not go into the lock. Four times Alexei checked to make sure he was using the right key and four times was able to assure himself of this. The fact that he was trying to put the right key in the right lock the wrong way up did not occur to him. Neither did the idea that he could have used the remote. He was far more concussed than he cared to admit.

Finally, the door opened to his tug, nearly knocking him to his knees in the driveway. It was only by the greatest exertion that he managed to stay on his feet, the half-filled bottle of Pepsi held tightly under his arm as though it contained either the elixir of the gods or nitroglycerine.

Without ceremony, Alexei sank heavily onto the front seat of the car, feet still planted firmly on the driveway, a distorted grin of proud accomplishment on his face, a glazed look to his eyes. Three minutes passed fully before it dawned on him that his task was not yet over. The goal he had established for himself in the kitchen was to get into the car and get the car out of the driveway. The realization came slowly that he had got in the car, but had yet to complete his task, and drive away.

Still behaving like a drunk, he hauled his legs in to the car by hand, almost falling forward head first onto the hard, unyielding asphalt. Once inside the car came the almost impossible job of closing the door. After three attempts, each almost ending in what would most certainly have been a fatal fall, head first to the asphalt, he abandoned the task. An inner memory, struggling to be heard via a distant synapse told him that the door would close of its own volition as the car surged forward at speed. The fact that he had first to back it out of the driveway did not register.

Throbbing all over, Alexei gave all of his attention to the next vital task, inserting the key in the ignition. This, of course, could only be accomplished after the ignition was located. The task was made even more onerous by the fact that he only had use of his left hand, the right wrist being broken by David Stone's swinging pipe wrench.

Several more minutes came and went in the slow-motion world of the blissfully ignorant. Alexei began to drift in and out of consciousness, losing the thread of his task, then, snapping awake, and tackling the insertion of the key on the right side of the steering column with a vengeance. For Alexei, three hours passed, for the ogling Mrs. Schultz, it was only three minutes.

Finally, the key went in and in a burst of cognitive energy, Alexei started the car and was then overcome with a feeling of satisfaction and accomplishment. He drank, painfully, the remainder of the Pepsi, dropping the bottle in the driveway through the wide-open driver's door. The bottle rolled out of sight beneath the car.

Concussion and shock were beginning to win out over the pain and Alexei had to struggle to keep awake now. The warm summer air was oppressive and perspiration poured down his face bringing salt to any open cuts it could find. He turned on the air conditioning inside the car, pointing all the vents he could find and manoeuvre directly onto himself. Slipping the car into reverse, the door swinging wide, he screeched out of the driveway onto the street with a loud popping sound as a rear wheel caught and trapped the Pepsi bottle, flattening it. Literally slamming the gearshift lever into drive, he lurched and then screeched down the street, the open car door closing tight with a bang. A feeling of satisfaction came over him to know that he had been proven correct about such matters.

* * * * *

Mrs. Schultz was so beside herself she stood immobilized, face pressed to the sheer curtains of her dining room bay window as the drunken stranger drove away in David Stone's car wearing David's grubby fedora. For once in her life Mrs. Schultz's ability to react was outstripped by events. She couldn't move.

Two minutes later, Mrs. Schultz's difficulties were exacerbated when yet another strange car slowed as it passed the Stones' house and then was parked in one of the vacant spots directly in front of her house. Mrs. Schultz finished off the last chocolate digestive and had another can of pop. She did not call the police as to do so she would have had to leave the dining room that meant ceasing to look out the window. She was sure she had seen neither the new man nor his car before. She was right. She then noted that the man was driving an unmarked police car. She was pleased with herself.

* * * * *

The injured man did not escape Superintendent Labelle's notice. The man had been driving an older model charcoal grey Camry, at a speed higher than appropriate for the residential neighbourhood they were in.

Since he was no longer on traffic duty in Prince Albert, the Superintendent limited himself to his best stern look. The man with the damaged face continued on unabated, almost oblivious to Labelle's attempted projection of his policeman's authority.

It was only later that it dawned on the Superintendent that he had unwittingly witnessed the escape of a Russian agent and had merely attempted to make him follow the traffic rules, and not even that successfully.

The peering eyes of Mrs. Schultz did not go unnoticed by Labelle as he cautiously pulled his car to a halt in front of her house. The Superintendent determined to have her questioned when the men from Toronto arrived.

"Funny," he thought to himself, "that all seems so quiet at the suspect house. Funny too, how different the spy business seems from the police business. Why, if this had been the closing of a ring in a CID case we'd have had men all over the place, both ends of the street and down the adjoining side streets and over the backyard fences. What the hell are they going to do here, just walk up to the door and ring the bell?"

Labelle knew he was exaggerating a typical police arrest procedure—describing a television version rather than real life, but still there would have been more precautions and certainly backup cars ready at hand if he had been in charge of this situation.

However, Superintendent Labelle was right about one thing. When Jerrow, Pasquale and Wilson arrived a few minutes later, Wilson pulled the car into the Stones' driveway, parking it so it would catch whatever shade the black walnut tree on their front lawn could offer. Labelle opened his car door, resisting the temptation to smile at the woman who was now blatantly staring at the whole scene, her entire head between the front window curtains, eyes bulging, mouth working, the head moving back and forth slightly between him and the new arrivals like someone anxiously waiting for match point at a table tennis tournament. The performance confirmed for Labelle that the woman was going to be questioned at length, and not by him. Labelle had interviewed his fair share of such busybodies.

Looking toward the newly arrived car, Labelle could see the men inside talking animatedly. He walked in their direction. A somewhat slender, bespectacled, bearded man got out of the front passenger door and advanced toward him. The two met halfway down the length of the rear bumper.

"I'm Jerrow, Superintendent."

Labelle seized and maintained eye contact with what he realized were very penetrating brown eyes. They were eyes that missed nothing, revealed nothing. The only humanity Labelle could find in Jerrow's eyes was in the faintest hint of laugh lines at the corners that may only have been the crows' feet of impending age.

Labelle held out his hand, the return grip was firm without any implication of turning this common method of social greeting into a macho contest.

"With your permission," said Jerrow, releasing the grip and the eye contact and nodding in the direction of the house.

Suppressing his urgent, policeman's need to conference, Labelle almost unperceptively allowed a slight incline of his head. Together, Jerrow and Labelle left the other two men standing one on each side of the car staring after them, Wilson moving instinctively to the passenger side next to Pasquale, putting the car between himself and the house. His old RCMP training was coming to the fore.

"So, it really is done like this," Labelle told himself, as he walked beside Jerrow up the front walkway of the Stones' house. Together, the two men climbed the front porch steps like a couple of friends dropping in for a quick beer while they were in the neighbourhood.

Proving Labelle's joke about prediction and with a familiarity he did not feel, Jerrow rang the bell. There was no answer. Jerrow was not surprised. He tried the door. It opened, but the main wooden door behind it was clearly locked. Without hesitation he reached into his pocket and took out his picks.

They were not unlike those used by Mikanovich on a hotel room door in Buffalo. Indeed, they were both from the same manufacturer in Trenton, New Jersey. Conveniently, while Jerrow worked, Labelle found himself fascinated by the hanging geranium plant nicely centred over the front railing of the porch.

The lock liberated, Jerrow and Labelle stepped into the front foyer. In the same tone he would have used if he had entered a friend's home unannounced—if he had any friends with homes—Jerrow called out "hello, anyone home." Silence was the answer.

Jerrow moved to the bottom of the stairs, which gave him a better vantage point from which to look around, and called again. No answer came. Nodding to himself, he looked at Labelle. The Superintendent strode authoritatively to the still open front door, opened the screen and waved in the general direction of Wilson and Pasquale.

There was a bit of a scuffle as the two men attempted to decide the best way to reach the porch. It was Wilson who finally took the lead and established the route—around the grass, not over it, and up the sidewalk. Jerrow held the two men to the foyer and then looked to Labelle affirming that everyone expected the Superintendent to take command. For his part, Labelle had every intention of assuming command—he was the senior Canadian official present. However, he was inwardly pleased that he did not have to wrest control away from the strange, slight American.

Assuming the man who had been driving the car was Wilson, Labelle turned to him. "There's an exceedingly nosy old bitch next door," Labelle said to the CSIS man, indicating which side with his thumb, "go see what she can tell you, keeping in mind, of course, that whatever you say to her will be exaggerated beyond all recognition and appear even more exaggerated on the front page of the rag they call a daily newspaper around here."

"I'll be discreet, Superintendent," Wilson replied and unhesitatingly moved between Jerrow and Pasquale and out the front door. It had obviously not occurred to the man to question Labelle's right to issue the orders. One could only admire his courage in so unflinchingly facing alone, what would be by now the slobbering figure of Mrs. Schultz. It could, of course, be naiveté. Unless, of course, she was overwhelmed by chocolate and caffeine.

Turning to Pasquale Labelle said, "You are?"

"Pasquale, Manuel Pasquale," the American agent found himself responding under the gaze of the soft brown bushy-browed eyes. He realized he was almost feeling guilty because he had stopped at his name and did not reveal his identification number.

Labelle nodded, as though he knew the information just imparted to him by Pasquale was incomplete. Another nod. This time it successfully implied that any additional details about Pasquale's life would only represent a mere formality anyway since Labelle already knew all there was to know including that incident in the candy store when Pasquale was ten-years-old, poor and possessed by an unrelenting sweet tooth. Pasquale was visibly relieved when the Superintendent seemed willing to let the matter rest, at least for the time being, and focus his full attention on the blank-faced Jerrow.

"Possibly four men," Jerrow began, repeating the story he had told Wilson earlier. "All believed to be Russian agents, two international, one from Ottawa and one a consulate type from Toronto.

"Yesterday, two of these men—the internationals—killed a blonde, thirty-five year-old woman SVR agent who we believe was planning to defect to the West. Evidently, the agent, whose body is missing, had something valuable that belonged to the Russians. She was planning on buying sanctuary with the item. We believe a microchip of some kind. Naturally, the Russians wanted it back.

"We don't know what the microchip contained, but we believe the information was important enough that the Russians were willing to go quite far to retrieve it. Somehow, again we are not quite sure how, though we believe it happened at Buffalo airport, David Stone, whose house this is, came into possession of this valuable item and the Russians have come after it.

"Our task," Jerrow inclined his head in the direction of Pasquale, "has been a somewhat unrelated one as we have been tracking the international agents who we have only recently identified after over two years of digging and probing.

"The Russian agents led us inadvertently to the defecting woman who had actually been negotiating with a different section of our department. That man is following another lead and his name is Gardiner. You'll be meeting him soon."

Jerrow stopped. He waited patiently for the Superintendent to analyze, ponder and then make his response. Labelle simply nodded. Apparently, he was now waiting for Jerrow to continue, offering Jerrow the same gaze he had graced Pasquale with a few minutes before.

Pasquale was both impressed and made nervous by how sincerely Jerrow had lied. It was a skill he hoped he could acquire for himself. His nervousness enhanced his already shuffling feet into a general fidget. Repressing a sudden desire to stamp heavily on Pasquale's instep, Jerrow was not to be drawn in by Labelle's tactic. He waited, along with the Superintendent—after all, this was his territory and he was in charge. Having told as much of his tale as he intended, Jerrow knew that if he kept talking without prompting he would be disbelieved. No professional ever volunteered anything to anybody unless it was unavoidable. The American agent knew that if Labelle was half the cop he seemed to be he would not believe all that Jerrow had told him, but he wouldn't know what the truth was and what was a lie, since all was plausible.

To the now antsy Pasquale's great relief, the Superintendent spoke. For Labelle it was not a matter of giving in and breaking the silence. Like Jerrow, he knew it was his move. He was in charge. It pleased Labelle that Jerrow was no rookie ready to fill silence with the sound of his own voice hoping to impress a senior officer with the minuscule pieces of wisdom that their naive, inexperienced minds could fathom and then manage to articulate, albeit without any perception of the value of brevity.

Certainly, Labelle did not believe half of what Jerrow had told him, but saw no point in peppering him with questions. Action would give him time to think while perhaps revealing some shard of truth.

"I would suggest a walk-through first. Three of us, three floors," he said directly to Jerrow, "you up, me down and Pasquale here, the main."

Jerrow did not miss the fact that the Superintendent was making a suggestion, and appreciated the oblique invitation to offer an alternative course of action.

"Fine," was his inflection-free response. "Easy," was what he turned and said to Pasquale. The nervous fidgeting diminished significantly and the young agent moved cautiously toward the living room standing in the entry way and scanning carefully the whole room before moving into it. Jerrow went upstairs, noting the shattered newel post and the various splinters scattered all over the place as if many shoes had picked up and kicked the various pieces. Once on the second floor he began the same room-by-room inspection of the house already done once before that day. Labelle went for the basement, not missing the blood trail leading down the stairs and also leading toward the back door.

Like the visitor before him, Jerrow noticed the possible tell-tale signs of violence from the stained sleepwear on the bathroom floor. He observed, but touched nothing. The bathroom told Jerrow that someone in the house was a home handyman. The pine tongue and groove wall coverings and louvered cabinet doors, while well done, were not professionally done. Jerrow appreciated the old wood taste of the place.

An odour that was obviously working itself up into a stench began to assail Jerrow's nostrils, clamouring for attention. It was coming from further down the hallway, and it smelled as if someone had defecated and not bothered to clean up the mess, or like a bathroom after a particularly lengthy and strenuous bowel movement. Jerrow entered the room from which the odour was emanating.

For the first time in a long time Jerrow was surprised at the sight of a body. Perhaps it was the fact that Mikanovich's particularly gruesome remains lay in the untidy, but nevertheless feminine ambience of a girl's bedroom. Cautiously he spent some time moving around the room, missing nothing—yet not quite seeing what was out of place. Something was wrong in the room, something was not where it should be, but the exact nature of the anomaly remained hidden to Jerrow's conscious mind.

He went over the details again, standing stock still, eyes roaming the room sector by sector. There was the cast-aside girl's clothing covering the hardwood floor—the bedspread and top sheet, the stuffed animals of childhood still trying to hold their own against an intrusive array of rock-star posters. There were other miscellaneous memorabilia of a fading girlhood still living comfortably alongside the signs of approaching womanhood. Make-up and make-up light, the toes of the panty hose used to tie Sara's wrists peeping over the edge of the mattress at the head of the bed. Even through the stink coming from Mikanovich there was a faint whiff of perfume in the air and, of course, the arrow sticking prominently out of the dead man's anus. Nothing. He would have to wait. From experience, Jerrow knew that whatever it was he had seen would reveal itself in his mind's own good time.

He moved on to the other rooms, an unusually tidy boy's room showing the same effects of the childhood and adulthood struggle as the girl's. Here the signs of childhood had faded almost entirely, demonstrating to Jerrow how quick men are to deny their childish side as though it were a sign of weakness. The boy's room, while it did not display the whole gamut of growing up, clearly showed the tension between grasping a hold of adulthood and savouring the more carefree days of adolescence.

Unlike the previous room, the floor here was carpeted, a rich chocolate brown, the walls a pale coffee, giving the whole room a warm earthy, womb-like sense about it. On the walls was an assortment of athletic, rock and cheesecake shots. A partial weight-lifting set was neatly arranged in one corner. Jerrow moved on; there was nothing here for him except his own boyhood.

The master bedroom was a warm, comfortable place. A place he would never have with any woman. Certainly not Rita. The room was dominated by wood. It was in the floor and in the furniture. Even the rich, though small, Oriental rug on the floor, seemed to ooze wood. A pine cannonball waterbed came off one wall leaving the others to antique dressers, one with a mirror. The room was untidy. One of the dressers, presumably the man's, was literally piled high with a vast array of papers, coupons, nuts, bolts and a veritable plethora of things. A man's clothing covered an old-style oak chair at the base of which was blood-stained clothing. One side of the bed was littered with a woman's clothes and old discarded Kleenexes. There was nothing here for Jerrow except things that could never be.

As he descended the stairs to the foyer it hit him. He found it necessary to fight the temptation to rush back upstairs into the girl's room and validate his conclusion. Jerrow had his clue and continued down the stairs, stopping to examine the bullet hole in the closet door and the splintered newel post finding a piece stained with blood.

CHAPTER 29

Superintendent Labelle had more clues than he knew what to do with. Just as Sara's room gave up a significant clue to Jerrow, the basement treated Labelle equally well.

Twenty years ago, when he had been a somewhat green, but know-it-all new detective sergeant, Labelle had not only come perilously close to destroying evidence in a double-murder investigation, the incident would not have benefitted his career a whole lot either. Instead, he had succeeded in making himself the butt of many jibes for months to come.

Like today, he had taken the basement of a house as his area of search and carefully, ever so carefully, went down the basement stairs, turned the corner into a family room and slipped and fell into a still-drying pool of blood. The accident, which put Labelle in hospital for a week with a broken tibia, was not made easier to swallow by the fact that he had found the two bodies. His startled cry, as his feet went out from under him, followed by the loud thump his body made as it landed and the painful scream which emitted from Labelle's mouth as his tibia snapped, brought three other officers into the basement, weapons drawn, to share in his discovery. They were also provided an opportunity to snicker and spread the word of the tight-assed Labelle's misfortune.

The now Superintendent never made the same mistake again. Twenty years after Labelle was able to take some pride in the fact that his experience was held up at detective training school as an example of how not to enter a basement when you suspect a crime, particularly a bloody murder, has been committed.

With the same caution as twenty years before, Labelle descended the basement stairs, having put on all the lights. On the way down he noted what appeared to be still moist blood droplets on the stairs, a blood smear on the banister and bloodied fingerprints on the adjoining panelling. He kept going. Forensics would give him the answers he needed.

Like déjà vu, without the accompanying thump and broken tibia, he found a patch of blood on the sleeping bag on the floor at the bottom of the stairs. More smears were evident on the wall panelling and a trail could be seen clearly heading to what was surely a coagulated pool by a door off the rec room, glinting almost black in the incandescent light.

Superintendent Labelle was a good cop. He quickly looked around the remainder of the basement and was able to identify a half dozen of what he believed lab work, or a good wash in warm soapy water, would reveal to be teeth from both the upper and lower jaw of a human being. Blood and what appeared to be blond hair on an obviously hurriedly cast aside pipe wrench made his next conclusion an easy one. He had seen enough for now. From just a cursory inspection, Labelle was satisfied that he had gleaned a great deal of information. If the two Americans had been equally lucky then it would not be too difficult to piece together what had taken place here.

Of course, that was only an ideal. Chances were that the other two floors of the house would reveal nothing immediate. Under these circumstances they would be left with all the clues to what was at least a severe beating with no victim and no perpetrator. But then, that was why God provided police officers with the Mrs. Schultz's of this world.

"Thank God for busybodies," he told himself as he went back upstairs. Thinking also "Thank God Wilson was interviewing her and not me."

"We'll need forensics," said Jerrow, simply making a statement while thinking forensics would take time they didn't have.

The Superintendent nodded. Jerrow knew it was not the nod of agreement, merely one of recognition. Labelle had heard what he had said. Jerrow kept his anxiety under control and certainly out of sight. There was a dead man upstairs with his pockets turned out. There had been a murder.

When all this got revealed, Jerrow believed it would be time to call in the locals. This would cloud the jurisdictional lines and Jerrow could see the current cooperative information sharing coming to a rapid end.

"Let's see what we've got first," finally came the answer from the Superintendent, as though he had been reading Jerrow's mind. Labelle moved in the direction of the kitchen, looking to Pasquale to indicate if it was safe.

"I suggest the dining room table," he said, "The kitchen has possibilities."

* * * * *

Mrs. Schultz hovered between the telephone and the door. The telephone would bring the police, for she was certain she should phone them. "Just in case." On the other hand, the handsome young man at the door was obviously intimately involved with the strange goings-on next door and she did not want to miss out on this excellent, once-in-a-lifetime opportunity to get some inside facts. She moved to the door, making a futile attempt to straighten out her flowered housecoat over her 220 pound frame.

On reaching the door she hesitated, "supposing the man is a criminal?" she asked herself "and I am the only witness whose testimony could transform the evidence to be presented by the Crown."

She attempted to frizz up her short, permed hair with the nail bitten ends of her pudgy fingers. "Totally oblivious" would be the way an outside observer would describe how she dealt with the fact that Pookie was frantically tearing at the door as though Sergeant Wilson was likely to be his last supply of fresh meat for many months to come.

"The young man looks like a police officer," she hurriedly told herself, reaching for the door with her best crooked-tooth smile forward and her powerful left hand hauling Pookie back by the collar as though he were a pet gerbil rather than a forty pound dog.

Pretend RCMP Sergeant Wilson inwardly rolled his eyes. He had interviewed many a neighbourhood busybody and their assortment of yapping and sometimes ripping dogs. Mrs. Schultz looked no different to Wilson than all the others. He suspected that busybodies bought their flowered housecoats on some kind of discounted bulk purchase deal. Definitely none of them were permanent members of weight-watchers. Also, their dogs all went to the same disobedience school and probably all had the same lineage.

Experience taught Wilson that the woman would be more than eager to help, but for all the wrong reasons.

"This woman will tell me everything she can about the Stones," he said to himself, "not because she cares about them or is concerned about their welfare, but because she can have an accomplice to justify her nosiness and share the distorted, sordid truths she believes she has garnered. Of course, there is always the fact that she is doing this because she can have my undivided attention and possible admiration for the next thirty minutes, if I'm lucky, or an hour or more, if I'm not, depending on what information she really has."

Wilson knew, again from experience, that once the woman had answered his questions and then answered some questions he didn't ask and then volunteered some information that she believed might be useful, even though it is third-hand and highly speculative to boot, and then proffered her opinion on law and order in the streets and then attempted to impress him with her vast knowledge of police work learned either personally or through a close relative taking advanced courses in criminology at a local college, or through a close personal friendship with a high-placed personage in the local police department —Wilson knew that after all this would come the agonizing task of isolating the real and useful facts. All this would take place, naturally, while the dog would do everything except pee on him. Wilson's best estimation was that the dog was too big and too much of a mongrel for that. Besides, there were no tell-tale signs on the front door mat. Throughout the interview, however, he knew the dog would be occasionally choked and severely reprimanded verbally. Inwardly cringing, Wilson proffered his identification to the hauteur "yes?" of the woman.

Instantly, Wilson saw she was suitably impressed—"they always are"—by the fact that he was from the RCMP.

"This is the big time, lady," he said to himself as he accepted the invitation to "come in." Mrs. Schultz was too titillated to notice the look of resigned boredom on the handsome sergeant's face.

Geraldine Schultz knew that this was the big time and if she played her cards right she would be able to regale friends and family alike with tales about this day for years to come.

CHAPTER 30

David had never seen a police car there before. In all the times he had come to this roadhouse there had never been a police car in the parking lot. With little difficulty he found a suitable parking spot somewhere other than the vacancy next to the patrol car.

After the bright sunshine outside the darkness of the roadhouse was overwhelming. It was very difficult for the Stones to look over the place to see if the police were inside. David had to suppress questions that were clearly idiotic under the circumstances such as, "How did the cops figure out we'd come here?" There was no need for David to use his clinical skills to realize the beginning symptoms of paranoia, or was it just plain fear?

The family saw an empty booth down one side that had a window on the parking lot and from which the restaurant entrance could be observed. They began to make their way toward it when David spotted the uniformed figure sitting, at the bar no less. There was something wrong, but he was unable to identify specifically what it was. Then it struck him.

It was highly unlikely for a uniformed police officer driving a clearly marked patrol car, to stop at a roadhouse and sit at the bar drinking beer on a late Saturday afternoon, no matter how badly he wanted to. David looked closer and realized that the uniform belonged to some military unit of some kind—les Forces Canadiennes. He smiled to himself and felt the deceleration of his heartbeat.

The heart's deceleration was only momentary. It accelerated right out of control as David's arm was seized and held firmly from behind. Switching to clinical mode, and introducing total lack of expression to his face, David forced himself to turn around. As he did so, he saw his family beginning to sit down in the booth. Whatever might happen in the next few minutes he decided he would do something in order to give his family a chance to get away. Completing his turn, David focused a portion of his mind on tensing his muscles and preparing himself for action. Adrenaline began pumping into his system, amazing that any was left, and David could feel his body react. He faced the owner of the arm that held him.

"Hi, Dave, how are you?" It was Sheila Preston, a reporter with the local daily newspaper. "I didn't know you frequented places like this?" It was meant as a joke. He had seen her in the place the week before.

David grinned, hoping the thin veneer of sweat he knew was forming on his forehead would not be noticeable in the darkness of the restaurant. "Slumming," he smiled. "I'll talk to you soon," he said a little too quickly, indicating his family, "good to see you again."

A touch of the hand still on his arm, "take care," she smiled back, a slight frown on her forehead, and went toward a table where she had obviously been sitting with some colleagues.

David knew he had been too brusque. He had violated the socially acceptable time a person was to devote to the meaningless chitchat, which accompanied such unexpected encounters. Quickly, he realized he didn't care. Gladly, he joined his family in their booth.

The cold, dry conditioned air in the restaurant was hitting David's sweat-soaked shirt and he was grateful for the coolness it was bringing.

When the server came, neither David nor Mary resisted the temptation to order alcohol. They would attempt to temper its affects with coffee when the meal was over.

Without exception, they were all ravenous and waited impatiently, or was it nervously, for the food to arrive. No one broached the all-important question, "What now?" Though before the drinks had arrived David and Mary had excused themselves to go to the bathroom, seizing the opportunity to talk.

"I think we should call Steven," David said.

"I agree." So he had gone to the pay phone outside the bathrooms and having looked up the lawyer's number on his cell phone he called Steven Greene. David was in luck. Steven was still in his office.

The fact that Steven worked a number of Saturdays was known to David. As a rising young lawyer, Steven intended to stay rising. Steven was more than willing to see him and certainly expressed the kind of concern about his well-being that David would have expected from Steven, who was also a friend. David had told him that he and Mary had to meet with him about an extremely urgent matter, indeed, a matter of life and death. While he and Mary and the kids were all perfectly fine, something terrible had happened and they felt they needed a lawyer as well as a friend. David demurred on giving Steven any further information until they met and was relieved when Steven didn't press the matter.

For his part, Steven had indicated that he could see them immediately and suggested it be at his office as that was where most of his reference books were. In concluding the call, David said they would be at Steven's in forty minutes.

The ravenousness melted away when the food arrived, and with the exception of Michael they listlessly picked at it, all the time talking of inconsequentials until Sara brought them back to reality.

"So, what are we going to do? We can't sit here forever. I'm scared." She was fighting back tears, the kind that lead spiralling down into the heart of hysteria.

With this prompt, Mary and David told Sara and Michael of the plan to see Steven. The children both knew Steven, and liked him. They were pleased that they could involve him in helping the family work out what to do. There were obvious sighs of relief when the family emerged into the bright sunshine to see the police car gone.

* * * * *

Alexei Petrovsky had no choice. Since he could barely open his mouth, let alone speak, he did not see any chance whatsoever of renting a car without being remembered. Furthermore, car rental agencies would be high on the list of his hunters. He could not take a chance driving David Stone's car very far. He was sure the police would be looking for it in earnest in no time at all. The stern look given to him by Labelle as the latter arrived on the Stones' street did not go unnoticed. Alexei easily recognized it as the look of a policeman. His best bet was public transit. He would less likely be remembered among the hundreds or thousands of customers passing through each day and it would require a police presence, not just a phone call, to get him identified.

Even though it meant walking a longer pain-filled distance, Alexei pulled the Camry into an empty parking spot in the middle of the crowded cars in the Aldershot GO Transit station parking lot in the hopes it would take longer to find. The GO trains were commuter trains feeding the towns and cities outside Toronto into the city. While Mikanovich had slept at the hotel, Alexei had used Google on his cell to study the various transportation options out of Stoney Creek and Hamilton should they have to abandon their car and go on the run—standard operating procedure when in foreign territory and being hunted.

Once out of the Camry, Alexei did his best to ensure that David Stone's ill-fitting raincoat, which he had found on the backseat and wore like a cape because of his broken wrist, hid his blood stained clothing. Somewhat drunkenly walking across the back of the several hundred parked cars, Alexei waited until he was approaching the GO station entrance from a completely different direction from where he had parked the car, he managed to concentrate enough to steady his walk as he approached the ticket booth. The old fedora pulled down and looking vaguely like some escapee from an old Bogey movie, Alexei purchased a ticket on the next train to Toronto. Because it was difficult to make himself understood, he had had to write his request on a slip of paper handed to him by the mystified and frustrated ticket seller in response to Alexei's wild gesticulations. He thanked his training on learning to print with his left hand.

From Toronto, Alexei would catch the Aeroflot flight to Moscow. It was very likely that the bi-weekly flight out of Toronto's Lester B. Pearson airport was watched, but there would be nothing that Canadian authorities could do. Surely they would rather he leave the country and, thereby, be rid of him forever than to tangle with Russia over the sanctity provided him by a diplomatic passport.

The first thing that Alexei did once he had purchased his ticket was to go to the single unisex bathroom. Not just for the usual reasons, but to also shred and flush all identity papers down the toilet. Because of his broken right wrist he was forced to tear up his papers by holding them down with his foot and tearing with his left hand—he was aided by the fact that the floor in the lavatory was wet, making the papers easier to rip or screw into a ball. Blood rushing to his head every time he bent over made his head pound even more and the agony in his jaw almost unbearable.

Down the toilet too went his false police badge. Clearly there was a strong chance that the badge and the poorly torn passport cover would clog the drain, but by the time that was noticed, reported to the right person, and something was done about it, Alexei would be well on his way to Moscow. On the other hand, the trash could be emptied in ten minutes and the badge and papers spotted immediately.

Alexei had no gun to ditch. The weapon had been missing when he came to after David Stone had walloped him with the pipe wrench. Alexei also took the opportunity to let water from the cold tap pour over his pain-racked head. He was able to do this for a full three minutes before someone rattled the bathroom door in an attempt to enter. It was not pleasant toweling himself dry with the harsh paper towels, but he managed. With effort he was able to mask the worst blood stains on his dark blue suit jacket. The shirt was a write-off, though fortunately, with his jacket closed, the ill-fitting raincoat pulled across and the tie slightly askew to the left, he could hide most of the dark-red stains.

To further prove that God was not going to go easy on Alexei, the only escalator was travelling up and he had to face the forty steps down to the underpass. The GO train platform for the eastbound trains, of course, was at the far end of the underpass and once there he faced another forty steps back up to the surface. While struggling through the underpass he could hear the bells of his train entering the station. While the trains ran every half hour he wanted to avoid hanging around the station any longer than necessary. As he limped onto the train the beep sounded, the doors closed and the train began to pull out. Luck hadn't completely left him.

Except in weekday rush hour, Aldershot is not an especially busy station and the long double-decked green and white train was not very crowded on this late Saturday afternoon. Alexei struggled his way up to the top deck of the train hoping that it would give him a better view of the stations the train would stop at en route. The higher view would perhaps give him some warning of police coming on board in search of him.

It only took Alexei three minutes to get the cell phone out of his right side trouser pocket, a task he had to stand up to accomplish, managing to only fall over once as the train hit an uneven piece of track. If they noticed, the three other people in the compartment with him said nothing.

The cell phone liberated and turned on, Alexei saw the red flashing signal for a low battery. Luck had left him again. With great difficulty and with several repeats with the background beating tone of his dying battery, Alexei managed to provide the code required and get his needs communicated. Within two minutes he got an answer and shut the phone down—the red eye of low battery still blinking. Luck had come back.

The one thing Alexei knew he couldn't do was fall asleep, in spite of the comforting rock of the train. He was helped a little in this regard by the man two seats over speaking in a loud voice into his cell phone about some real estate deal he was involved in. At Burlington, a young woman got on with cheap earphones allowing her music to be shared with all those around her.

With this background support, Alexei forced his mind to the man who had all but left him to be caught in the Stones' house. Alexei believed he knew who he was. One of the first things he would attempt to check out once he was home would be this belief. If it turned out that he was correct about the identity of the man, whose only assistance was to give him an air rifle for a crutch, then he was confident that he would have an opportunity to repay the favour, albeit in time. The thought of this, coupled with the stopping of the train and the increasing noise around him as more passengers boarded, kept him from falling asleep as his concussed brain so desperately wanted to do.

CHAPTER 31

Deputy Police Chief Fred Smallwood listened. Superintendent Labelle talked.

"I'm claiming a national security one, Fred. Now, how long can you sit on it. Note, I'm not saying 'cover it up', just 'sit on it'?" Labelle kept talking. He wasn't yet ready to let the Deputy Chief respond.

"We've got what we believe is a Russian national involved in espionage, and kidnapping, to name just a few. We don't know whether he was killed by another Russian agent, a private citizen or person or persons unknown." Labelle believed he did know exactly what went on in the Stones' house, but he was not prepared to share his knowledge with his good friend Fred Smallwood.

Labelle saw no reason to be any more honest with Fred than he suspected Jerrow was being with him. He was only reluctantly directly inserting the RCMP into the middle of the situation at this stage. Of course, he was astute enough to understand that their involvement was probably inevitable. Claiming a national security issue would buy time for the various powers above him in the food chain to mark their territory and sort out areas of responsibility.

Then there was the public to whom a plausible explanation would need to be given. There was also a need to possibly prevent some very innocent people from ending up in some very serious trouble. Beyond that, there were the political overtones that left his mind in a whirl.

Deputy Chief Fred Smallwood of the Regional Police was no dummy. He was certainly out of his league when it came to counter-espionage, however. Murder he understood. Counter-espionage was brand new territory and he thought it was new to Labelle too.

"Michel, I can keep this from the press for as long as it takes to keep the body away from a funeral home. Let's say twenty-four to forty-eight hours. And that's if no one on the coroner's staff talks. The main problem is the neighbours. How do we remove a body from an average house in an average residential community without the neighbours getting suspicious?" Before Labelle could respond he answered his own question.

"We'll call an ambulance and pretend the man is not yet dead. I tell you frankly Michel, I don't like this, and the more I think about it the more I think the federal authorities have to take full responsibility."

This was the reply Superintendent Labelle expected. Fred Smallwood was too honest a cop to come to any other conclusion. The Chief was not about to let the Regional Police take a public beating for any hanky-panky with a dead body. If the RCMP wanted to play espionage and counter-espionage with their friends at CSIS then they would have to explain their own bodies to the public. Cover-ups like this happened in spy novels, not in real life—or, at least, Labelle was sure that this was the trend of Fred Smallwood's thinking and experience. This was, after all, Canada.

"Give me a couple of hours, Fred, and I'll call you back with the answers you need. You know I appreciate your forthrightness. I expected nothing less." After the mumbled reply, Labelle hung up. He was beginning to have serious second thoughts about involving himself in intelligence work. Already he was beginning to feel tainted.

Instinctively he knew that it was a state of life in the espionage trade, where "tainted" went with the territory. It was the same with dishonest cops. It left a bad taste in the mouth and a twinge in the stomach.

"Good cop," said Jerrow "can't fault a guy for being a good cop." This after the Superintendent had related the details of the telephone conversation.

Labelle nodded and forced deeper the feeling that he was rapidly getting out of his depth. He looked at Wilson. After all, there may be some rules to this game that Wilson could pull out of his pocket. Wilson accepted the unspoken invitation to speak.

"I'd recommend a straight, down-to-earth public statement, subject, of course, to some clarification about the American's involvement," Wilson stopped.

Jerrow nodded appreciatively. Labelle waited. He could see that this was going to be worse than talking to a politician. He looked expectantly at Wilson, feeling some relief when he noticed out of the corner of his eye that Pasquale wasn't sure what the hell Wilson was really saying either.

"What I'm suggesting, Superintendent, is we simply say that a foreign agent on the run from the United States authorities was accidentally killed while trying to hold the Stone family hostage. Further, the foreign agent, whose nationality is still uncertain, had mistaken Mr. Stone for a Russian physicist who defected five years ago from Russia and who the agent wrongly believed was now doing research at McMaster University in Hamilton.

"We will, of course," Wilson went relentlessly on, "deny having any knowledge of such a scientist and be quite ardent in our statements about the inaccuracy of the foreign agent's beliefs. I'm confident that the University and the Department of Foreign Affairs, Trade and Development usually referred to as DFATD—the Canadian equivalent of a State Department or Foreign Office—will help us with the denials.

"Naturally, this story is only designed to deal with what we now know. In my opinion, it is imperative that we find the Stones. It would appear to me that they are in grave danger."

Labelle was speechless. The cleverness of Wilson's recommendation was immediately apparent. The essential facts were true and would certainly stand up to examination, providing David Stone actually did the killing in defense of his family and did not suffer from some strange passionate desire to contradict it all as a way to assuage any guilt he might feel over the death. The red herring in Wilson's fabrication appeared faultless—the only danger being if there really was a defected Russian physicist at McMaster University—a risk Labelle saw as practically non-existent.

Jerrow was very impressed. He suddenly saw Wilson in a different light. Jerrow made no comment, however, that was Labelle's position—he was in charge. Pasquale nodded eagerly, grinning with appreciation at Wilson's handiwork. One look from Jerrow and his face became instantly passive and expressionless.

Before anyone responded verbally, Wilson added, "If the body upstairs is actually that of a Russian agent, which seems likely, there is always the chance that the Russians would very gratefully accept the body with no questions asked and no answers given. Of course, that would solve all our problems. An ambulance could deliver the body to them." He stopped and faced Labelle with as much aplomb as though he had been talking about arranging a surprise party for a mutual friend.

From a strict RCMP perspective, Labelle knew that this was Wilson's case. Labelle was only involved because this was his territory. Murder and other crimes had been committed and it was far better to involve the district Superintendent from the beginning than haul him in in the middle of a mess and a crisis and expect his help and cooperation. Besides, CSIS, as all intelligence agencies, much preferred the shadows and had no policing authority in any event.

When all was said and done, however, this was really not Labelle's problem. If he went along with Wilson and the whole thing fell apart the worst he could expect was a weak reprimand and a possible transfer to another post. This latter would come only if there was a serious public outcry. As a good, honest cop, in the traditional sense that all those words implied, Labelle was appalled, but he was also a realist. The Superintendent knew that the rules in the game of espionage were different from those in police work. There was no doubt in Labelle's mind that if David Stone had killed the Russian upstairs then for him to stand public trial was a serious miscarriage of justice, let alone a possible breach of national security. Superintendent Labelle, however, was not inexperienced at making statements either.

"Well, Wilson, I appreciate you informing me of what you intend to do and while on the surface it seems a little unorthodox, I have to assume you have your orders and you certainly have more experience in these matters than I."

Once again, Jerrow was impressed. Labelle's equivocation was as artful as Wilson's. It was time for him to ensure his own livelihood.

"I'm sorry to say sergeant," Jerrow turned to Wilson, taking advantage of the fact that Labelle's statement, among other things, had opened the way for Jerrow to deal with Wilson directly, "that Pasquale and I will not be in a position to assist you in making a public statement as we have urgent business elsewhere.

"Insofar as the Russians are concerned you may very well be right. I've known them to do it before, indeed, as have we. There is a certain integrity in collecting our dead and bringing the bodies home, no matter how disgraced. I'm sure you will find the Russians will want their dead, quietly and quickly."

"Naturally, I understand your situation," responded Wilson blandly. He had hardly expected undercover CIA agents to make public statements. "Of course, we will expect private, high source support, for our public statements."

Jerrow hesitated. He had hoped Wilson would have let things ride. "Naturally," he said with a smile, and the deal was done.

Both Wilson and Jerrow knew that all they had done was to cover their respective arses. The Governments of Canada and the United States would spend years haggling over the exact interpretation of the words Jerrow and Wilson had used to make their agreement. The two agents could care less, they had done their part.

All this time Labelle had pretended to be interested in the design of the kitchen tiling or the whorls in the marble counter.

"Right," he said, suddenly, "let's review what we've got one more time." Obviously eager to push behind them the clandestine, conspiratorial atmosphere of the last several minutes, he was eager to press onward into the relatively clean, unambiguous ambiance of a police investigation.

The four men toured the house together sharing observations. In the daughter's room they agreed one of the Stones had dispatched Mikanovich. It was in Sara's bedroom too where Jerrow had found an important clue.

Evidence suggested that someone, probably one of the Stones, had covered the body using the bedspread. The spread was smeared in blood about where it would have covered Mikanovich's head, soaking up the oozing blood from his mouth. When Jerrow had first entered the bedroom the cover had been thrown back, this was the clue that Jerrow almost missed—someone had wanted to look at the body and had not bothered to recover it.

There was not a great deal of deductive reasoning involved for Jerrow to theorize that it was highly unlikely any of the Stones would want another look at the grisly scene. It had to be the unidentified mystery man Mrs. Schultz had mentioned to Wilson. Although the busybody's descriptions were obviously running over into each other, it was clear that there was a fifth person. Possibly a tall muscular man with close cropped hair.

It was during the basement discussions that it occurred to Labelle he may have seen a badly injured Russian agent driving, erratically, down the street when he arrived at the house. Labelle mused that if he had suffered the kind of injuries and amount of blood loss as the Russian seemed to have he would not have been driving at all. The information provided by Mrs. Schultz easily lead to the conclusion that the fourth Russian had taken David Stone's car.

On the main floor was one more clue—a significant, disturbing one that once again suggested the presence of a mystery man.

Pasquale had noticed the closed personal telephone directory on the arm of the couch next to the telephone. Rifling through the pages he noticed that a page had been torn out. It was in the "G" section.

The whole was purely speculative, a page could be torn any time out of a personal telephone directory, but that train of thought left them with no answers to their questions. Hopefully, a more plausible explanation for the missing page was that it could also have been the mystery man removing a clue. Even more likely, taking a clue with him. The existence of a fifth man was increasingly indisputable. If anyone had an answer to his identity, they weren't saying.

Labelle made a phone call that began mobilizing RCMP resources, followed by another to Fred Smallwood. The Superintendent was able to arrange to have other neighbouring Regional police forces—Halton, Niagara, Peel, Haldimand and Waterloo, as well as the OPP—to be on the lookout for David's Camry. Labelle assigned two of his off-duty men to cover the bus station, Hamilton rail station and airport. Another two constables were given the task of calling the area car rental agencies starting locally and circling out to the airport and the surrounding towns. It was his on-duty sergeant who asked about the GO stations at Aldershot and Burlington. "Arrange it," was Labelle's reply.

Arrangements were also made to have someone call all the hospitals in the area looking for a case of injuries that appeared caused by fighting. One of the Stones could have been injured in their struggle with the invaders. Having done that Labelle and Jerrow headed to the movie house where Mrs. Schultz had told Wilson that Michael worked.

For his part, Wilson took on the task of calling Ottawa and beginning the process whereby someone from DFATD, utilizing informal contacts, would see if the Russians wanted Mikanovich's body. Because it was Saturday late afternoon, Wilson knew it could take time and would result in some poor senior bureaucrat being rousted away from his weekend BBQ in the Gatineau Hills. As he dialled the number in Ottawa, Wilson found it difficult to muster up any sympathy.

The phone was answered at the other end, "Special Services, bonsoir. Mailloux." Wilson began his story.

CHAPTER 32

The movie house was the best lead they had. There was nothing for Jerrow and Labelle at the Stone house except waiting. Action suited Jerrow and Labelle better. Chances were that Michael Graves had long since joined the Stones, but one never knew. Before they left Jerrow had ordered Pasquale to track down Gardiner. He had been silent too long. While Jerrow was confident that Gardiner could take care of himself, a sliver of worry was beginning to penetrate his tired mind.

Insofar as the escaped Russian was concerned, Jerrow's bet was that Alexei Petrovsky—it was assumed the blond hairs on the pipe wrench belonged to him—would not be found. Jerrow had encountered Petrovsky several times and knew him to be extraordinarily resourceful and persistent. When it came to his own personal survival the Russian would use all the skills and resources his experience placed at his disposal. He had too many options. There were so many airports, bus and rail stations within a one hundred kilometre radius that the SVR Colonel could be anywhere.

As Labelle drove the three kilometres to the cinema, Jerrow reviewed his, the CIA's, priorities. Revenge aside, he had to put it aside for now, catching Petrovsky was secondary. It was Rita's body that Jerrow wanted. Not for sentimental or humane reasons, that too was suppressed, but so he could get the microdot, and with it the identity of the mole. With the mole came the security of Canada, the United States and the other three nations in the Five Eyes (FVEY) intelligence-sharing agreement. Getting the microdot was, of course, the best way to honour Rita. It had been to acquire and then protect the microdot that Rita had sacrificed her life. The Stones were the key.

The police would get the Stones soon enough, "after all," Jerrow told himself, "they are only ordinary people, who would not know how to go to ground."

As they turned a corner and the mall came into sight the two men were greeted with the flashing lights of a fire truck, ambulance and three police cars. Instinctively, both men knew that this did not augur well for their search.

Labelle, identification held up to the open driver's window, drove as close as he could to the burned out shell of a car, still smoking from the intensity of the fire. The air stank with the mixture of burned and melted plastic, rubber, metal and human flesh. To the experienced cop and the experienced espionage agent it was painfully obvious that this was no accident.

"Hello, Murphy," said Labelle, walking up to a slightly overweight, freckle-faced man with thinning red hair—the stereotypical image of the Irish cop one usually finds in Boston and New York.

Labelle did not introduce Jerrow, who meandered away casually inspecting the still smoldering car and peering at the charcoaled remains of Prokanin and Talinsky.

"Michel! I thought this looked like your kind of fun. Got here a little fast though, didn't you?" Murphy did not ask who the stranger was. He simply made a lot of false, though useful to Labelle anyway, assumptions.

"What makes you think it's mine?" Good cop technique answering a question with a question.

"You've got to be kiddin'? Two men blown to bits in a parked car on a nice quiet Saturday afternoon in a shopping mall parking lot full of people. This is hardly the actions of a discontented spouse, enraged employee or swindled Canadian Tire customer. This one's yours all right." As a coup de grace he pointed to the badly bent but easily identifiable red diplomatic license plate some three metres away from the car. The bright blue eyes stared into Labelle's which were an innocent puppy dog brown.

"The way I figure it Michel, this is connected to your other problem. You know, your missing person. Unless you're really having a bad day an' have set yourself two shit-loads full." Murphy had obviously heard radio chatter about bus stations and airports.

"Well?" it was the kind of resigned question that one cop asks another when he is acknowledging that he is about to assume responsibility for the case. In the distance, Labelle could see Jerrow talking to a uniformed officer and a fireman.

"Well," Murphy smiled satisfactorily, inwardly pleased that he, at least, would be home tonight for the monthly poker game. He was also disappointed, but not surprised, by the lack of response to his prompting about the goings on with the missing man.

"The way I figure it," this was one of the limited number of ways in which Murphy was able to begin a story, "someone blew up the gas tank. The whole car was converted into a giant Molotov cocktail." Labelle was unable to stop a slight ironic smile crossing his face. "The trunk lid was found two hundred metres away at the other end of the mall. It landed on top of some poor bugger's antique TR7, flattened the windshield and almost welded itself to the body. The car's steering wheel now looks like one of those half wheels they have on commercial airplanes," he stopped, glancing sideways at Jerrow who was now down on his hands and knees looking into the surprised face of Talinsky, his head facing the wrong way because of the snapped neck.

"Who were they?" asked Labelle innocently, "any indication?"

"You tell me," came the ready reply.

"I haven't a clue," Labelle lied, knowing the whole time that the lie was being seen for what it was.

Murphy didn't honour the falsehood with a response. He was dying to know how Labelle got there so fast. How had the Superintendent known? Not wanting to embarrass him by forcing another lie, he kept his peace.

Jerrow came back from his examination, nodded at Labelle, almost imperceptibly, and kept walking into the gathered crowd. Murphy remained silent, following Jerrow through his peripheral vision until he was swallowed up in the chattering and pointing knots of people.

Labelle took control. It dawned on Murphy that the unintroduced man's nod was all the Superintendent needed.

"Right, Murphy, if your people can handle crowd control and, of course, send us all written reports and interviews, we'll handle it from here. I'm not sure what this is all about, but I agree it looks a lot more like mine than yours."

"Like hell you're not sure," Murphy thought to himself a touch angry that having turned the case over that he now wanted it back. Well, n

ot back exactly, not in the "responsible for" sense but in the information sense.

"Naturally," he said out loud. "I'll just finish off a few things and pass the word. Enjoy," and he moved away as Labelle reached into his car and pulled out the mike for his two-way radio. By the time he had finished giving instructions, instructions that cancelled all leave and guaranteed lots of overtime, Jerrow was back. Labelle looked at him.

"Yep," Jerrow said. "Today's the day the Stone family have learned how to kill. I checked the movie house and the Stones' son left early when some teenage girl came and got him claiming a family emergency."

Labelle said nothing. There was, after all, nothing to say. At least not for the once-innocent Stone family. Like Labelle, they had entered a foreign world. A world where different rules applied. Rather, a world where there were no rules at all, only missions. A world where the only colour was grey. Full of lies and obfuscations directed out of Ottawa, Yasenevo, or Langley.

Abandoning his ruminating, Labelle turned to Jerrow. "We have to find the Stones."

"Right," said Jerrow. "Exactly what I was thinking."

"There's someone else out there," Labelle said, "someone we don't know about, someone who was in the Stone house and he knows something we don't." Labelle stopped and stared directly at Jerrow, almost challenging him to debate the truth of this statement.

Jerrow was not easily nonplussed. He appreciated Labelle not demanding to be told information that he had evidently deduced Jerrow possessed.

"The man described by Mrs. Schultz and who presumably tore the page from the personal phone directory." Jerrow offered it as a statement, not a question. If Labelle had figured it out, then it was better that they work together. Labelle smiled and nodded.

"Do you think it was another Russian or a new player with unknown motives?"

"That is a very good question."

* * * * *

"Yeah."

"The boss is looking for you."

"What's up?"

"We now know where the body went when it left Buffalo. Rita's not here, the car that had the body in it isn't here, but we have a dead Russian. The boss wants you here pronto."

"Where's here?"

"The Stoney Creek address. Where are you?"

"Actually, I'm on my way to you. I've finished with St. Catharines and Dunneville. I'll be there in an hour at most." With that Gardiner hung up.

CHAPTER 33

Steven Greene was startled. He had not expected the knock on his office door so soon after the phone call from David Stone. He opened his outer office door. The well-dressed man showed him some identification and asked if he could talk to him about a matter of national security. Taken aback, Greene nodded and moved aside so the man could enter.

His quick, agile mind already making a connection between David's mysterious phone call and the stranger, Steven Greene closed the door and turned around.

"I must talk to you about a client of yours, David Stone," the man began.

"Oh?"

"It is vitally important for me to know if he has been in touch with you today. You see his life and that of his family is in grave danger and

I must locate him so that we can protect him. He has disappeared, you see.

"Actually, he has taken his family and is attempting to hide, but those chasing him will find him—they are professionals. If we do not help him then they will all be killed. Now, please, have you spoken to him today?" The burly man with the Marine haircut knew his act well. He knew that if he overloaded the lawyer with a good mixture of fact and feeling the lawyer would tell him what he wanted to know.

"Yes," said Steven, "he called me a short time ago."

"Thank God. Was he...er...they, alright?"

"Yes. He said he was in some kind of trouble and wanted to see me."

"Good, good. Somehow I knew he'd come to you." It was too late. The man had made a mistake. He had taken the focus off the Stones and put it on himself with his "I."

"Do you know David?"

"No. I only know about him. It is a long story, most of which is blanketed in the National Security Act and I couldn't tell you anyway. In brief, however, David Stone was mistaken by the Russians for one of our agents, a man who they desperately want to kill because of some information he has. My job is to get to Stone, tell him this and then protect him and his family, until the Russians discover their error."

"You mean David doesn't know what's happening?" The man had switched the focus back.

"No. All he knows is that he is in danger and he can't go to the police because he has killed two Russian agents. Of course, he doesn't know that they were Russian agents." He added hastily.

Steven sat down behind his desk, at a loss for words.

"Will you help us?"

"Of course." Steven snapped out of it. "The Stones are on their way over here right now. They should be here any minute."

Gardiner smiled and said, "Thank God," and sat down in one of the chairs in front of Steven's desk. It would not be long now. He would have the Stones and, through them, what he knew was a microdot still attached to Rita Brickston's long-dead body.

Gardiner had been working for months behind the scenes carefully planting seeds and arguing that Jerrow was a likely candidate for mole. He was adept at working Langley politics, something that Jerrow was hopeless at. In fact, it was Gardiner's political skill that had gotten him trusted enough to be assigned to the mole search team. Indeed, it had been implied that he discreetly keep an eye on Jerrow. If Jerrow didn't recover the microdot his mission would end in failure. The mission failure would be another straw helping to convince Langley that Jerrow was the mole. Then when Gardiner turned in a microdot and it revealed Jerrow as the mole, a life-term in Leavenworth would be the best Jerrow could expect. Gardiner's position in the CIA would be secure and a long overdue promotion would surely come his way. Taking a cigarette pack out of his pocket, Gardiner waved it in the general direction of Steven. Steven shook his head but pushed the dirty ashtray toward Gardiner. The CIA man lit up and the sweet scent of the Turkish tobacco from his American cigarette began to fill the room. A puzzled look crossed Steven's face as he began to fumble his way toward a question. Gardiner watched the process and knew what was coming.

"What government agency are you with?" Gardiner had been right.

"National Security Service." He exhaled more of the sweet smelling smoke.

"That's not Canadian." Steven thought his voice did not sound as confident as he would have liked.

"No, no. I work for the United States government. David Stone was visiting the United States until yesterday and it was there that the Russians mistook him for one of our people."

That was the right answer. Steven now felt stymied. He knew David was going to Boston because they had discussed it three weeks ago over lunch. So far, everything the American was saying hung together and made sense. That is, if you accepted two premises.

First, that Russian agents ran around mistaking your ordinary citizen for a well-known, to themselves at least, American agent. Second, that a lone member of the United States National Security Service would be running around Hamilton, Ontario *sans* RCMP, to protect a Canadian citizen.

As he thought about it Steven Greene, lawyer, had increasing difficulty with accepting these premises. Then there was a most important question—"Where did the American get his name?" Steven began to wonder just how it was that the American agent knew that Steven Greene, barrister and solicitor, was David Stone's lawyer.

Steven got up from his desk and moved around it to where Gardiner was sitting and stubbing out his cigarette.

"Excuse me," he said, "while we wait there are a couple of things I need to do. Please make yourself comfortable." He left his office heading for the desk of his secretary. Once there he saw the local telephone directory stacked on a shelf with other similar books—Postal Code and Zip Code Directories, Toronto phone book, Oxford Shorter English Dictionary and the Secretary's Handbook, as well as a legal dictionary.

As he reached for the local directory, an unseen and unheard Gardiner stepped out of Steven's office—his left hand reaching up inside his jacket behind his back—there was a scuffling noise in the hallway outside the main office door followed by a knock. Gardiner froze. He saw Steven hesitate, then let the phone book drop back in place as he went to the door. Gardiner went back into Steven's office, but remained standing just inside the door, out of visual, but well in audio range.

The Stones entered Steven's outer office like a group of frightened refugees. David avidly pumping Steven's hand while his left kept squeezing the lawyer's right shoulder. All four looked somewhat dishevelled and they had dilated pupils as if they'd just come from a pot party. David was telling him how good it was to see him and Mary was reinforcing it with how much they all appreciated it.

Silence fell instantly. David's pumping hand froze in mid-pump when Gardiner emerged from the inner office with the smile of a vacuum cleaner salesman on his face. For an instant no one moved except Gardiner who continued coming the short distance toward them, the smile replaced with words.

"Thank God you're safe. We've been very worried about you. I know you've had a terrible ordeal, but you are safe now. It's all over." Briefly, he paused, then pressed on.

"My name is Jenkins, Arthur Jenkins. I'm with the National Security Service—the United States National Security Service. Don't be afraid. I know, we know, what you've been through and my job is to tell you what it's all about and then to take you to a safe place once you've taken me to the body."

David removed his hand from Steven's and moved his body in front of his family.

"You'll forgive me if I'm skeptical Mr. Jenkins, but my family and I have had a rather rough eighteen hours. You do have some identification I suppose?"

Gardiner handed it over with a smile. "It's quite genuine I assure you." One of the few wholly truthful statements Gardiner had made so far since he had entered Steven Greene's offices.

For the second time in just a few hours, David examined an official looking plastic-coated card as though he could identify a false ID if he saw one; this one with a picture of a stone-faced Gardiner on it. He wanted to believe it was real, but he didn't. Already he had believed seemingly genuine official identification documents and been taken in. He handed it to Mary who repeated the process, comparing the small coloured picture with the real life person before her. As equally dissatisfied as her husband, she handed it to Gardiner. The only thing about which there could be no doubt, Mary thought to herself, was the fact that the picture on the plastic card was of the man standing before them.

"Thanks," she said to Gardiner/Jenkins and then turned to Steven. "You know?"

"I know you've had to kill two men and are afraid to go to the police."

"Four," Mary said calmly, "we've had to kill four men. Do you have any idea, any at all, what we've been through? Do you...?" She was cut off as David gently placed a finger over her lips. Mary was building herself into a hysterical outburst, which she fully deserved but this was neither the time nor the place.

"Four?" the words were out of Gardiner's mouth before he knew what happened. Before the response came he was already chastising himself for this second verbal mistake.

"Yes. Two men at our house," she said, having gotten a semblance of control, "and two more outside the movie theatre where Michael works." She smiled at her son who blushed at the sudden attention given him.

Gardiner nodded knowingly, and asked Steven if they could all sit down in his office. This accomplished, he set about his primary task, which was to locate Rita Brickston's body and its tiny, precious cargo. The fact that David had ignored Gardiner's previous statement about the body he had read in the psychologist's eyes that David knew full well where the body was.

In spite of the time pressing down on him, Gardiner knew he had to win the Stones' trust. He needed to repeat his story to the Stones about the Russians misidentifying David as a hunted CIA agent. Next, came the truth—all four of the dead men were Russian agents.

By the time Gardiner finished his tale, David was back in clinical mode. Desperately, he wanted to believe what the American was telling them, but his finely honed intuition told him not to. All the signs were there. He could feel it. It was precisely the same sensation he got when the client opposite him was covering up some fact from fear of rejection or the truth or both. Only this man was covering up for his own dark purposes. The man in front of him seemed too eager;

there was an undercurrent of impatience as if there were a hurry. Of course, the man did want to find a dead body before God knows what else happened to it, but there was something more, David was certain. He had to prepare himself.

"So what do you suggest now, Mr. Jenkins?" David asked calmly.

Gardiner was ready. "Not yet, Mr. Stone, as you know there is more. There is the matter of the body in the trunk of your car."

Steven Greene gasped involuntarily. He had not understood Gardiner before when he alluded to a body in his introduction to the Stones. "Body? Trunk of the car? You did not mention that." It was clear he was using the collective 'you', equally accusing of Gardiner and David for neglecting to mention this "insignificant" little tidbit of trivia.

"I'm sorry, Mr. Greene, but it was not information I felt I could share with you until I knew for sure that you could put me in touch with the Stones," Gardiner said smoothly. "With Mr. Stone's permission I'll explain?" He looked to David, who stared back with a blank expression.

"It was all part of how the confusion around Mr. Stone's identity happened. We had accidentally killed a Russian double agent, a woman, who had resisted our attempt to take her alive. She poisoned herself before we could get to her in the parking lot at the Buffalo airport. We put the body in the trunk of your car, Mr. Stone. Not knowing, of course, that it was your car, but rather believing it to be that of someone else."

"Also a Canadian?" David asked, clinical tone in place, a trace of skepticism slipping in.

Gardiner hesitated the prescribed amount of time, then stumbled. "Well, er, no, Mr. Stone. We did not know, or rather I did not know—there was no one else involved. I had no idea whose car it was. I had a dead body on my hands and the Russians were nearby and I had to do something until help could arrive. It seemed a reasonable chance to take given your car was in the long-term parking area."

David looked at him impassively. The psychologist telling the client to "go on" with his story. The man's apparent ability to lie over a small matter to protect his own ego, but to sacrifice the embarrassment for the far more important scruple of honesty, was causing David to question his doubts. Gardiner was human after all and David Stone, clinical training notwithstanding, was a sucker for human error and a marshmallow in the face of human honesty. However, David knew the difference between accepting what someone tells you and believing it. The part about the Russians being nearby made sense. Had he not seen the fraudulent Inspector Brown and his hairy friend, both now dead, in the airport parking garage?

Gardiner went on. It was a good tale, one sufficiently laced with truth and discretion to be convincing—the truth reluctantly and confidentially given, the discretion to protect the innocent and matters of national security. It was, by all accounts, an extremely convincing performance by a professional whose entire well-being depended upon his ability to perform, night after night, like some computer-programmed Christopher Plummer, blowing away a different audience every night with different lines to a different play.

When he had finished, Gardiner was convinced that there was little doubt in anyone's mind that he was a real life version of the Hollywood spy—an espionage agent who was human. Who erred and had fears and knew loneliness and cared and felt deeply about fundamental human values. It was, of course, bullshit. But then, everyone knows that bullshit baffles brains. Or so it's said.

Chapter 34

Wilson was pleased with his good fortune. The right person had been on duty at Special Services. Quickly they had grasped Wilson's, and therefore the agency's, dilemma, and had agreed with Wilson's plan of action and promised to make the arrangements. As for contacting the Russians, that was passed up the line to the power mandarins. If all went well, Mikanovich's odiferous remains would be removed by ambulance in the next hour. There had been much discussion about getting a hearse to remove the body, but Wilson had been able to convince HQ that it would be easier for the Stones, should they survive the day, to say a visiting friend got taken ill than to explain who died.

Off the phone, Wilson was confronted with a badly fidgeting Pasquale. A rookie with nothing to do but wait. Wilson had vague memories of being a rookie waiting, feeling at loose ends. Useless. Pasquale had completed his assignment. He'd called Gardiner. That seemed a long time ago.

"Listen," said Wilson, "while we wait, let's do another top to bottom search. Something could have been missed and it's better than standing around with our thumbs up our arses."

Pasquale readily agreed.

"Up or down?"

Pasquale chose down. So down to a dried pool of Alexei's blood.

It was about thirty-five minutes later that the former experienced cop in Wilson led to a major discovery in the upstairs bathroom. A most important clue. A clue which could well blow the entire case wide open.

* * * * *

Once at RCMP headquarters Jerrow and Labelle had not wasted any time. The Superintendent had quickly discovered, or rather one of his men had discovered, that no one answering to Alexei's description had rented a car, at least, not locally. Based on the assumption that the man Labelle had seen driving down the Stones' street had been Alexei driving David Stone's car, he and Jerrow concluded that he hadn't ditched it, at least not for another rental. Another conclusion was that the Stones must then be driving the Russian's car. Jerrow had its description and license number from the car rental at Pearson International.

The Provincial and local police had been notified and were already on the lookout for Alexei driving an older model charcoal grey Camry license plate LMZ239 and for the Stones driving the rented cream Chrysler. That piece of the process was taken care of.

Jerrow and Labelle reviewed what had been done. Labelle had arranged for two of his men to go to the local bus and train stations to look for the charcoal grey Camry. In the meantime, RCMP officers from Toronto were covering all train and bus arrivals in Ontario's capital, and the men already at Pearson International were doing the same with departures.

Toronto was the most logical destination for the missing Alexei according to Labelle. But Jerrow had his doubts. Alexei was not a criminal. He did not think like a criminal. Alexei was an espionage agent and Jerrow knew he personally would not head for Toronto if he were in Petrovsky's shoes and he didn't think Petrovsky would either. When Labelle nodded for Jerrow to elaborate, all the CIA man could do was shrug and say "Somewhere we don't expect. A small remote air field where he could rent a plane, perhaps." In his near-exhausted state, Jerrow had forgotten that sometimes there was no choice but to do the simple and easy thing, even if it is more risky.

RCMP officers were on their way to Hamilton's airport, but flights from there would mostly take the Russian agent to western Canada or Kapaskasing in northern Ontario. Arrangements were being made to cover other smaller airports within a seventy-five kilometre radius. There was nothing more that could be done. Besides, in the end they both agreed that capturing the Russian was a bonus, not a necessity. It was the Stones who had to be found.

Without a great deal of hesitation, the two men then focused their energies on identifying the contents of the missing "G" page from the Stones' personal phone directory. Labelle had produced it from his jacket pocket. The deductive reasoning necessary to figure out that the missing page contained the name of a person the Stones had gone to see was minuscule.

"Who?" asked Labelle out loud, "Goddamn it, who?" He and Jerrow reviewed the obvious.

"If you were the Stones, who would you visit under the circumstances?" Labelle had asked.

"I don't know. My best friend, my family, my doctor, my lawyer," had been Jerrow's easy reply.

It was the same list that Labelle had ticketed off for himself and seemed to lead them nowhere. More slowly the two men reviewed it all again.

"What was the name of the doctor?" asked Jerrow.

"Woods," came the answer.

"The relative who's listed under emergency?"

"Marshall. However," came Labelle's voice raised in excitement, "the goddamned lawyer's name is Greene." Conveniently, the Stones had filled in that section in the front of their personal directory that was available for listing important phone numbers—doctor, emergency, police, fire, hospital, poison control centre, lawyer.

As Labelle pulled his cell and dialled the number from the phone directory, Jerrow dove for the local directory and found the address in the yellow pages listing. No one answered the telephone at Steven Greene's office. No home number was listed in the personal directory. Jerrow went straight to the white pages, only to discover that there were three S. Greene's listed. He briefly realized he had been lucky, there could have been ten.

Labelle took a different route. He called Bell Canada. Using his police authority he requested the immediate home number and address of Steven Greene, lawyer. Politely, Labelle was informed that it would take some time. Not so politely, he said he didn't have any time and that lives were at stake. The Bell Canada supervisor said she would hurry.

Meanwhile, Jerrow had begun calling the three Greene's listed in the white pages. There had been no answer at one of the numbers and he was working on the second listing in Ancaster, a nearby community, but not fast enough. Bell Canada beat him to it, or rather their computer did. It had moved through its bytes of information faster than Jerrow's fingers could walk through the telephone directory.

Superintendent Labelle hung up his phone and said, "Try 519-723-5555."

A woman answered.

"Mrs. Greene?" Jerrow hazarded.

"Yes?" the suspicious voice of a woman expecting to be given a chance of a lifetime to have her rugs cleaned.

"This is the RCMP," he winked at Labelle, who shrugged, "we're trying to locate your husband. We have reason to believe that one of his clients is in some difficulty and we wish to notify him."

The woman quickly told them that her husband was working late at his office—seeing a client, in fact. Worry showed in her voice when told that they had already called his office and got no answer.

"Then he must be on his way home and I'll have him call you the minute he comes in."

"Is there any reason he might not come straight home?" Jerrow asked.

"What do you mean?" the leading edge of insecurity creeping into the voice.

"Is there anywhere he might have gone, like a store, a bar, someone's house, a fitness club, anywhere. It is extremely important that we speak to him right away."

There was no place. The couple were going out to dinner and a late movie together and she expected him home by six thirty at the latest. He lived twenty minutes from his office and she could only say she would have him call the minute he came in.

Labelle mouthed "Does he have a cell?" Jerrow asked and Mrs. Greene supplied it, nervously offering to call her husband for them. Jerrow, still pretending to be a member of the RCMP told her he would call and that she needn't worry. Briefly, Jerrow was happy that he was a spy and not a policeman having to be kind and supportive to the average worried citizen.

Jerrow dialled the cell number. It went to voicemail.

All Jerrow and Labelle could now do was the one thing that all policemen develop a knack for: wait. Wait for the men checking the parking areas, wait for Steven Greene to come home, wait for the highway patrol cars, wait for the men going to the airport, wait for something to turn up. Wait for anything.

* * * * *

Jerrow's thoughtful waiting was interrupted by a call from Pasquale. He had spoken with Gardiner and the agent was on his way from St. Catharines.

"How long?"

"He said about an hour."

"Thanks. Good job." After a brief moment of relief, Jerrow turned to Labelle.

"How long from St. Catharines to Stoney Creek?"

"Depends on traffic. I would say forty minutes at the outside." A questioning look entered Labelle's face.

A frown came across Jerrow's. He remained silent, ignoring Labelle for his own thoughts.

*   *   *   *   *

The two RCMP officers were bored and hungry. Neither being unusual conditions for working police officers. The two had just spent the best part of an hour and a half driving and sometimes walking through parking lots and along side streets at the bus and rail stations in Hamilton and the adjoining City of Burlington. Now, they were almost at their final stop before they could at least rectify one of their conditions, hunger.

The Aldershot GO Station has a large parking area which, on weekdays, is generally filled with parked cars. On this particular Saturday there was a Blue Jays game going on in Toronto and many fans preferred the GO train to the crowded highway. The charcoal grey Camry took ten minutes to find even though it was where a police officer who knew his stuff would expect it to be—in the middle of the lot surrounded by cars.

Suddenly, the officers were no longer bored and their hunger had gone away. With considerable care they got out of their own car and moved on either side of the Camry. Nothing. There was the possibility of a blood stain on the head rest of the driver's side of the front seat. That was it. The car was locked. They radioed in and were sent by the duty sergeant to the station proper to find out if anyone could identify the missing Russian.

They were in luck. The ticket seller remembered the strange foreigner with the battered face and stained fedora. He bought a ticket to Toronto some thirty-five or forty minutes before.

Without asking, one of the men reached over the counter and grabbed the telephone and began dialing frantically.

* * * * *

As he brought his mind back to the present and focused his eyes on his immediate surroundings, Jerrow realized that Labelle was staring at him. Studying him with his policeman's mind would be a better statement. Jerrow smiled a little weakly. Labelle broke eye contact and answered his ringing phone.

The caller reported that David Stone's Camry had been found at the Aldershot GO Station. The ticket seller clearly remembered a strange man with a battered face, speech impediment and an old fedora who was wearing an overly small raincoat. She remembered the Russian had bought a ticket for Toronto.

"When?"

The answer came back "about forty minutes ago."

"Good work. Stay by the car until relief comes."

Jerrow listened as Labelle nodded and "uhuhed" and gave orders. Hanging up he said "Your Russian, we've located him on an intercity train."

Labelle had kept the phone in his hand and called a counterpart in Toronto and gave instructions to contact GO, have the train stopped wherever it was and have a four-man team board the train and take the Russian into custody. He also asked to have the train conductor, if he hadn't already, go and check tickets and see if the Russian's location could be identified. Finally, teams were to converge on every station still left for the train to visit. His instructions agreed to, Labelle turned to Jerrow. "I think we should go to Steven Greene's office, if nothing else it's better than waiting here. If your men are lucky and the Russian is caught, we still have to find the Stones."

"I was thinking the same thing," said Labelle.

Chapter 35

Time was closing in. Gardiner was getting nervous. Reassurance was taking too long. Not that it showed. Outwardly he was the calm, humble professional American agent and he had succeeded in convincing David and Mary Stone to go over, in detail, what had happened in the last eighteen hours. They did. After all, they had their lawyer present.

Having established with David that he knew about the woman's body in the trunk of the car, it was not difficult for Gardiner to demonstrate the genuine nature of his concern for them by asking them to take their time and go over what had happened from their side of things.

Gardiner longed for the detail of where the body was and to be gone to it. But he knew that he should not rush things too unreasonably. When the time came and the actual location of the body was revealed in its proper sequence, that would be the place for him to put further explanations on hold while the body was recovered. For now he lived through the initial finding of the body, the narrow brush with discovery when the police constable arrived to lend a hand with the flat tire. The terrible drive home and then the revelation to Mary and Mary's reaction—this latter laced with vast quantities of praise for Mary's common sense and a couple of jokes about David not always thinking things through. While irrelevant to Gardiner's goal attainment, the agent took it as a sign that the Stones were more relaxed and, therefore, more trusting.

Gardiner sat through it all. The peppering of questions from Sara and Michael who were learning new tidbits they had not heard before. Gardiner, smiled and frowned, nodded and "tsk, tsked" and smoked his sweet-scented American cigarettes and kept his growing excitement at bay.

When he was able to finally close his dropped jaw, Steven Greene had questions too and the whole thing took longer than Gardiner would have liked, but finally it came.

"So, we took it to the freight yard, you know Steven, by the old brick factory? We hauled the body up into an empty coal car. We figured it could be days before the body would be found, but even if it wasn't, no one could implicate us. Why would they?"

Gardiner agreed. No one would. Except, of course, that someone did. The Stones would not be in their current predicament otherwise. Gardiner deferred pointing this truth out.

Without hesitation, Gardiner said, "I think it is very important that I get to the place where you've disposed of the body. I know it's not pleasant," he appealed directly to Mary and David with this remark, "and I guarantee there will be no legal proceedings against you, but it is extremely important that we get there before anyone else."

Mary smiled wanly and David nodded, sternly.

"Do you think you could take me there?"

"Yes," said David.

Gardiner saw Steven Greene ready to interfere with what would undoubtedly be a typical lawyer's comment and caution. Perhaps the nature of the so-called guarantee.

"Good," Gardiner said, all business, and pre-empting Steven's speaking. "Now I need to have a private word with Mr. Greene. I need him to make a phone call for me to ensure that the RCMP are sent to the freight yard. I'm sorry to be so mysterious but it involves giving Mr. Greene a piece of information he shouldn't really have, but because he is a lawyer and an officer of the court I can assume it is safe with him."

"Of course," said David and he and Mary began ushering Sara and Michael out into the hallway. "We'll wait in our car out front."

Gardiner was all smiles and apologies as he and Steven went with them to the main door. Steven said, "Call me. Tonight." The door closed and the Stones were gone.

"Well, Mr. Jenkins?" Steven asked Gardiner, all lawyer and businesslike.

"Let's go into your office shall we?" said Gardiner, moving ahead of Steven down the short hallway and through the doorway into his private office. Steven followed. He was shocked to enter his office, a few steps behind Gardiner, and find the American agent pointed a gun at him when he turned to face the lawyer. The barrel looked huge because of the silencer screwed into the end.

"Please, sit down Mr. Greene," the smile of the vacuum cleaner salesman was gone, replaced by the cold, bleak smile of a North Saskatchewan winter.

Steven Greene did not move. He wasn't even sure himself whether it was out of bravado or temporary paralysis.

"Please, Mr. Greene, your sitting down will not hurt and it will ease things considerably." There was gentleness and calming reassurance in the voice, only the eyes remained unchanged. Steel cold.

Steven Greene moved to a chair in front of his desk and was about to sit down heavily when Gardiner stopped him.

"Behind the desk, please, Mr. Greene, then with the desk between us I can put this stupid gun away."

The lawyer moved to the chair behind his desk and sat down. As he looked up, words of protest forming on his lips, Gardiner shot him twice in the chest. Steven Greene was dead before his head hit his desk top, his words trapped forever between his tongue and his lips.

Deftly, Gardiner pulled his back up gun from around his ankle, wiped off his fingerprints with a pocket handkerchief and placed it on the floor in front of the desk. He unscrewed the still hot silencer using the same handkerchief and dropped it into his jacket pocket. The gun went back behind in its rear holster. It was only after this that he actually checked to make sure the lawyer was dead. He was.

Gardiner quickly opened Steven's appointment book, which was on his desk just to the right of his vacant, staring eyes, and after briefly studying the writing style made a two-word notation "David Stone." Satisfied, he left quickly so that the waiting Stones outside in their car would not get too nervous about the amount of time he had spent with their lawyer.

As he closed the office door behind him, Gardiner could hear Steven Greene's phone ringing. He ran easily down the stairs to the street door well-satisfied with his accomplishments over the last hour and a half. He had been very lucky, and he knew it. He needed his luck to continue to hold. At the freight yard, if the body of Rita Brickston was still there, undiscovered, he would recover and destroy the microdot, take care of the Stones and appear at the house in Stoney Creek—ready for action and full of apologies for getting lost and being late, unable to call because his cell had lost its charge while secretly pleased with the success of his mission and relishing the deposits put into his numbered Swiss bank account.

The vacuum cleaner salesman smile was back in place as he came out into the street, saw the Stones in the car the now dead Mikanovich had rented, waved and headed for his own vehicle which was parked a half block down the street around a corner, and three cars down. Gardiner had not wanted to take any chances of having his New York state license plate being seen by anyone in the vicinity of Steven Greene's office.

Gardiner had been right to worry about how long he had taken. David's level of suspicion had risen. Gardiner had been too perfect. The humane spy. The active listener. The smile that never reached his eyes. It was all just a little bit too perfect. Not exactly at the used car salesman level, definitely better than that. The man was hiding something and whatever it was, it coloured everything he said. There was something going on that didn't fit. David Stone pulled out in front of Gardiner and started out for the freight yard.

Michael asked first "What's wrong?"

"Nothing."

"No, what's wrong, you sure look like there's something wrong. You know how your lips get tight and you get this weird look on your face."

"All right. I don't know. There is something, but I don't know what it is. And I'm nervous as hell."

"I agree," said Mary. "I was thinking the same thing. There is something about Mr. Jenkins that doesn't fit, but I don't know yet what it is."

"We need to be on guard. Don't trust him, no matter how nice he seems," concluded David.

In these respective frames of mind Gardiner and the Stones made their way to a hopper, empty except for the now rigid body of Rita Brickston.

* * * * *

"Blatantly conspicuous," described admirably how Alexei had felt in the increasingly filled second floor of the GO train car. Alexei had noted the look on the face of the ticket checker when he asked Alexei for his ticket—a suspicious frown appeared on it as he handed Alexei's ticket back to him. Alexei was left to wonder if the conductor would forget and leave well enough alone or would his suspicions niggle away at him and lead him to make a phone call that could be disastrous.

* * * * *

Back in the communications car, the conductor acted on his suspicions and called the GO Control Centre. When he had finished telling his story and describing the suspicious, battered-looking man he was told to hold on the line as there might be a problem but they were just getting information as they spoke. While he held on, the conductor announced the train's arrival at the Mimico Station—two stops away from Union Station, the main Toronto station and the one on Alexei's ticket.

As the train lurched to a stop the conductor was told that it was possible the man he had described was someone of interest to the police. If that were the case, he was also told that the man should be considered armed and dangerous, that under no circumstances was he to approach the man. Too late, Control told him to hold the train at Mimico. The train was already picking up speed as it left the station behind.

Looking out the window the conductor saw the strange-looking man moving painfully along the platform toward the exit, guided by a burly man with a firm grip on the limping man's arm. As the two men faded into the distance, all the Control could tell him was the police had been called and were already on their way. The further the train sped its way toward Long Branch, the next station, the more colour returned to the conductor's cheeks. "I think they arrived in time," he told Control.

* * * * *

As the train pulled into Mimico, the station where Alexei had arranged to be picked up, for the first time he began to feel the ordeal was almost over. He had estimated the drive to Pearson Airport would take twenty minutes where an Aeroflot flight would be waiting, having been delayed on some trumped-up excuse.

It had been both painful and difficult placing the cell call to the Embassy in Ottawa. In his thoroughness he had fortunately memorized the special number which gave him a direct line to the now dead Prokanin's office where it was only necessary for him to give a code, a time and the airport needed for a flight.

Alexei had had to repeat "Pearson" three times before he was able to make himself understood. Unbelievably, the person at the other end of the phone had been well trained and asked no questions—silently Alexei praised the professionalism of Prokanin, noting to give the agent a positive mention in his report to Moscow. Alexei did not know that such a report would only be helpful to Prokanin's family.

The man in charge of Aeroflot had already been ordered to arrange for a natural-seeming delay for the daily flight out of Toronto in case Alexei and his team needed a quick getaway. Immediately after talking to Alexei, Prokanin's efficient staffer confirmed that Aeroflot would need to make room for one important passenger in the business section. The airline could expect the special passenger between six and six thirty.

It had taken longer to arrange for a car from the Toronto Consulate and the Embassy official had almost had to resort to ordering a member of the Aeroflot crew to go to the Mimico GO Station—a practice definitely frowned upon by Moscow as there was always the danger of a defection.

However, the problem had been resolved when the agent on duty had been found in the soundproof white noise room with one of the secretaries. Both men's clothing was somewhat in disarray.

CHAPTER 36

With Labelle driving at speed, siren blaring, grill lights flashing in his unmarked car, the two professionals, the policeman and the spy, left for the six kilometre ride to Steven Greene's office.

It took them eight minutes. From the outside the offices looked closed, though it was difficult to tell from the street. On the second floor windows they could see the stencilled letters "Steven Greene, Barrister & Solicitor" on them. The offices were above a men's clothing store, the small single business variety which one can still find in old neighbourhoods. The store was open. They noticed an elderly man inside behind the counter while a teenage boy was stocking shelves.

Too many times the two men had learned that appearances can be very deceiving. Jerrow and Labelle decided to go and see for themselves, first hand. They were encouraged to find the street door to the stairway unlocked. It was a good sign, possibly indicating that Steven Greene was in fact in his office. It seemed highly unlikely that anyone would leave the door unlocked for the weekend. Of course someone could be working in the accountant's office or the dentist's, both of whom shared the second floor with the lawyer.

Their encouragement did not run very deep, and Labelle put his hand on his holster and pulled out his gun.

Seeing Labelle's reflex reaction, Jerrow took his Glock 26 from a holster fitted above his belt into the small of his back.

"After you, I believe this is your jurisdiction," he smiled.

Labelle eyed the gun in Jerrow's hand.

Jerrow shrugged and smiled again.

Labelle nodded and checked his own gun to see that the safety was off and preceded the American agent up the stairs.

The light was on in both the stairwell and the hallway at the top, making the two men perfect targets for any would-be assassins. There were none. The two men reached the top of the stairs alive. Hesitantly peeping around the corner at the top they could see the door to Steven Greene's office down the hallway on the left. To the right were the accountant and the dentist.

Cautiously, with Labelle still in the lead, gun at the ready, they moved up to the door. It was a wood panelled door and presented no clue as to what might be on the other side. It did give a suggestion for action, however, for just below the sign giving the occupant's name and profession was a smaller one which read "Knock and Walk in."

Labelle and Jerrow did, though not exactly in the manner anticipated by the author of the sign. The knock part was slight and the "enter" somewhat hurried with one man moving rapidly to the right, the other squatting down in the doorway. Had the office been occupied by normal working people pandemonium would have broken out. The wild-eyed, furtive glances made at their surroundings by the two men, brandishing hand guns, would have been enough for anyone to suspect a terrorist attack. As it was, Jerrow and Labelle were met only with silence and the sound of their own breathing. That and a faint hint of cordite.

When they entered Steven's own private office the silence remained, but there was a greeting of sorts—Steven Greene's dead body slumped down on the desk top, the left side of his face flat against the hard surface, the unseeing eyes, staring in surprise at the diploma on the wall proclaiming Steven Paul Greene a graduate at law from York University, Osgoode Hall.

Holstering his gun, Labelle matter-of-factly walked over to the desk and placed his finger on Steven's neck. There was no pulse, but the body was not that cold. The blood from the wound was still coagulating on the seat of the chair and the carpet beneath where it had dripped from the wound. They were perhaps no more than half an hour, maybe less, behind the killer. The faint odour of cordite in the air confirmed, if any confirmation were needed, that the killing was not that long ago. Jerrow scanned the room and knelt down to examine the gun on the floor. He recognized it immediately as Russian made and standard issue for the SVR. He pointed at it and said, "Russian."

Labelle nodded and looked at the appointment book open on the desk top. "David Stone, five p.m.," he said.

It was Jerrow's turn to nod. At that moment, Labelle's phone rang.

* * * * *

Exactly forty-six minutes after the Toronto-bound GO Train left Aldershot, ostensibly carrying Alexei to safety and home, Toronto's Pearson airport witnessed a flurry of activity by RCMP officers. There were only four on duty at the airport on this late Saturday afternoon, but it was thought to be enough to capture one unsuspecting and injured Russian agent.

* * * * *

The distance was not long between Steven Greene's office and the Lawrence Road freight yards. With the Stones leading the way, they and Gardiner pulled through the entryway and turned right. David could see the line of coal cars in the distance and was greatly relieved.

They could have been on their way to the harbor to be filled with coal. The chances then of finding the correct car would have been one in several hundred.

There was no crowd of people, no flashing lights, no guards. The body must still be there. There were also no RCMP, a fact that worried David. He brought the Chrysler to a halt near where he thought the hopper was in which he and Mary, about twelve hours ago, had dumped the woman's body.

Dust flying, Gardiner pulled up behind the Stones still fearful that time was running out. It had taken him half an hour to find the goddamned lawyer's office, more time gone while he waited for the Stones to arrive and another forty or more minutes to get the Stones to agree to show him where the body was. He got out of his car. The Stones stayed where they were. As Gardiner approached David rolled down his window. Instinctively Gardiner knew what was wrong.

"Funny," he said, through the open window, "Though I suppose they haven't had a chance to get here yet. We were not that far away."

"What?" David looked perplexed but knew what Gardiner was on about. He just wanted to stall for time, to avoid acting directly on the decision he and Mary had made on the drive from Steven's office to the freight yards.

"The RCMP," Gardiner said patiently, "they must have had farther to come than us."

"Right, I'm sure they won't be long," answered David, not moving.

"Well, we may as well get started," tried Gardiner, though he had a feeling that things were going to get difficult sooner than he would have liked.

David did not move, even though Gardiner had moved back to let him out of the car.

"I think maybe we should wait until they get here, Mr. Jenkins. I know I would feel much better about it all," the tone of his voice was gentle but the resolution in the message was unmistakably clear.

Gardiner bowed to the inevitable and pulled out his gun.

"Get out of the car very slowly Mr. Stone, if you don't I shall shoot you. You will get no second chances with me. Tell your family to do the same." It was their living room all over again, except this time David wasn't as surprised.

David nodded, Mary flushed, Sara went white and Michael's mouth hung open. David could feel the anger rising inside of him and he could sense the same reaction in Mary. A person can only tolerate so many people pointing guns at them in any one day before you either cower and plead for your life or you tap into your anger and bide your time. David reached out and touched Mary's hand, giving and receiving support, love and like-mindedness. For now, pleading and cowering were not on, except to save the children.

David knew that just inches away, under the front passenger seat was the weapon he had taken off the tall Russian whose head he had caved in in the basement recreation room of his own home. Mary, anxious to get the weapon out of her purse, had put it there after they had left the burning car in the mall parking lot. It was near his son's toes. The psychologist knew that he could never reach the gun and survive. He prayed that Michael understood that the same was true for him.

The Stone family got out of the car, a mixture of anger and fear on their faces. Mary and Michael were on the far side, the cream Chrysler between them and the man with the gun. Mary left her door open believing it might afford extra protection for her son if shooting started. Sara left her rear door open, copying her mother.

Using his gun, Gardiner indicated that Sara and David were to move away from the car in the direction of the hoppers ranged in a line behind them. At the same time he indicated that Michael and Mary were to join them. As the five moved closer to the coal cars their nostrils were assaulted by the sting of coal dust and their ears were assailed by an unusually distracting buzzing noise.

Having got the family Stone positioned where he wanted, Gardiner laid out the ground rules.

"Mr. Stone, you and your son are to climb onto the coal car with the body and remove it and place it in the trunk of my car. Now I have no intention of harming any of you," he lied so glibly, "if you co-operate this will all be over for you and your family in an hour." In this, he was not lying—it would all be over for all four of them.

"When the body is in the trunk of the car, Mrs. Stone will get into my car and drive. The rest of you will get into the Chrysler and follow us. So long as you arrive where we do and you don't try anything funny Mrs. Stone will be all right.

"There is a genuine matter of U. S.'s national security involved here and you must understand that I am in deadly earnest. Your cooperation will be greatly rewarded." That, of course, assumed there were a God and a heaven, not to mention the assumption that the four Stones were part of the faithful and deserving.

Gardiner stopped to observe the effects of his words. "Useless," he thought to himself. "Oh, well, either way they'll all be dead in the next forty-five minutes." Out loud he asked, "Any questions?"

"You don't need the children Mr. Jenkins. They could be tied to the coal cars and left behind. Even if found they wouldn't say anything until we came back for them. They're just children, Mr. Jenkins. Just children." This plea came from Mary.

"I'll think it over, Mrs. Stone. I promise I'll think it over." He actually managed to sound human, as though he really was going to think it over. Gardiner knew that hope, like everything else, could be used as a two-edged sword. Sometimes it gave a person the will to hang on, to survive, sometimes it gave the person an excuse to co-operate and do things they didn't want to do.

Mary didn't believe him. She desperately wanted to, but didn't.

"Now please, Mr. Stone, you and your son go and get the body."

It was not difficult to identify the coal car in which Mary and David had dropped the body. The flies made identification easy. There was no longer any trace of Rita's perfume.

As soon as David and Michael began climbing up the side of the coal car flies began to circle their heads looking for places to land.

David was the first to reach the top of his ladder and was also the first to puke, all down the one side of the car. Michael, a fraction of a second behind David in reaching the rim, was likewise a fraction of a second behind David in emptying his stomach. Flies descended in hordes on the vomit, bringing dry heaves to the father and son. Gardiner prevented Mary and Sara from running to the coal car to help them. Sara fighting not to throw up herself.

"The sooner you get on with it, the better it will be," said Gardiner, sounding sympathetic, but his eyes were like ice. David, tears streaming down his face from the force of his retching, nodded and jumped over the side of the hopper to land at the feet of Rita Brickston's rigid body. A cloud of flies buzzed around his head and once again began to settle on him and the body.

To Michael he said, "Don't really look and you'll be all right."

Michael nodded, not very enthusiastically, but then the task was not one even an undertaker would be able to generate much enthusiasm for.

Since he was there, David grabbed the cold stiff ankles intending to lift the legs to pass them up to his son. Rigor mortis prevented this plan. Nothing would bend. Rita was like a human board. A one hundred and twenty-five pound board. David dropped the legs to the bottom of the coal car, flies swarming all around. An image from TV's CSI flashed across his mind of the medical examiner having to break the legs of a body in order to free it from where it was lodged. It was not for him.

Notwithstanding the fact he wasn't an athletic man, David went down on his haunches and pushed his hands and arms under the body, scraping and scratching his bare hands on the sharp-edged pieces of coal on the car bottom. In spite of his great motivation to have the whole thing over with, he did not have the strength to raise himself up with the body.

After what seemed an hour, but was barely a minute, David decided he could roll Rita's body up the side of the hopper and with luck his son would be able to haul it over the edge. Sometimes, good ideas turn out to be stupid and David's idea of rolling the body up the side was such an idea. Stupid. Because of the height of the car David couldn't get enough leverage to roll the body high enough for Michael to reach. While he tried to let the body down easily Rita's corpse landed with a thud, face up on the bottom of the coal car, sending coal dust and flies billowing into the air.

With blackened face and between coughs David told Michael to find a rope, or chain or anything because they were going to have to haul the body out. Leaving David alone with the resettling dust and flies and Rita's vacant stare, Michael went to explain to Gardiner's gun what he needed.

Gardiner was increasingly on edge. Time was running out. After explaining the situation, Michael asked Gardiner if he had a rope in the trunk of his car. Gardiner exploded, calling him a fucking moron for thinking rental cars came with ropes in their trunk. It was Mary whose usual common sense saved the day. She and Sara had gathered around Michael as he approached and listened in as he explained the problem to Gardiner.

"Maybe there's rope in that rail shed over there," she said tentatively, pointing to a stained and dirty shed not far beyond where David and Michael had been struggling with the body.

Of course, the shed was locked. A more relaxed and humorous man would have laughed, but Gardiner could barely contain his rage. Ushering the Stones further along the tracks, he attached the silencer to his gun and fired two shots at the old lock shattering it and freeing the shed door.

As Michael entered the shed he could hear David screaming to find out what was going on and scrambling to get up the side of the hopper in fear that his family was being murdered. As he reached the hopper top he was in time to see Michael emerge from an old rail shed with a rope passing between his mother and sister.

It took another six minutes for David to tie the rope and lift the body while Michael pulled before Rita's corpse reached the lip of the hopper and tumbled not too gracefully to the ground at Michael's feet. Rita's empty eyes stared into the lowering sun.

Gardiner could feel his heart race as he saw first the legs and then the naked buttocks emerge from the coal car. He knew he was close. In ten minutes, perhaps less, he would be gone from this place and on his way to a country road. As David, pale, dishevelled, filthy and reeking, climbed over the coal car rim, Gardiner threw his own car keys to Mary so she could open the trunk.

A look of satisfaction crossed Gardiner's face as the long-sought body of Rita Brickston was being carried by David and Michael toward the trunk of his rental. Because the body was in full rigor the not very pleasant task of carrying the body was easier. Lowering it into the car trunk however, was an entirely different proposition.

"It won't go," yelled David still gasping from the coal dust in his lungs and the struggle to get out of the hopper, not to mention carrying his share of the body's 125 lbs.

"Wedge it, force it, just fucking do it."

Gardiner watched while the two Stone men tried to wedge the rigid body in, and by some stroke of luck they succeeded. "Good job," he said trying to sound generous, "Now close the lid."

That done, the horror of the corpse was sealed in by the closed trunk lid. A large number of frustrated and jealous blow flies were left buzzing frantically on the outside trying to find a way into the trunk to continue their feast and egg-lying with their brothers and sisters trapped inside.

"All right," said Gardiner, suddenly cold and all business. "Mrs. Stone, you can get into my car, the rest of you into the Chrysler. And remember, if you want Mrs. Stone to live, your wife, your mother, if you want her to live, you'll do only what you are told, which is to follow me. Understand?" David nodded, white with rage. He was still hoping for the one opportunity he believed he needed to save his family.

Imperceptibly, as she moved passed Gardiner toward his car, Mary nodded at Sara. Without warning Sara let out a frightful, ear-piercing scream and fell to her knees. Mary yelled "my baby" whirling around and knocking Gardiner off balance—this was to be the only chance the Stones were to have. David's opportunity had arrived and he seized it. For the second time that day he threw his out of shape, inexperienced body at a professional with a gun.

CHAPTER 37

When his feet touched the platform Alexei felt his arm caught in a vise-like grip as a burly, well-dressed man in an immaculate suit began forcibly propelling him to a stairwell about 50 metres away. It wasn't until his companion said: "You'll soon be home, comrade," in Muscovite that Alexei understood the man hurrying him along was from the Russian Consulate.

As they hurried down the stairs to the underground tunnel to the car park, Alexei was grateful for the man's strength. As they neared the top of the stairs leading to the exit and parking lot, Alexei heard the approaching wails of police sirens. When they emerged Alexei, now almost being carried, saw the diplomatic plates on a large black Ford. His companion flew open the rear door and not so gently shoved Alexei into the back seat. At the parking lot exit they had to miss the green light as two police cars screamed their way into the entrance, lights flashing. They almost missed the next green as an unmarked police car chased after the others now congregated around the station exit.

As the car pulled out onto the highway leading to Pearson International and home, Alexei had mixed feelings. His mission was in tatters and for that he felt deeply sorry. In the world of espionage, there are many losses and occasional wins. He had no immediate way of knowing if the body had been found and if found the microdot and its container had survived all the vicissitudes that the body had experienced. Or whether the mole would thereby be exposed.

Alexei thought he might have met the mole. The man in the basement of the Stones' house should have shot him or at least handcuffed him instead of offering him a superior smile and a toy gun as a crutch. Then again, he could have been a CIA agent on a hunt for the mole himself and with no interest in Alexei except to show his superiority. The SVR had its own share of such agents. They usually never made it to retirement, dying with their superior smiles frozen on their faces.

As for what was facing him at the airport, while there was no guarantee, Alexei was confident that the Canadians, having failed to take him at Mimico would not interfere with him boarding the waiting Aeroflot flight. After all, what would they do with him in the end anyway, except deport him with a strongly worded diplomatic message pinned to his jacket lapel.

Past experience had taught him that no one, the Canadians included, would want a public trial. Politically it was not good to have heavy media discussion about the number of Russian and American spies roaming freely in Canada and holding Canadian families at gunpoint. With Mikanovich dead at the hands of Mary Stone, the Canadians could easily rationalize that justice had already been done.

No, the Canadians would be glad to see the last of him and choose to interpret his departure as a well-deserved act of self-exile. He hoped. There were always other, more unpleasant possibilities. Not a morbid man, Alexei turned his mind to other things. Specifically, he printed out a shaky question to hand to the man in the front passenger seat if anything was known of Talinsky and Prokanin.

"Nothing," was the simple verbal answer.

While he didn't say so, Alexei hoped they had not hurt the Stone boy, or interfered when the Stones went to get their son. Alexei knew that neither Mary nor David believed him when he had told them that their son was not being watched. With the same conviction he knew that Talinsky and Prokanin would do their job if the Stones showed up. The prospects were not pleasant. Indeed, they were tragic. All was now beyond anything that Alexei could do—his feelings and wishes now made irrelevant by time and circumstance.

* * * * *

"What do you make of this?" Wilson asked. Holding up a turquoise-coloured woman's track suit, a pair of man's blue jeans and a short sleeved three-buttoned man's cotton shirt, original colour tan.

"Really dirty laundry?" Pasquale questioned back.

"Really dirty laundry covered in coal dust."

"That seems a bit unusual, right?"

"Maybe in this household, but not in this town. Hamilton has some of the largest steel mills in Canada. Where there is steel, there's coal. Where there is coal, there is a bounty of coal dust.

"If you wanted to dump a body, why not in a coal car? There must be freight yards around here somewhere full of empty hoppers ready to be filled with coal for the hungry mills." As he finished, Wilson dropped the dirty clothes back in the open basket, pulled out his phone and punched in some numbers.

"Fuck! Not now," he said as a voice message came through the speaker.

* * * * *

Labelle stepped back from the prostrate body and answered his phone as though he had been expecting a call. After his initial "yes" he said very little, just listened and grunted occasionally, presumably to let the talker on the other end of the line know he was still there and paying attention. "Good work sergeant," he said and hung up.

"It's Petrovsky," he said to Jerrow, "he got off the train three stops before Toronto and was last seen being assisted to the station exit. The most logical thing is that he's on his way to Pearson International where there's been an Aeroflot plane with so-called technical difficulties sitting on the ground since four o'clock. It must be waiting for him. We're going to have a crack at meeting him, but I wouldn't count on success in holding on to him. No doubt his friends driving him to the airport came equipped with the proper diplomatic papers."

Jerrow only nodded. There was nothing to add to the truth. Another call attacked Labelle's phone.

"Yes," Labelle expecting another call. This time he was more verbal though the conversation didn't last half so long.

Jerrow actually witnessed excitement race across Labelle's face and settle in his eyes. He told the mysterious caller about finding the still warm body of the lawyer. He ordered the caller: "Get there." Then it was over.

"Let's go, Jerrow," was all he said when he had hung up "we may have just hit pay dirt." And he walked out of the office dialing another number, Jerrow running behind to catch up. As the two men raced down the stairs, Jerrow heard the Superintendent mutter something about "good police work winning out every time." Into his phone Labelle ordered someone to come and sit with Steven Greene's body.

"Not that I won't follow you anywhere Superintendent, but just where in the hell is the particular anywhere you're taking me to?" asked Jerrow as he clambered in the car and Labelle tore away from the curb at speed, rapidly leaving behind the squeal of brakes of the car he cut off.

"The freight yards, Jerrow. I'm going to show you some of the local choo choos," and for the first time Jerrow actually heard Labelle laugh—not a cop's controlled laugh, but an honest to goodness real human laugh.

CHAPTER 38

Mrs. Schultz was in for another treat. Just when she had decided that she had had her fill for the day and that the best she could hope for was the return of the Stones, something happened. The arrival of an ambulance sans siren and flashing lights in the Stones' driveway was almost more than she could bear.

The Stones' driveway just kept on giving. Just after the ambulance had left with someone Mrs. Schultz couldn't identify, the two men, whom she knew were still in her neighbour's house, came running out of the front door and into their car.

To Mrs. Schultz, the sight elicited from her a jealous reaction. Convinced the two policemen—"who else would be allowed to walk around someone's home so freely and for so long?" and besides, the nice handsome RCMP sergeant was one of them—were on their way to another crime. Mrs. Schultz envied the next-door neighbours of the new crime victims. Still she had been provided with a first-hand look at how the police responded to emergencies. They certainly did not waste any time.

* * * * *

Once in the car, Wilson surveyed the evidence as he saw it. Indications were better than fifty-fifty Rita Brickston's body could be found in the freight yards. This he shared with Pasquale, who nodded agreeably. Wilson also thought, on the basis that David Stone had had an appointment with his lawyer and the lawyer was now dead, it was no longer reasonable for them to overlook the possibility that David Stone was far more intimately involved than had been first suspected. Perhaps he was not just an ordinary citizen who had got himself and his family accidentally caught up in the middle of some Russian-American espionage game. Maybe David Stone was one of the key players in the game and not a playing piece being moved around the board with every throw of the dice. These thoughts Wilson did not share.

"We'll soon know. I hope!" Wilson told himself as he and Pasquale pulled out of the driveway.

Wilson called the RCMP office to get directions to the freight yards as neither he nor Pasquale were familiar enough with the streets of Hamilton to get there by the quickest route. As it turned out, they were not that far away. Wilson wheeled his vehicle through the often congested, one-way-streeted city at the best speed he could.

* * * * *

It was unusual. Given that Aeroflot used modern Boeing 767s and no longer the increasingly unreliable Tupolevs, it was definitely unusual that a technical difficulty had arisen with the 16:30 flight out of Pearson. It was this flight that had just resolved its technical problem and was now allowing its passengers to board in preparation for take-off, some hour and a half behind time.

Normally an overly suspicious, bureaucratic bunch at best, on this particular occasion the Russian officials responsible for the airline were bordering on the downright surly. They were trying to claw their way into the highly competitive Canadian airline market flying the Moscow-Toronto-Moscow route three days a week. Luring some of the members of the large Toronto Russian community onto the airline was going well, in part because of the upgraded aircraft and the reliability of the schedule. This so-called technical difficulty could set them back. The orders for the difficulty had come directly from a highly placed SVR General in Moscow. Not someone an airline official in a Western provincial capital would want to argue with if he wanted to keep his overseas assignment.

The official's nervousness about the delay was increased to paranoia when confronted by the increase in the number of uniformed RCMP officers present—ordered there at Labelle's request—near the loading gate as well as the presence of a senior official from the Toronto Russian Consulate who had arrived unannounced and in a foul mood just ten minutes before. The bad mood of the official had a great deal to do with the BBQ he had abandoned in his back yard.

When Alexei Petrovsky arrived, the stage was definitely set for a confrontation, or so it seemed. When his car pulled up, it was greeted by the official from the Consulate and a uniformed RCMP officer. The official demanding to know, none too politely, just what the imperialist policeman thought he was doing. A "diplomatic incident" of giant proportions was threatened. The Consulate official emphasizing that one of the consequences of such an incident would undoubtedly be the Mountie spending the rest of his professional career, if not his entire life, as the only police officer in some remote Canadian Arctic community on Resolute Bay.

Having been adequately briefed, the threats and scathing remarks of the Russian in no way ruffled the exterior calm and equanimity of the Mountie. Using a lot of diplomatic language of his own and keeping his own anger well in check, he informed the Russian official that he had been asked to personally check the papers of the tall, very pale and battered-looking gentleman who had just arrived.

"Furthermore," he calmly stated, it was his "intention to ask the gentleman to please come to the RCMP offices at the airport, there being a number of questions which Canadian authorities would like some answers to."

Now ensued a routine with which Alexei had some familiarity and he knew how to play his role. He was gracious. Since he couldn't speak he was hardly able to behave otherwise. He was cooperative in so far as the showing of his papers was concerned—papers just recently handed to him after his arrival in Mimico. Naturally, he was not about to submit to questioning, but it would not be up to him to take a firm stand there, that was the Consulate official's role. And he played it to the hilt.

Alexei was justified in his belief that the Canadian authorities were not prepared to make any more of his departure than would be normally expected under the circumstances. In non-diplomatise, that meant they would find his diplomatic passport in order—which it was—and would ask him to voluntarily surrender his rights under it—which he would refuse. The Canadians would appeal to the Consulate official—who would, in the strongest terms, tell them to go eat maple syrup. Finally, the Department of Foreign Affairs, Trade and Development—whose official was unaccountably delayed—would eventually deliver a relatively mildly worded note to the Embassy in Ottawa and through the Canadian Embassy in Moscow to the Russian government.

Publicly, the Russians would ignore it all as so much Western propaganda. Privately, they would agree that Alexei Petrovsky would never again enter Canada—the kind of statement which would have been sought by Canada and which the Russians would make while crossing their fingers behind their back.

Whether or not the Russians took a beating over their dead Mikanovich, Prokanin and Talinsky was as yet unknown. There was always the possibility that their presence, though strongly denied by the Russians, could lead to a major diplomatic hoopla. These things took time and for the moment were of no concern to Alexei. By the time they were settled, Alexei Petrovsky would be safely home, recuperating and preparing for his next assignment. For the moment, and out of genuine ignorance as to the fate of Talinsky and Prokanin, he chose not to ponder too seriously the fact that he would have a great deal of explaining to do to the old men in Yasenevo or even worse Lubyanka.

If he had not been in so much pain, Alexei would have enjoyed more the accuracy with which he had predicted the turn of events. He showed his passport, it was in order. He declined to waive his rights. The Embassy official talked about maple syrup and Alexei was hustled out to the aircraft that closed its doors and headed for the runway in an unusual display of Russian efficiency.

As the Boeing 767 gained height, Alexei felt a genuine sense of freedom. For the first time in many months he was safe. He knew that within weeks he would be longing for a different kind of freedom—the freedom to be away from Moscow, away from the ever-watchful eyes of the FSB directorate, the kind of freedom only an operative can find at the end of a long string with the scent in his nostrils and a secret mission to fulfil. But for now, Alexei Petrovsky would enjoy this freedom, and savor the anticipation of home. He would also flinch to the ministrations of the doctor assigned to attend him on the long flight.

* * * * *

The sound was unmistakable. As Labelle had squealed the car onto the gravel entryway to the freight yards Jerrow heard four distinct gunshots. He did not need to be told by Labelle that there were four members of the Stone family. Then there was nothing. Silence. In a plethora of oil and coal-soaked dust and flying gravel Labelle brought the car to a skidding stop.

To the left, in the distance he saw what he was looking for—coal cars. Next to them two parked cars, the one in front was a cream Chrysler. He knew this was it.

As Wilson ground his car to a halt behind him, Labelle took off to the left, his tires spinning wildly in the gravel before biting into the hard dirt beneath. The car leaped forward suddenly, throwing Jerrow off balance as he had undone his seat belt ready for action.

* * * * *

David Stone threw his five foot ten inch one hundred and sixty-pound body at the off-balanced two hundred and twenty-five pound six-foot-two Gardiner. It was not that David took advantage of Gardiner's distraction with Mary and Sara that surprised the American—it was the force with which David knocked him to the ground. Gardiner was a big man and unused to being knocked over as though he were a bundle of sticks. All the deep-felt rage surged into David's muscles making him seem to be a far more powerful man than he actually was.

Gardiner fell heavily to the ground, his arms splayed out on either side, the gun still firmly grasped in his left hand. Training had its benefits. David had fallen on top of him, but like the amateur he was he was not in full control of his current advantage. Had Gardiner allowed a man like Jerrow or Alexei Petrovsky to do this to him his chances of remaining alive could be comfortably placed in a thimble no matter what the size differential. The man on top of him now was only an enraged untrained light-weight ordinary citizen.

David took a wild swing at Gardiner's face, hitting him a glancing blow as in one movement Gardiner's left arm swung up off the ground, the silenced barrel sending shooting pains down David's shoulder as it smashed onto his collar bone. Gardiner's right knee, which was free, came up throwing David further off balance in the opposite direction. As David attempted to recover his equilibrium and numbness began to spread into his arm, Gardiner threw his own body to the left, causing the psychologist to fall hard onto the already injured shoulder.

Gardiner rolled upward, gun in hand, but he had made a mistake. In his anxiety he had pushed too hard in the wrong direction and failed to disentangle himself from David's legs. The two men began to roll over and over in the oiled, coal dust soaked gravel, each time sending lances of pain down David's right arm. Throughout the gun stayed planted firmly in Gardiner's left hand.

Because he was double jointed, David had a surprise advantage over Gardiner. It was an advantage he could only use once. He did, bringing up his legs so that he caught Gardiner in a scissor hold. It was useful while both men were relatively off balance, but once Gardiner stabilized himself with David on the bottom, he was once again able to use his gun to effect, smashing the butt end into David's left kneecap. David let go and Gardiner jumped lightly to his feet, leaving the citizen to writhe in agony on the ground, on the verge of fainting from the excruciating pain in his knee. The fight was over. The professional had won, easily.

When the first bullet hit him in the right shoulder a look of complete surprise came across Gardiner's face. The force of the bullet spun him sideways saving his life. Easily he identified the hot wind below his chin as the passage of the second bullet. As the third bullet passed through his left hand and into his abdomen, Gardiner was still attempting to regain control. Still holding tenaciously onto the gun, he was beginning to pivot in the direction of the shots. Instinct and training overrode shock and pain.

The third bullet assisted him in his pivot, bringing him face-to-face with his executioner. The fourth bullet, struck him full in the chest, puncturing the heart muscle and severing the hinge of the left ventricle. Gardiner was dead before he hit the gravel, a half-formed look of surprise frozen forever on his face.

The only sound was that of a distant car skidding on gravel and the still persistent buzzing of flies.

Michael dropped the gun to the ground and was immediately overcome with the dry heaves, tears streaming down his face. Mary threw her arms around her son, calming him. David staggered to his feet as Sara rushed, sobbing into his open left arm—his right now completely numb, hanging uselessly down his side. It was in this pose that the would-be rescuers finally found the four Stones and the rigid corpse of Rita Brickston. Unseen and unfound were the shattered remains of Rita's cloisonné earrings still sparkling through the coal dust in the rays of the sun. The microdot hidden in the pattern forever lost.

Acknowledgements

This novel would not have been possible without a great deal of help from family, friends and Deux Voiliers Publishing's dedication to promoting the works of new Canadian writers. Gratitude must go to Ian Marquis in Toronto, Pat Hopkinson in Yorkshire and David Rossi in Marblehead for their invaluable help in providing encouragement and most importantly incisive constructive criticism; to my partner Karen McCutcheon who not only provided encouragement, editorial skills and constructive criticism, but listened patiently to the agonies of the dark side of writing. Also significant were the invaluable suggestions and editorial insights provided by author Mike Young who embraced the early role of editor in behalf of Deux Voiliers Publishing, to Bill Horne who did a sterling job as copy editor and to Ania Szneps for her patient proofreading. Finally, all would have come to nought without Ian Shaw of Deux Voiliers Publishing who endorsed the work from the beginning and contributed to its final formulation with his knowledge and perspicacious recommendations.

About the Author

Norman Hall was born in Yorkshire, England. As a pre-teen he moved with his family to St. Catharines, Ontario where he attended high school. As a young man he moved to Massachusetts where he received undergraduate and graduate degrees. He is an ordained minister and as such served a parish in Dedham, Massachusetts before leaving parish work to head up an adolescent residential program.

After returning to Canada he worked as an Executive Director of a large social service agency in Hamilton, Ontario for thirteen years. He has also worked as a certified adult ESL instructor and as a Personnel Officer. While at Seneca College he co-authored two text books on English pronunciation and edited several text books on English grammar and conversation. He has two children living in Massachusetts and currently resides in Toronto with his partner Karen.

About Deux Voiliers Publishing

Organized as a writers-plus collective, Deux Voiliers Publishing is a new generation publisher. We focus on high quality works of fiction by emerging Canadian writers. The art of creating new works of fiction is our driving force.

We are proud to have published *Four Stones* by Norman Hall.

Other Works of Fiction published by Deux Voiliers Publishing

Soldier, Lily, Peace and Pearls by Con Cú (Literary Fiction 2012)
Kirk's Landing by Mike Young (Crime/Adventure 2014)
Sumer Lovin' by Nicole Chardenet (Humour/Fantasy 2013)
Last of the Ninth by Stephen Lorne Bennett (Historical Fiction 2012)
Marching to Byzantium by Brendan Ray (Historical Fiction 2012)
Tales of Other Worlds by Chris Turner (Fantasy/Science Fiction 2012)
Romulus by Fernand Hibbert and translated by Matthew Robertshaw (Historical Fiction/English Translation 2014)
Bidong by Paul Duong (Literary Fiction 2012)
Zaidie and Ferdele by Carol Katz (Illustrated Children's Fiction 2012)
Palawan Story by Caroline Vu (Literary Fiction 2014)
Cycling to Asylum by Su J. Sokol (Speculative Fiction 2014)
Stage Business by Gerry Fostaty (Crime 2014)
Stark Nakid by Sean McGinnis (Crime/Humour 2014)
Twisted Reasons by Geza Tatrallyay (International Crime Thriller 2014)

Please visit our website for ordering information
www.deuxvoilierspublishing.com

CPSIA information can be obtained at www.ICGtesting.com
Printed in the USA
LVOW11s1838241115

464028LV00002B/384/P